Why are we, Thy creation, so eager to believe the worst of each other, Lord? So quick to judge what we don't understand? And now all I can do is cry out, "Father, forgive me!" I know Thou will. But I fear that poor girl will forever hate me for the role I've played in all this.

Prudence Willard
Marietta Ohio
May 5, 1862

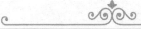

SECRETS OF WAYFARERS INN

Family Secrets
River of Life
All That Remains
Greater than Gold

SECRETS OF
WAYFARERS INN

Greater than Gold

ROSEANNA M. WHITE

Guideposts

New York

Greater than Gold

PROLOGUE

Marietta, Ohio
April 28, 1862

"Pru."

Prudence jumped, splaying a hand over her chest, where her heart tried with valiant energy to escape its confines. Her brows knit, even as she chuckled and spun to face her husband. Dawn was barely a kiss of rose and gold on the highest tips of the mountains to the east. What would bring him to the kitchen door of the Riverfront House when he ought to be in their own barn, milking and mucking and feeding? "Jason. What is it? Is something the matter with Moses?"

"No, all is well." He darted a look over his shoulder and then over hers, stealing silently across the stone floor until he could lean close to her. "Can thou come home? Only briefly? I have a...gift for thee."

"A gift?" They rarely had money to spare on such things—and though Jason had been known to pick her a bouquet of spring's first flowers, he wouldn't feel the need to come to the inn on this morning, one of the few when she was here helping in the kitchen while the usual cook was sick, and tell her of it. Unless…

His smile bore the strain of danger. "A…*package.*"

Try as she might to catch her breath, it wouldn't slow. A package—a runaway slave. But why would her contact have brought the poor soul to the farm, to Jason? She pitched her voice to the barest of whispers. "I don't understand."

Her husband leaned closer still, slid a warm hand into its familiar place on her waist, and rested his lips against her ear. Perhaps, if anyone came upon them, they would look like any other couple whose love was as deep as theirs—exchanging a few secret words about nothing but their own affections. "She was alone, my love. Not delivered by anyone. I found her hiding in the haymow. Or rather, Patience found her."

For a moment, a grin chased away her frown. She could well imagine her pet goose startling the poor creature with a loud honk of greeting. But amusement could not hold out long against the worry. She reached behind her back to untie the apron she'd tied only ten minutes earlier. "Give me just a moment to find Elizabeth. She will have to get the bread mixed up while I am gone."

Twenty minutes later, Prudence followed Jason into their barn. Morning had crested the mountains while they made their way home from the hotel, and now it spilled golden and sweet through the open barn doors.

Her husband cleared his throat and whistled a three-note tune. Seconds later, the rustling of hay drew Prudence's gaze to the shadows of the back corner stall they used for storing hay. Jason had said nothing on the short journey here about the unexpected visitor he had discovered. But she was always prepared for the worst—people half-starved, their feet bleeding, frostbitten in the winter or suffering heat stroke in the summer.

The young woman who stepped out into the half-shadows, however, was none of those things. She wore a dress the equal of any of Prudence's, or even superior. Had hair a shade lighter than her own. Skin so pale it barely hinted at any African heritage. And a face so beautiful that a stab of jealousy pierced Prudence before she could even think to guard against it.

Jason touched a hand to the small of Prudence's back. "Sweetheart, this is Tilla."

CHAPTER ONE

The adventure had begun. LuAnn Sherrill stood by the staircase, unable to wipe the grin off her face as Tess Wallace checked in their first-ever guests at the Wayfarers Inn. People who were even now handing over a credit card to be swiped. People who stood with smiles as they craned their heads back to take in the gorgeous ceilings. People who would go home in a few days and tell their friends what a beautiful place the bed-and-breakfast had been.

They were really doing it. Had *done* it. Against all odds, they'd opened their doors in time for the Sternwheel Festival. Despite all the headaches and false starts, they'd embarked on what was sure to be the greatest adventure of their lives.

"LuAnn!" Adventure sounded an awful lot like panic in the voice of Janice Eastman. The third member of their trio gripped LuAnn's arm and tugged her back a few steps, out of sight of the guests. "The elevator's broken."

"What? That can't be. It was just working an hour ago when I took the café's linens down." True, it had been making that strange grinding sound, but that was to be expected in an elevator so old it still had gates and had to be hand-operated, right?

Janice gave her a look that LuAnn knew well—one they'd both perfected after years in the public school system. A look that said, *Are you really questioning me?* As if she would make that up.

LuAnn sighed. "Do you think Thorn will know how to fix it?"

"I already called him." Though she didn't exactly look confident as she said it. Running her fingers absently through her platinum curls, Janice sent her gaze back down the hall, toward the apparently cantankerous machine. "Though I highly doubt he's ever had cause to work on a hundred-and-fifty-year-old elevator before."

They'd brought a professional in to get it working again after they'd discovered it hidden behind a false wall, but the professional didn't exactly live in town to help them out in a pinch. But Thorn had watched him working, hadn't he?

"He's worked on plenty of other things," LuAnn said. "Surely the skills are transferrable—gears are gears, right?"

"Let's hope so. Thorn said he'd be here in five—oh, and then he said to remind everyone he has that surprise coming. To meet in the sitting room at one."

In the excitement of the day, LuAnn had spaced on the promise he'd been grinning about last night. "Any hints as to what it is?"

"No, but he sure sounded happy about it."

"He's been in a good mood for weeks." LuAnn smiled just to think of it.

Janice turned away again. "Go tell Tess about the elevator, will you, to make sure she doesn't send the guests there? I'll see if I can find someone to help them with their bags on the stairs.

"Sure." And if Janice failed to round up any younger arms to play bellhop, they'd manage it themselves. Heaven knew they'd all lugged their fair share of loads up those stairs in the last few months. LuAnn slipped around the corner to the front desk, where Tess had smoothed out a brochure about the Sternwheel Festival.

While the couple had an on-the-spot debate about which band to see first that evening, LuAnn slid to her friend's side and whispered the latest conundrum into her ear. Not that such news visibly frazzled Tess Wallace after years in the hospitality business. She just gave LuAnn a discreet nod and renewed her smile.

"I bet we can see them both, if we make it a point to keep moving," the young wife on the other side of the desk said. She aimed a bright smile at Tess. "Thanks again for the early check-in."

"It's our pleasure," Tess said with the ease that LuAnn was tempted to practice in a mirror to learn to emulate. Not that she couldn't look calm and collected too, but there was a reason they'd given Tess front-desk duty on opening weekend. "If you're ready, LuAnn will show you up to your room. This weekend we'll keep the front doors unlocked until midnight, but if you happen to return after that, just ring the bell and someone will be down to let you in. Breakfast is served from seven to ten, and if you've had enough festival food at any point and want something a little different, don't forget to check out our soup café. We're open for lunch from eleven to three."

The couple beamed and reached down for their bags just as one of the servers from the café slid into view. LuAnn let out only one small puff of relief and motioned him forward. "Taylor will help with your luggage. You two just follow me." They only had a wheeled, mid-size bag and a toiletry bag, so really, they wouldn't even miss the elevator.

Now, that family due to check in at three with a baby and a toddler would be another story altogether. As soon as she had a moment without watching eyes, LuAnn would offer up one mighty prayer that Thorn could work his skills on that elevator before it became necessary to haul the foldable crib and cot up the staircase.

She led the way around the hand-carved bar that now doubled as the reception desk and toward said staircase, polished to a gleam and looking absolutely beautiful when one had only to haul *oneself* up it. "Have you been here for the Sternwheel Festival before?" She glanced over her shoulder at the couple. They must be the Prescotts—Scott and Emily. The family with the kids was the Kellys, and the other couples to be checking in were all older.

"Yep, we were here last year and just loved it," Emily said, touching a hand to the shining mushroom-shaped newel cap. "The funny thing was that we were walking by this building and Scott was seeing all the potential and saying what an awesome B&B it would make, weren't you, sweetie?"

Scott ran an appreciative hand up the banister. "Lot of beauty in this old place. I couldn't believe it had sat empty for so long. If we'd had the cash, I would have bought it then and there."

Emily gave an enthusiastic nod that sent her blonde curls bouncing. "When Laura told us the inn would be open for the festival—well, we couldn't resist."

LuAnn didn't have any idea who Laura was, but any word of mouth was welcome. "And we're so glad you came."

Once on the third floor, LuAnn led the way down the hall. "We put you in Moonlight and Snowflakes. You have a gorgeous view of the river." And a gorgeous view of the room itself when she opened the door for them. The novelty of opening one of those doors and seeing their vision come to life before them definitely hadn't worn off yet.

This room sported a sleigh bed in dark wood that contrasted beautifully with the whites and silvers and blue accents they'd used to decorate it. It was one of her favorites. Of course, so was Woodbine and Roses. And Lilacs and Sage. And, if she was being perfectly honest, all the others.

"Here we are. You two get settled, and if you need anything at all, just let us know."

She stepped out of their way with a smile that felt permanently affixed to her face. Their first guests. Opening day. Dreams coming true.

No broken elevator could possibly ruin this day. Nothing could.

A familiar masculine voice pulled LuAnn from the kitchen an hour later. It had been a while since she'd seen Bradley Grimes, but she somehow wasn't surprised he'd found time to stop by on opening day. The Realtor had proven himself a friend, and LuAnn palmed one of the wrapped truffles for him that she'd been arranging in a bowl as she headed through the swinging door to say hello. This time of day, the café had only two tables filled, so she could slip easily through it and around to the parlor.

"There she is." Janice's eyes twinkled as LuAnn followed their voices into the front room. "I had a feeling you'd come join us."

LuAnn smiled back and held out the offering of chocolate. "Every guest gets one of these today."

Brad accepted with a grin. "Don't mind if I do. Thanks."

"And look what *he* brought." Janice pointed to a lavish bouquet of flowers on one of the end tables. "Wasn't that sweet?"

Sweet and thoughtful and extravagant—that arrangement had to have cost a hundred bucks, at least. "Well now my truffle looks paltry. Those are gorgeous, Brad. You didn't have to do that."

"I wanted to." His voice was warm. "You ladies deserve it after all the hard work you've put into this place."

"Speaking of which." LuAnn lifted her brows toward her friends. "Did you two need any help? My list is just about completed."

"Nope, I think we're all caught up." Tess slid a finger along the mantel, though there couldn't possibly be so much as a speck of dust on it. Not with the once-over they'd given everything that morning.

She then turned back to the flowers. "You know what? Those don't belong in here—they belong on the front desk, where everyone can see them the moment they walk in." She charged toward the end table, scooped up the colorful vase, and vanished.

"I had better check on Thorn," Janice added, pivoting toward the door.

LuAnn held up a hand. "If he's in the basement, I'll check on him—I was headed down there next anyway. The linens from the café ought to be dry."

Janice didn't argue. "Perfect. I need to call Stacy back. Thanks again for the flowers, Brad."

He tipped an invisible hat and then leveled his smile on LuAnn. "Mind if I walk down with you? I've been wanting to see how the basement renovations are coming along."

"Of course I don't mind." She led the way, motioning for him to follow. "Not much more than the last time you saw it—but now that the main floor and guest rooms are finished, I imagine we'll focus more down here."

"I'm still amazed at the progress you all have made in such a short time. I thought you'd be lucky to be open by Christmas."

There had been plenty of moments when LuAnn had thought the same. She chuckled. "Never underestimate the power of three determined women—or a small town determined to help them." And here they were, open by the second week of

September for the town's biggest festival. Sometimes it didn't seem real.

Then the piles of laundry hammered the reality home. She listened as they descended the steps but didn't hear the tumbling of the dryer. Good. She could get the linens out and folded and delivered back to the soup café before the flood of guests arrived for the three o'clock check-in.

Though come to think of it, she also didn't hear any tinkering or thumping or humming coming from the elevator shaft—and Thorn was seldom quiet when working. Usually a whistle or hum filled the room around him.

"Hmm." She felt her brows pull down as she headed through the dim stone chamber, toward where she imagined he'd be working. "Thorn? Are you down here?"

No answer came. She aimed herself toward the elevator doors, knowing her frown was in full force by now. The gate was open, proving the elevator car was still down here—probably from when she'd come down with that load of laundry earlier, and then went back up by the stairs for the exercise. And the panel in the wall beside it was open, proving Thorn had accessed the innards somehow or another. But he was nowhere in sight. "Where could he be?"

Brad stopped beside her. "Maybe he had to check out something on another floor? Or run out to the hardware store?"

Either was a reasonable possibility. Then a strange glint caught her eye as she angled toward Brad to agree with him. "What's that?"

"What's what?"

"That?" she asked as she crouched down—careful to keep her specially chosen opening-day outfit well clear of the not-so-pristine floor—and reached for what certainly didn't look like an elevator part. Its gleam was far brighter than the age-patinaed brass of the lift, and accented with green as deep as a forest. As deep as...well, as emeralds. "What in the world?"

She closed her fingers over the links and lifted up what was obviously a bracelet. Obviously old. And possibly more expensive than any piece of jewelry she owned, given the lavish diamonds on each side of every emerald. Not to mention the ornate goldwork that cradled all the gems with a flair absent from any of her department-store purchases.

She could see it so easily on the ivory wrist of a Victorian lady, perfectly set off by the deep green silk of an evening gown. The woman would flutter a fan with that hand, letting the gaslight catch the bracelet and set the diamonds shimmering, while she dimpled and batted her eyes at a man in a top hat.

Brad let out a low whistle, pulling her out of the scene, and crouched down beside her. "Methinks something new was unearthed yet again at the Wayfarers Inn."

No excitement could fill her veins at the prospect of more "urban archaeology" though. Not given the shop rag soaked through with blood that she pointed to next—and the trail of dried red that led toward the exit. Their big adventure had just developed another wrinkle, and it tied her stomach in knots. Because the simple question she'd asked a minute ago felt rather ominous. "Yes but...where's Thorn?"

CHAPTER TWO

The opening day buzz had vanished from LuAnn's veins, leaving in its place a foreboding sense of worry. She walked to the door that led from the basement to the garden—overgrown and impassable just a couple of months ago but now an easy way in and out—and held her cell phone to her ear.

Pick up, she willed Thorn. *Please pick up.* But it just rang. And rang. And rang.

Brad shook his head as he jogged back down the stairs into the basement. "I didn't see him upstairs anywhere or hear his phone ringing. Though he could have it silenced, I guess."

"He doesn't usually do that when he's working." He too often needed to communicate with them or his team of construction workers. And, for that matter, with the scads of friends he'd made through their church in the last couple of months. He'd come a long way from the depressed, homeless former teacher they'd first met on the so-called haunted fourth floor of the inn back in June. In these last couple of weeks especially, he'd really bloomed.

The phone, yet again, kicked to voice mail. "This is Tory Thornton. You can leave a message if you want. Or I'll just see you called and call you back. Whichever."

She hadn't left one the first time she called or the second, when Brad decided to run upstairs and see if he could hear Thorn or his phone. This time she did. "Hey, Thorn, it's LuAnn. I came downstairs to check on you, and it looks like you got hurt. Just wanted to make sure you're okay. Let me know, please. Thanks." She ended the call and slid her phone back into her pocket, her eyes still on those telltale drops of dark red that speckled the floor.

Brad slid closer. "Mind if I look at that bracelet?"

She'd nearly forgotten about the gold and emeralds in the face of the blood. "Oh. Sure." She fished it from her pocket and handed it over, her gaze tracking back to the shop rag. It was soaked in blood, but the trail wasn't that bad. Did that mean Thorn was okay? Or just that whatever wound he'd suffered was dripping through a second rag?

Was he even capable of answering his phone? "I'm going to check outside. See if his truck's still there."

"I'm coming." Brad's footsteps echoed hers, though at a slower pace. "This is really a remarkable piece of jewelry. Reminds me of some things the aunts have. Old, I'd bet."

She glanced over her shoulder to see him squinting but didn't pause. She was already turning the old knob, and she pushed it easily open. "Somehow that wouldn't surprise me."

The door had been firmly closed. If Thorn came out this way, he was apparently not so injured that he didn't think to shut it behind him. But...

"There—another blood drop," LuAnn said. It glistened slightly on the flagstone of the walkway, otherwise she might not have seen it. "Must be pretty fresh, right? It's warm enough that it would dry quickly."

"Agreed." Brad stepped up beside her and shook his head as he handed the bracelet back. "You head left at the sidewalk, I'll head to the right, and we'll meet around front. He's surely either around or there's an indication of where he's gone."

"Good plan." But as she followed the flagstone path toward the sidewalk, her stomach tightened.

If he'd been hurt, why hadn't he come to them for help? Called for them? Why would he go outside alone?

She could well imagine what happened—he'd found the bracelet somewhere in that elevator shaft or its panel and had been so excited he jerked up, smacking his head. Head wounds always bled like the dickens, right? He'd grabbed his ever-present shop rag to stem the flow and... That was where her story unraveled.

Following the sidewalk along Front Street, LuAnn's gaze swung ahead, to the parking lot by the inn. Some of the cars she recognized, some she didn't—customers of the café or their newly checked-in couple. But her gaze sought one vehicle in particular.

The old, dented blue pickup that Thorn had been driving sat in the lot. Still there, tucked into its usual corner. He hadn't driven anywhere. Which meant Brad was right that he couldn't have gone far.

"Excuse me," a woman said as she bumped into her.

"Oh! My fault. Sorry." LuAnn offered a smile, but the woman had already walked on. The sidewalks were busier than usual by far. The whole town would be, with the influx of tens of thousands of visitors for the festival. What a day to misplace a friend.

"No luck, I take it?" Brad sidestepped a few more pedestrians who had halted in the middle of the path to point at the river, and rejoined her.

LuAnn shook her head. "Usually I'd say I'd just walk around a bit and see if I can spot him, but today..."

"That would be quite a task." Lips pressed together and blue eyes scanning the crowds, Brad shook his head. "You're right. I say we head back inside and let the others know what's going on. Maybe one of them saw him while we were trying to call."

"Yeah, maybe," she said, though the knot in her stomach didn't loosen any, which made it impossible even to smile at the group of forty-something women who were gathered in front of the inn, reading the historical marker and exclaiming over how gorgeous the place looked.

A fine day to lose a friend indeed.

She led the way up the walk and back through the front doors. Tess looked up with a practiced smile, but her smile faded as she looked into LuAnn's eyes.

"Lu. I thought you were checking on Thorn in the basement."

"He isn't down there." She kept her reply quiet as Brad closed the door behind them. "Looks like he's injured—there was a bloody rag. And this." With a glance over her shoulder to make sure no customers lingered nearby, she placed the bracelet on the table.

What had looked ornate and expensive in the dim basement light looked downright regal against the deep wood of the bar.

"What in the world..." Tess lowered her head to study the bracelet. "Obviously not Thorn's. Where was this?"

"Just on the floor, by his toolbox. I think he found it and was so surprised he hit his head and..." The "and" still stymied her. Why wouldn't he have gone to the sink down there, or up here to fetch them? Ask for help? Granted, he wasn't the type to want to ask for help, but he wasn't foolish enough not to ask when he needed it. And that rag said he needed it.

"Maybe he didn't want to disturb you guys on opening day." Brad leaned an elbow onto the bar to study the jewelry.

"That can't be it. He had some surprise scheduled for us in..." She checked her watch. "Any minute now. Hey, could he maybe have just stepped out to take care of that?" Hope bubbled.

Brad's phone rang, and with a glance at the screen, he muttered, "Gotta take this, if you'll excuse me." A moment later he was out the door.

Tess's face relaxed into a relieved smile. "He must be working on whatever the surprise was. We're fretting over nothing. Worst-case scenario, he cut himself and had to get it taken care of or something. But I bet it's his surprise." When she glanced back up, her expression moved into a welcoming smile a beat before the door opened, bell chiming. "Good afternoon and welcome to Wayfarers Inn. Will you be dining in the café, or are you checking in? Mrs. Kelly, perhaps?"

If so, the family was two hours early. LuAnn picked up the bracelet and slid it back into her pocket. Then she turned to see a sleek, lovely young woman with auburn hair, a stylish outfit, and a little boy clinging to her hand.

The mother smiled. "No, sorry. I'm Laura Getty, and this is my son, Noah. And we're not here to eat. We're, um…actually, I was told to just wait in the sitting room. Is that okay?"

Laura—why did that sound familiar? Oh, that was the name their guests had mentioned. They must have asked her to meet them here. LuAnn renewed her smile and nodded. "Of course. So good to meet you, Laura! Go on in. We have a few puzzles and games for the little guy in the corner with the bookshelves." She motioned to the left.

"Thanks." With a bright smile, Laura led her son away.

Tess lifted her brows at LuAnn. "Do we know her?" she whispered.

"The Prescotts mentioned that a Laura told them about us. That must be her—meeting them, I'm assuming."

"She brought us customers?" Tess grinned. "Well in that case, go offer her some chocolates or something."

"I'm on it."

LuAnn hurried through the café and past the swinging door. The soothing bustle of the industrial kitchen surrounded her. The white tile floors gleamed, the white cabinets stretched upward, and Winnie Washington hummed her way from one kettle of soup to another on Big Red, the antique stove, without looking up.

Winnie had been in her element since the café opened.

LuAnn headed for the table tucked into the corner, well away from busy servers or cooks. Her bowls of truffles still sat, ready to be taken out. She scooped one of the bowls up and was soon back through the café, across the entryway, and into the sitting room.

The young mother had settled her son onto the floor with a puzzle and had her phone to her ear, her back to LuAnn. "Hey, Dad, it's me. You did say the sitting room, right? Not outside? Because you're not in here, so…I'd ask you to call me, but I'm sure you'll just come in before you could. See you in a few."

Maybe this wasn't the Laura who had referred the Prescotts. Or maybe her dad was meeting them too, how was LuAnn to know? Regardless, she cleared her throat and then lifted the candy with a smile when Laura spun around. "I brought some treats for you and your son, if he likes c-a-n-d-y."

Laura smiled and slid her phone into her trendy purse. "How sweet of you. Hey, Noah, you want some chocolate?"

The little boy didn't look up from the large wooden puzzle piece he had in his hand. "Minute."

Laura, her smile turning a bit strained, rubbed her hand on her leg, as if her palms were damp. Then shook her head and breathed a laugh. "Wow, I can't believe how nervous I feel. Especially since you already seem to know who I am. I guess I could just ask you if my dad's here yet, huh?"

"Um." LuAnn slid the bowl of candy onto an end table and tried not to look clueless.

Noise from the doorway drew their attention, Janice and Tess laughing their way in. Janice was checking her watch. "Only two minutes late. Is Thorn here yet?"

Laura stepped forward, her smile back to bright. "That's what I was just asking."

Wait…what? LuAnn couldn't keep the frown away any longer. Laura hadn't asked about Thorn. She'd asked about her dad.

The woman held out a hand toward Janice. "Guess he let the cat out of the bag at some point, huh? It's so good to meet you guys. Dad's been telling me all about you for months. I've really been looking forward to seeing all the work he's done on the inn. And, well, to thanking you." She made a show of peering out into the entryway. "I wouldn't say this with him here, but since he's late—I can't tell you how much I appreciate what you guys have done for him. If you hadn't hired him, helped him get back to his real life, I don't think he ever would have contacted me again."

Janice and Tess were both staring at the young woman, their eyes wide. LuAnn knew her own expression matched. Math had never been her subject, but this was a simple two plus two. "Wait a minute. Are you saying that Thorn is your father?"

Now panic settled on Laura's pretty face. "You mean he hadn't told you? Oh no! I've ruined his surprise." With a muted, dramatic scream, she covered her face, then laughed. "You seemed to know who I was! Oh man, he's going to flip. He had this big reveal all planned out."

Tess and Janice both looked at LuAnn, questions brimming in their gazes. LuAnn gestured with her hand for a moment, trying to usher some words into her mouth. "I just—the Prescotts mentioned you. Or someone by the name of Laura, anyway. I figured you must be their friend, meeting them here."

"I am—I did." Still chuckling, Laura lowered her hands again. "But it didn't occur to me you'd know me from *that*. I just figured Dad had been too excited to keep the secret any longer."

Janice had wrapped her arms around her middle. "Apparently he has no trouble with that. So far as we knew, he only had one daughter. She was killed in that accident, along with her mother."

Serious again, Laura nodded. "His second wife. And my half sister. I've been with my mom in California ever since their divorce, right after he got back from Desert Storm. I honestly hadn't even seen him since then, not until last month. He finally came out to visit, and that's when Jake and I—my husband, Jake—decided we'd relocate, so I could get to know him. We just got to town two weeks ago."

It lined up with Thorn's unfailing good mood the last two weeks. And, for that matter, with his mysterious trip over the summer. Still.

Tess voiced the question hammering on LuAnn's thoughts. "How could he not have told us for so long?"

To that, Laura shrugged. "You know him—he plays his cards close to his chest. Probably didn't want to say anything until he was sure I was coming. And these last two weeks have been pretty crazy. We were getting settled in at the new house, and I know Dad was super busy here. But he said it should calm down a bit once the inn was open." She raised her brows. "Though maybe not. Is he working somewhere around here?"

"He's in the basement, yeah. Fixing the elevator," Janice said.

"Actually..." LuAnn looked to Tess, seeing if she had any newer information to interject. But when only silence met her pause, LuAnn continued, "...he's not. When I went down there, he was gone. I was honestly a little worried—his shop rag had blood on it, and he wasn't answering his phone. But then I realized it was almost one and thought he'd just come up here for this big surprise."

Laura frowned, only brightening a bit when her little boy— he must be around three or four—bounced over, asking for chocolate. LuAnn passed him a piece from the dish, grinning at his polite thanks.

Laura shook her head. "It's unlike him to be late. Isn't it? I mean, it seems like it—he's always early, whenever he calls or when he's come by these last couple of weeks to help us move in." A melody from her purse interrupted her. "Oh, I bet that's him. Or, no. Jake. Excuse me for a second."

She partially turned away and answered with a cheerful, "Hey, honey, what's up?" A moment later her expression went from expectant to frustrated. "She didn't! She always sleeps for at least two hours...no, I know. Dad's late anyway, I'll just run home and get her." She held up her wrist. "I can be there before your class starts."

As she disconnected, she was wiggling her fingers at Noah. "Come on, buddy. We have to go get your sister real quick. She won't go to sleep, and Daddy has his class on the computer." As she scooped up the chocolate-lipped little boy, she offered an apologetic smile to the Inn Crowd. "I'm so sorry. I thought for sure Paisley would sleep the afternoon away, but of course, the one day I need her to—here." She fished a card out of her purse and handed it over. "This has my cell number on it. Could you just give me a call when Dad comes back? I'll see if I can get her settled again or if I need to bring her with me."

Almost before Tess could take the card and say, "Sure, of course," Laura and Noah were out the door in a flurry of energy.

The door had no sooner closed than one of the servers filled the doorway. "Hey, Tess, got a minute?"

"Sure." With a grin for LuAnn and Janice, Tess followed the teen out.

LuAnn turned to Janice. "Wow, huh?"

"I'll say." Janice passed a hand through her hair, still staring at where Laura had been. "When that man says *surprise,* he means it."

LuAnn chuckled. "So. Get everything all ironed out with Stacy?"

Janice nodded. "Dinner plans are all set. Are you sure you guys don't mind manning the inn without me tonight?"

LuAnn dismissed that with a flick of her fingers. "Of course not. Go, have fun, see your family. We'll check out the festival tomorrow."

"Great. I promised Larry I'd get him cotton candy." She laughed and clapped her hands together. "Get him sticky and hyper and send him home. Goodness, I love this grandparent thing."

LuAnn smiled, though all her grandparenting came vicariously through these friends of hers. "So where do you think Thorn could be? Think maybe he lost track of time or something?"

Janice pursed her lips. "He was awfully excited about this. Maybe he's at the hardware store?"

"Maybe." One would have thought that if he went to get a part or something and was running late, he would have let Laura know, though. "I'm sure he'll get here soon. In the meantime, look what he must have found. It was lying beside his tools." She fished the bracelet out again.

And nearly laughed at how wide Janice's eyes grew. "Goodness gracious goat! Where did *that* come from?"

"Couldn't tell you. I'm guessing somewhere in the wall beside the elevator. Or maybe in the elevator itself, who knows?" She placed it in Janice's outstretched hands. "I'd wonder if it belonged to a guest, if any had checked in before the elevator broke. Gorgeous, huh?"

"Very. Looks a bit Victorian in style, doesn't it?"

"Or older, even." Like the kind of piece a Victorian lady would wear with pride, telling any who would listen about how it had been in her husband's family for generations, since the first Earl of Something or Other commissioned it for his beloved wife to commemorate the birth of their first son.

Janice chuckled. "More urban archaeology. I can't wait to hear how he found it when he gets back."

"Agreed." LuAnn jumped when her cell phone squawked, and Tess's voice came from her pocket. Their walkie-talkie app. She pulled her phone out. "Yeah?"

"Did you bring the café linens back up?"

"Oh, phooey. I got distracted by the bracelet and then everything else. Be right there!" Flying back out of the sitting room and down the stairs, she pushed aside all the questions for now.

Thorn was a grown man—he was fine. He'd come back soon with a bandage, maybe a few stitches, and a whopping story to tell. He'd introduce his daughter to them officially, they'd tell about the mix-up with her. They'd all laugh about it over a bowl of peanut soup.

Nothing to worry about.

After fifteen minutes of folding towels, tablecloths, aprons, and dishrags at the sorting table by the laundry machines in the basement, LuAnn fully expected to walk back up those stairs with her basket in her arms and find Thorn and Laura laughing with Tess and Janice in the sitting room.

Instead, when she slid the linens into their place on a shelf in the kitchen, she turned to find Brad coming back inside, his gaze on something he cradled in his palm. She'd half assumed him to have left while she was downstairs on laundry duty. "Hey."

His returning "Hey" was subdued. No, more distracted. He glanced up after nearly running into the doorframe, shot a look around the kitchen that she would have classified as suspicious—or perhaps cautious—if that weren't a bit too dramatic, and motioned her to follow.

Curiosity piqued, LuAnn trailed him to the front of the inn once again, where Janice stood leaning against the bar, laughing with Tess over something Larry had said to her on the phone. A glance at the grandfather clock in the parlor told her they had maybe half an hour before the rest of the guests began arriving. The café would close at the same time, freeing their attention for this new portion of the business.

Brad managed to silence the other two women without saying a word. All he had to do was drop a small something onto the dark wood.

LuAnn drew near enough to see what it was. A pebble, maybe? A rock? No. A stone, but not that sort. She sucked in a breath.

Tess did too. "Is that...?"

"Another emerald." Brad turned his arrow eyes to LuAnn. "Bigger than the ones in the bracelet, isn't it?"

She pulled the bracelet out of her pocket by way of answer and set it there alongside the loose gem. To her untrained eye, they looked to be the same clarity, were certainly the same color and cut. But the loose stone was at least three times the size of any of the ones in the bracelet. "Where'd you find that?"

"Outside, between the flagstones."

Janice leaned close while Tess tapped a finger on the wood and said, "How would an emerald that size have landed in our walkway?"

"If I were to guess..." Brad hesitated, drawing in a long breath and looking at each of them in turn. "The only thing I can think is that Thorn dropped it. Which, of course, begs the question..."

"What question?" LuAnn didn't know exactly what he was implying, but she was pretty sure she didn't like it.

He cleared his throat, and his shoulders edged back. "Why was he carrying it out of the inn? And what else did he have in his hands, if he didn't notice dropping *this*?"

CHAPTER THREE

The kitchen was warm, bordering on hot, the air fragrant with the peanut soup Winnie had just finished up. It was stored in the fridge, ready to be heated and served tomorrow. They'd opened the windows, and music from a band somewhere a few blocks away drifted in on the late afternoon breeze.

LuAnn drew a finger through the condensation on the outside of her iced tea glass and looked from Tess to Janice. They'd checked all the guests due to arrive today into their rooms, had gotten everyone settled, left the bell on the desk in case anyone needed them, and propped the door between kitchen and café open so they'd hear any bell ringing.

But Thorn still hadn't shown up, and now that they had a moment to pause for breath, LuAnn had to admit to more than a little concern about it. He wasn't the type to lose track of time so totally—and especially not when he'd been planning a big introduction.

"I'm going to try calling Laura. Maybe she's heard from him." LuAnn slid over the card that Tess had set on the table.

"Good idea," Janice agreed with a nod.

After tapping in the number and double-checking it against the card, LuAnn put her phone to her ear. And nearly dropped it when a deep male voice answered with an obviously irritated, "Yeah?"

"Oh." She sat up straighter, squinting at the card. That was the number she'd called, wasn't it? "I'm sorry, I may have called the wrong number. I'm looking for Laura Getty—"

"Yeah, this is her phone. I—hold on a sec." Though whoever-he-was obviously tried to muffle the phone, she could still hear him saying, "Noah, give that toy back to your sister right now. I said *now*."

Usually that would have made her smile. At the moment, it simply made her shoulders relax a bit. This must be Laura's husband.

"Sorry. This is Jake. I just walked in to find that Laura had an unfortunate encounter with strained peas and had to jump in the shower." Amusement laced his voice.

"Ah. This is LuAnn Sherill—from the inn? Laura's dad still hasn't shown up, and we're a bit worried. We'd hoped he'd been in touch with Laura and she just hadn't had a chance to let us know."

Jake muttered something she didn't quite catch. Or care to hear, given its tone. Then, louder, "Figures."

"Pardon?"

"Look, ma'am, like I told Laura when she insisted we move back here—the dude's a flake. I don't know where he vanished to this time, but the fact that he disappeared the hour he's supposed to be introducing everyone—yeah, not surprised."

LuAnn sat up straighter, knowing her brows were furrowed. "I'm afraid he might be injured—"

"If that were the case, he would have let someone know, don't you think?" Jake grunted. "Look, I'm going to do whatever I have to do to get Lar out the door to meet our friends, like we'd planned. I'd appreciate it if you wouldn't bother her again about Thorn. He's not going to ruin our whole weekend with his drama."

"But—" LuAnn was interrupted with the chime of her phone disconnecting from the call. She pulled it away and looked at the screen. "He hung up. He thinks Thorn just ran off or something."

Janice rested her head on her hand. "I can't believe Tory would do that—there has to be some other explanation."

"Of course there is. He wouldn't abandon his plan to introduce his daughter. Plus he wouldn't leave in the middle of a job. And he certainly wouldn't take something he'd found in our walls with him. Assuming he *did* find the jewels in the walls." LuAnn set her phone on the table and stared at the puddle of condensation around her glass.

"Where else would they have come from?" Tess leaned back in her chair, closing her eyes. "Let's look at this reasonably, one subject at a time. First, the jewels. The logical assumption is that he found the bracelet and whatever item the larger emerald came out of somewhere in the basement. Probably near or in the elevator. Agreed?"

"Most likely," Janice said.

LuAnn sighed. "It seems like the best explanation."

"Okay," Tess continued. "We'll assume that and set it aside. We also know he's been gone for almost three hours, though he had every reason to be here. His truck is still in the parking lot, and he's not answering his phone, nor can we hear it anywhere around here when it should be ringing. So Thorn, logically, is no longer at the inn. Agreed?"

"Obviously. But I don't agree with Brad's insinuation that he found some hoard of treasure and ran off with the rest of it." Janice's face looked downright pinched at the suggestion.

Much like LuAnn's heart felt. "No way. He wouldn't do that."

"I would say we all agree on that part. So then, logical explanations for where he might have gone." Tess opened her eyes and leveled her gaze at LuAnn. "Madam List-Maker?"

A grin pulling at one corner of her mouth, LuAnn pulled one of her many notebooks from the center of the table. She flipped to a new page and uncapped the pen she'd left with it. "Okay. Option one—the hardware store."

Tess pulled out her phone. "I have them in my contacts. We can answer this question quickly enough." She stood as she told her phone to dial, pacing the kitchen as if she still had energy. Then again, she'd spent the last couple of hours behind the reception desk rather than carrying luggage up the stairs, so maybe she did.

LuAnn went ahead and added a number two to the list. "Another option—the hospital or an urgent care place. He could have cut himself on something, needed stitches."

Janice granted the point with a nod.

"Hi, Kip. This is Tess Wallace, from the inn. Has Thorn been by there lately?" She paced back toward the table, her face lighting. "Oh, great! When was that?" And down came her brows again. "Oh." *Last night*, she mouthed, covering the phone. "And he hasn't been by since?" She gripped the ladder back of her chair and sighed. "Uh-huh. He was?" Her eyes slid shut again. "No, we haven't seen him either, not for a few hours. He left in the middle of a job and...okay, thanks. And we'll let *you* know if he comes back here first. Thanks so much, Kip. Try to have a good evening."

LuAnn wrote an *x* beside number one. "That didn't sound promising."

"Kip was about to call us. Thorn was supposed to meet him at the store at four and then walk downtown with him and his dad to check out a band some former students are playing in tonight. Needless to say, he never showed. Kip couldn't reach him on his cell, so he wanted to check with us. Thought maybe he was just caught up in a job." Tess ran a hand through her coppery hair and blew out a breath. "Strike one."

"Let's hope number two is a strike too."

"What's number two?"

"Hospital," Janice said, her tone matter-of-fact. "But don't you think Laura should be the one to call them? He's her father. Apparently."

LuAnn obediently wrote the name in spot number three. "I don't dare try her again right now. Her husband sounds none too happy with Thorn. And if I tried to text her or something, I have a feeling he'd just delete it."

Jake was quickly topping her list of people she didn't particularly care for.

A question mark, then, beside where she'd written *hospital.* "Okay, so what other options do we have?"

Tess's mouth moved into a firm line. "Not that I think this is what happened, but to be thorough, we ought to include Brad's suspicions. That Thorn found something valuable and left with it."

LuAnn's fingers tightened around the pen. She didn't even want to commit that to writing. It seemed like a betrayal of a friend. "I'll put 'left willingly.'"

"Wait. Then...what about..." Janice pursed her lips and leaned in close to whisper, "What about *un*willingly? Is that a possibility?"

Tess looked dubious. "I don't see how."

"Well..." LuAnn gazed off and let her imagination run. "What if Thorn wasn't the one to find the bracelet? What if someone else was down there, already searching for it, and Thorn startled them? They could have hit him and then carried him out to keep him quiet."

"All right, Walter Mitty, I prefer your stories of romance and eras gone by." Tess gave an exaggerated shiver. "I do *not* want to think of strangers digging around in our basement."

Silence descended, heavy and long. Because as much as none of them liked to think about it, this old building had too many secret entrances and hidden mysteries to ever rule such a thing out.

Janice rubbed her arms. "Okay, well we've already ruled out ghosts in the house, so if someone spirited Thorn away, it would be a flesh-and-blood somebody. Which means we'd find evidence of them. But I don't think that's likely. With all the crowds around today, no one's going to try to sneak into the basement to dig for treasure."

"Or," LuAnn breathed, "with all the crowds around today…"

Tess finished on a sigh. "It might be the *perfect* time to sneak into the basement to dig for treasure." Their gazes met.

Janice shook her head. "Uh-uh. I am *not* digging around for clues right now. I have to meet Stacy in half an hour—"

"You're right. And finding clues is unlikely." Though at this point, her list was awfully full of unlikely options rather than likely ones. But if they wanted to go looking for evidence of intruders in the basement, she and Tess could do that once Janice left. There was no point in getting her upset and anxious before sending her off to the festival.

"In fact, you might as well go ahead and get ready." Tess offered her perfect hostess smile. "There's really not much we can do about Thorn. I'm sure he'll show up tomorrow morning with apologies and explanations. No need to get ourselves worried."

LuAnn nodded her agreement. "Tess is right. You go on up and then out and have a great time."

Janice didn't look convinced by Tess's professional face, but she stood. "Are you sure? I hate to leave when—"

"Just keep your cell phone on. If something comes up, we'll let you know. But really, what can we do?" Tess shrugged. "Lu and I will man the fort and wait for Thorn to come back. You go gorge yourself on funnel cakes and Italian sausages for the rest of us, okay?"

And try not to see Lawrence everywhere you go, LuAnn added silently. Last year, Tess had spirited Janice away for this weekend in September, all but forcing her to DC for a few days of touring the Smithsonian—all a safe five hours away from the iconic Marietta festival Janice's husband had always participated in.

According to Stacy, their family's plans for the evening involved staying far, far away from the little booth Christ Fellowship would be running. When Lawrence was pastor, they'd set up a table with tracts and other literature about the church every year. It was one of his favorite events—when he got to meet all those strangers and share the love of Christ with them. No way Janice would be able to see that booth without seeing Lawrence inside it, joking about taking a bite of the food people walked by with and drawing them in to talk faith.

Still, LuAnn would be surprised if Janice didn't shed a few tears tonight after she got home. It had only been a year and a half since Lawrence's death, and times like these—his favorite times—hit her hard.

"All right." Janice let herself be shooed toward the door. "Want me to bring you some cotton candy?"

LuAnn laughed. "Make it a snow cone, and you have a deal. Now go."

As soon as she'd padded her way through the café, Tess leaned close. "We're going down there once she leaves, right?"

"The very second. I can't think anyone was really down there, but there's no way I'll be able to sleep tonight if we don't check it out."

While they waited for Janice to head out, they found more chores to take care of. LuAnn finished prepping the cinnamon rolls for the guests' breakfast in the morning—Winnie had already gotten them started—while Tess took care of some bookkeeping and reviewed the reservations for the next day, since tonight they had a one-night-only guest, and a new one would be taking the room tomorrow. In no time, Stacy was jogging up the steps to the front door and Janice was jogging down the ones from the fourth floor.

LuAnn and Tess waved them out with smiles and jokes and a promise to call if anything came up.

The second the door closed behind them, LuAnn made a beeline for the basement stairs. "All right, let's hurry. Much as I want to check things out, my imagination will be far happier with the plan if we finish up before dark."

"Right behind you, sister."

LuAnn opened the hidden door behind the reception desk—they hadn't been willing to give that up during renovations, even though they kept it open a lot—and flipped the switch for the lights they'd had installed.

Darkness still clung to the basement.

"Not again—there has to be something wrong with that fixture or the wiring to it." LuAnn shook her head. "We'll have to get Thorn to—"

Reality interrupted her.

Tess cleared her throat. "We will. Tomorrow, when he comes back to work with his tail between his legs." She turned to the sideboard tucked against the wall the café shared with the kitchen and opened one of its drawers, where they kept a supply of flashlights. "We'll need these."

"Right." LuAnn accepted one but started down the stairs without switching it on, since the other lights in the basement seemed to be okay. She still couldn't quite come down this staircase without imagining the people from centuries past who had done the same. But tonight, her concern wasn't with antebellum daughters sneaking down for a midnight cup of cider, or even with Prudence Willard of the journal they'd found, sneaking down to help escaped slaves on their way to freedom.

She really only cared about what had happened in the basement today.

Once on solid ground again, LuAnn moved to the work lights still set up down here. After a minute of fumbling, she managed to flood the basement with their light. She then turned to the elevator and its still-open panel. Tess already had her flashlight on and aimed into the dark hole in the wall. It caught on a few stray cobwebs floating there, turning them to silver.

LuAnn wrinkled her nose. "Ew."

"And aha. That tells us Thorn wasn't in there very long, right? Or they'd be totally dislodged, not just loose on one end." Still, Tess didn't offer to stick her head in to see what else might be lurking.

"Shouldn't all of that have been cleaned out when the elevator people came to begin with?" LuAnn edged closer to the hole and peered in as far as she could without striking up a close acquaintance with the makers of those spiderwebs.

"Wait." Frowning, Tess flashed her light here and there through the opening. "There are no gears here. This isn't the elevator's access panel."

"Huh. You're right." LuAnn took a step back and tried to conjure up a memory of when the professionals were here getting it in working order for them. She'd come down to check on them and bring them some iced tea and had, in fact, seen the panel open. It was... "He opened the wall on the wrong side. The gears ought to be here." She tapped a panel on the other side of the silent elevator.

This was the only section of the basement with wood paneling over the brick walls, which is what clued them in to something being there to begin with. But it had never occurred to LuAnn that there could be secrets other than elevator gears hidden between this paneled wall and the bricks behind it.

Tess aimed her light into the darkness again. "He had to have realized right away that he opened the wrong side."

"So something must have caught his eye immediately, to make him put the panel down and poke around in there rather than correcting his mistake." LuAnn made another face at the silvery wisps. "Hold on. I can take care of this." She dashed over to the laundry area and came back with a broom, a few paper towels to wrap around the end, and some tape to marry the two. Within a minute, she had her weapon ready. "There we go. LuAnn Sherrill's Amazing De-Webber."

"Patent pending."

The laugh that tickled her throat felt decadent, proving again why she loved these friends of hers so much. Even in the midst of question and mystery, they could make each other laugh. She cleared the webs away and chucked the broom to the side. "There we go. Now let's see what else might be hiding in this wall."

Tess nodded and leaned forward. "And whether there's evidence of anyone other than Thorn looking in it."

The light from the work fixtures didn't reach much of the opening, and their flashlights cut only through a segment at a time. But even so, LuAnn was soon tapping Tess on the arm and holding her light steady on the beam of wood that ran along the ground, perpendicular to the wall. "Look. There's a brick sitting there."

"From...?" Tess flashed her light along the exterior wall until it caught on a hole. "That, maybe? Stick your De-Webber in there, will you?"

LuAnn obligingly used the broom handle to examine the hole. "It's deeper than just a brick would warrant. Seems to open up a bit. A secret storage place, it seems. For what, I wonder?"

"This, maybe?"

Pulling her head out of the hole, LuAnn followed Tess's beam to Thorn's open toolbox. Sitting there, among the wrenches and screw drivers, was a small gray metal box, its only defining characteristic being the layer of grime on it. "I didn't notice that earlier." Of course, it blended in with all the other grimy tools. And she'd been distracted by bloody shop rags and gleaming bracelets. "But maybe that's just a box he keeps nails or screws in." Although there were plenty of both scattered throughout the toolbox. "I guess there's only one way to find out."

She reached for it but then stopped. Thorn could have pulled it out of the wall and set it there. But they'd come down here to investigate unauthorized intruders, right? "Maybe we shouldn't touch it. In case there *was* someone else here who Thorn startled."

"I want to see if it fits in that hole though. Gloves?"

"Gloves." They'd stashed some work gloves down here somewhere, hadn't they? LuAnn headed over to the laundry area in search of some while Tess went in the other direction. They had gardening gloves somewhere in the cabinet, she knew. Those would do. Though before she could find them amid the trowels and hats and spades, Tess called out that she found some.

When she did an about-face, LuAnn's flashlight caught on something on the elevator. She couldn't tell what it was, but while Tess lifted the box by its corners, careful not to smudge anything with her gloved fingers, LuAnn shone her beam on the brass grate, folded open like she'd left it.

There was definitely something marring it, though they'd given it a thorough cleaning yesterday in preparation for guests. Could be grease—it was the same color as much of what covered Thorn's tools.

But he hadn't even opened the correct panel, so it didn't seem likely that he would have gotten greasy. Which meant those dark, fingerprint-shaped smears were most likely blood. Thorn's? Some mysterious assailant? The same person's as was on the rag? "Now would be a great time for someone's kid to become a CSI."

Tess snorted. "I think county coroner is as close as we're going to get. Do we need to have Janice call Stuart?"

"I sure hope not. But look at this."

"It fits in the spot, and there's some dirt on the bottom that would be consistent with it coming out of there." Tess straightened, box in hand again. "What am I looking at?"

"Fingerprints."

"Grease? Or..." She peered closer and then backed away again. "Blood?"

"That would be my suspicion." And here she'd been *ew*ing over spiderwebs. True, she'd already known there was blood down here, but somehow it was different, seeing it in fingerprints on a grate. Like Thorn had reached for it, grabbed hold of it. Was he holding himself up? Trying to fend off an attacker? Or was it just an accident?

A squeak drew LuAnn's gaze back to Tess, who had lifted the box's lid. "Empty." She set it back on the toolbox where they'd found it. "Let's check the tunnel entrance and make sure it's still closed up, shall we?"

"Yeah. But the basement door was unlocked. Someone could have come through there, and I don't see how we'd know it."

LuAnn and Tess headed for the hallway full of what had once been servant quarters and headed straight for the last one on the left. While Tess switched on the lights—these actually came on—LuAnn crouched down and pulled out the stool that hid the opening.

It was still locked, no evidence of it having been tampered with at any point. "Looks secure to me."

They backtracked into the main room, all the more cavernous since the old derelict furnace had been removed.

And screamed when a figure moved at the base of the stairs.

CHAPTER FOUR

The figure screamed too, slapped a hand over her chest, and then started laughing. "Sheesh, ladies, you about gave me a heart attack."

"Robin!" LuAnn splayed a hand over her own chest, heart racing.

Still laughing, Robin Rogers eased to a seat on the bottom step, shaking her dark curls. "I just ran into Janice and thought I'd stop by and see if you guys wanted me to man the front desk so you could join her. Didn't mean to give us all a fright."

Janice would probably have preferred that Robin herself join the family meandering through the festival—if she had her way, her son Stuart and Robin would fall head over heels in love. Robin's focus right now, however, seemed to be on finding permanent employment.

Tess leaned against the railing. "How'd you know we were down here?"

Robin sucked in a deep breath and motioned up the stairs. "I saw the door open and light coming up. Used my amazing powers of deduction."

Smiling, LuAnn exchanged a glance with Tess. Robin had been making no bones about her desire to be hired at the inn full-time, in whatever capacity they could find for her. She'd proven herself capable while on the construction crew during renovations but was apparently just as comfortable with a computer or a broom as with a hammer. And after seeing far too many young people who offered the bare minimum to get by in her years as a teacher, LuAnn was fond of Robin's method— to make herself useful and indispensable.

Hopefully they'd soon be in a position to hire her permanently. For now... "Some extra hands could be helpful this weekend, I'd think. Tess?"

The business end of their trio lifted a brow, but nodded. "Sure. If you wanted to take over the front desk this evening, I wouldn't complain. And we could use an extra hand tomorrow morning too, freshening the rooms. Maybe come around ten?"

"I'll be here. Anything else you need me to do tonight?"

"Nope, it should be pretty quiet. Just answer phones and be available to any guests who come in with questions. I have a feeling most of them will be out pretty late at the festival— except maybe the couple with kids. Do offer anything you can to help them out—I remember traveling with little ones."

And their primary goal for the inn, after all, was to minister to those staying under their roof. Any way they could show Jesus to people was top priority. LuAnn nodded her agreement. "There's a basket of granola bars and things in each room, but we're keeping the fruit basket stocked in the café area too. Tell them to help themselves."

"Will do." Robin pushed herself up again with a grin. LuAnn still wasn't quite used to seeing her in feminine clothes rather than the tank tops and cargo pants she'd favored while working construction. Tonight, however, she wore a cute floral skirt and a knit top. She'd obviously come dressed for the position she'd hoped to talk them into giving her.

Smart girl.

"Go on up then. We have a few things to put away down here. Thanks, Robin." Tess sent her up with a wave of her hand, then shifted closer to LuAnn. "Was that just because you wanted to help her out with some hours, or are we really going out?"

LuAnn shrugged. "Turning in early wouldn't exactly be terrible. But I admit I had the thought that we could try to find Laura."

The lift of Tess's brows was incredulous. "You expect to find one person in that crowd?"

"No, I expect to find four. They're with the Prescotts, right? Weren't they talking about which bands they wanted to catch tonight?"

Tess smiled. "As a matter of fact, they were. And…" She glanced at her watch. "Assuming they didn't change their minds, we have plenty of time to catch up with them. Let's put this stuff away down here and go change into some walking shoes."

The river was crowded with an eye-popping array of boats in dazzling style. LuAnn granted herself the indulgence of taking it all in while she and Tess strolled along, their pace slow, thanks to the crowds. As she watched, one of the majestic riverboats left the dock, its decks ablaze with light and its paddle propelling it into the Ohio with ease.

Laughter and chatter and the occasional shout from one friend to another colored the air. While Tess paused to say hello to someone she knew from the resort her late husband Jeffrey used to run, LuAnn watched the sternwheeler. On its side the words *Rufus B II* were painted, but her eye was drawn along the white sides to the brilliant red of the paddle wheel. After putting brochures for the festival in each room, she knew this was one of the oldest of the boats in town, most of them accurate replicas made in the last couple of decades. This one, however, was built in the 1920s, and it was said that the original owner hosted Al Capone on those very decks.

How well she could imagine a Roaring Twenties dinner party in full swing as the boat steamed its way up and down the river, jazz music spilling out of the cabin and across the sparkling water. There would be a flapper present in her scandalously short dress—still below the knee, though only just—and some more mainstream women in silk gowns that touched the floor. They'd be wearing glitzy headbands with feathers and brooches, and the men would look dapper in their tuxedos. How many were mafia that night? Just Capone, or was he perhaps meeting with another mafioso, trying to determine if he were a rival or an ally?

"Good seeing you. Enjoy the rest of the festival." Tess touched LuAnn's arm, pulling her out of her reverie. "Ready?"

"Mm-hmm." Though it was a shame they couldn't just *enjoy* the unexpected free time tonight. But hopefully Janice was having fun enough for all of them. And if LuAnn's prayers were answered, then tomorrow would be absent the worry about Thorn too. She pulled out the brochure she'd tucked into her pocket and double-checked where the band they were searching for would be playing. "We're just about there."

"Let's hurry. I see some folks from church over there getting barbeque, and while I don't want to avoid them, we could miss Laura if we get caught up in another chat."

"I'm with you. We can always say hi to them afterward."

A few minutes later they were scanning the crowd gathered to hear one of the bands the Prescotts had wanted to check out. LuAnn was about to declare them not here after all when Tess nudged her and pointed to the far side of the crowd. There, nearly hidden by the shadows of another vendor booth, were Laura, a man LuAnn assumed was her husband, Jake, and Emily and Scott Prescott.

The smile on Laura's face lit hope in LuAnn. Surely she wouldn't look so carefree and happy if she hadn't heard from her dad. With a nod to Tess, LuAnn led the way on a weaving path through the crowd. When only a handful of people remained between them, Laura looked their way and smiled anew.

Lifting a hand in greeting, she slid behind her husband and helped close the distance. "Hey, Miss Sherrill! Jake said you called and said Dad was okay, just got caught up in the repair."

LuAnn frowned. "Um, no." She hated to call anyone a liar, but… "I'd called to see if you'd heard from him. We haven't."

"What?" Green eyes glinting, Laura swiveled back to her group. "Jacob Getty!"

Jake turned with lifted brows, giving LuAnn her first full view of him. He was just above average in height but clearly spent a lot of time in the gym. Chiseled features, strong jaw, light blue eyes that clouded at the tone of his wife's voice. No wonder a cute young woman like Laura found him attractive. But good looks didn't make a guy likable.

Laura folded her arms across her chest, apparently having no problem facing him down. "Allow me to introduce LuAnn Sherrill and Tess Wallace from the inn."

Jake's face somehow combined frustration with a plea. "Look, babe, I just wanted you to be able to enjoy the evening with Emily and Scott. We've been planning this for months—"

"Do you not realize that my father is *missing*?"

The frustration overpowered the plea. "Gone, maybe. That's a little different than missing."

Laura stiffened and glared at her husband.

He folded muscular arms across his chest. "You know I don't want to be right about him. But I warned you, didn't I?" He turned to face LuAnn. "Tory Thornton is always just looking for the next 'something better.' He joined the military because it seemed better than life with Laura's mom when things got tough. He took up teaching because it seemed better than the military. He got remarried, had another kid, because apparently that seemed better than trying to fix things with the family he already had. He never once tried to get in touch with Lar—not until now, after his other wife and kid died, and then suddenly maybe his first daughter was good enough again?" He snorted. "You ask me, he found something better and he took it and ran, just like he's always done."

Face set in hard lines, Tess shook her head. "That's not the Tory Thornton I know."

"Yeah? Well the one I know has made my wife cry a few too many times for me to feel real favorably toward him." His face softened a degree as he looked at Laura. "I'm sorry, Lar. I know I promised you a year to put things right with him, here in Marietta. But if this is the way he's going to act… I know he's your dad. But you have to seriously consider whether he can be trusted around our kids."

Though the evening was warm, Laura wrapped her arms around herself like she was fending off a chill. She didn't meet her husband's gaze, or anyone else's. She just stared straight ahead as she said, "We've only been here two weeks, and already you've made up your mind never to trust him."

Jake let out a long breath, his arms falling back to his sides. "Babe, we've only been here two weeks, and already he's vanished. Again."

A faint jingle of music intruded into the conversation. Tess patted at her pockets and came up a moment later with her ringing cell phone. "It's the inn. Excuse me." She stepped away, plugging one ear with a finger as she answered.

LuAnn wasn't sure where to direct her attention. The arguing couple or Tess? She did her best to listen to both.

"—appreciate your willingness to move here but—"

"That can't be right. The couple in Woodsmoke and Pine already checked in. They're the ones—"

"—trying. You know that. But my top priority is the safety of our family. And I mean emotional safety too, not just—"

"—tomorrow. I distinctly remember, because it was our one reservation that didn't span the whole weekend. I'm certain I told him—"

LuAnn gave up on listening to both and focused entirely on Tess—just as her friend said, "Okay, we'll be right there. Shouldn't take us but ten minutes or so to get back." She disconnected and made a face at LuAnn. "First day, first scheduling snafu, apparently. Though I know I made sure he understood the room was only available Saturday and Sunday nights. I'm absolutely sure of it."

"Well we'd better get back to take care of it." LuAnn turned to inform the Gettys of this, only to find that Laura was already moving toward them.

"I'm coming with you. I want to see where he was before I got there this afternoon."

Jake huffed out his opinion of that. "Lar—"

"I'll catch up before the band even finishes." Barely sparing a glance for her husband, Laura motioned the ladies on. "Lead the way."

Seeing no point in arguing, they did.

The man loitering in the parlor would have made most people huddle behind the reception desk with a wary eye. He was huge. The kind of huge that was one part above-average height and five parts pure muscle. His gray hair was shorn in a flat top, the lines in his face looked chiseled in, and his T-shirt strained over his chest. It was the way he stood that made him look intimidating, more than just his size. He had to be around sixty, but he was the sort of sixty that men half his age knew not to mess with.

Robin looked perfectly at ease when LuAnn and Tess bustled up to her. She sat comfy-as-you-please upon the stool, elbows propped on the deep, polished wood of the bar, and smiled a greeting. "Nine minutes and twenty seconds—you are master estimators. Ladies, this is Marshall Bricker. Mr. Bricker, here are the illustrious innkeepers. Can I get you a refill on your drink while they assist you?"

LuAnn hadn't even noticed the glass of soda dwarfed by his massive hands. He smiled—effectively softening the brutal lines of his face—and held it out. "That would be nice. Thank you."

Okay, so maybe initial impressions couldn't be trusted. Could be that this Bricker fellow was a gentle giant.

Robin moved to take the glass and disappeared into the café—Laura had already gone that way, headed for the basement, and the two exchanged a greeting.

Tess turned on her pleasant-hostess face and moved toward Mr. Bricker, hand outstretched. "So sorry for this trouble, Mr. Bricker. I'm Tessa Wallace—we spoke on the phone last month when you made your reservation."

He nodded, smiling again. "Good to meet you, ma'am. Sorry if I've thrown a wrench in the works today. Now that I think about it, I did recall you saying something about coming on Saturday. Guess there are no rooms tonight?"

Well, this shouldn't be too bad, if the guy was already granting that Tess was right. Her shoulders relaxed a degree. "I'm afraid not. Though I'm happy to call one of the hotel booking services for you to see if there's another room available tonight somewhere in the area."

Mr. Bricker dipped his head. "That would be mighty kind of you, ma'am. Again, I'm sorry for upsetting things tonight. Maybe I'll just give my friend a call and see if he has a couch I can crash on—Thorn? I think he works for you, he's the one who recommended the place."

The stiffness came right back to Tess's shoulders. "He does, yes. But I'm afraid he hasn't been answering his cell phone tonight. You're welcome to try to reach him, of course, but in the meantime, I'll just call up that booking site, okay?"

"Sure. Thanks." Something flickered in Mr. Bricker's dark eyes. Concern? Disappointment? LuAnn couldn't be sure. But while he pulled a cell phone out of his pocket, she scurried back to the front desk to answer the ringing phone.

"Good evening, Wayfarers Inn, this is LuAnn speaking. How may I help you?" It only took her a minute to remind the couple staying in Sunshine and Daisies how late the front doors would be open tonight. She could hear Tess in the office behind the bar, talking to whichever booking service she'd called, and Robin was returning to the parlor with a refilled glass.

LuAnn headed for the basement door, reaching it just as Laura was coming back up the stairs. Her face was tight, her eyes a bit misty when she reentered the café. "He really just left everything out like that? The job unfinished?"

LuAnn nodded. "It's not like him. I don't know where he could have gone, but..." She debated a moment and, voice low, added, "There was a bracelet down there, and an emerald on the walkway. He must have found them."

Laura folded her arms around her middle again, looking more like a little girl than a mother of two as she let her gaze wander the dim café. "Seriously? So what if Jake's right? What if he just saw something that looked better...and took it?"

Not having any idea how to answer that, LuAnn simply wrapped her arms around Laura and held her close. "He wouldn't. You *know* he wouldn't. Cling to that."

But her own mind couldn't help but click through the possibilities and the questions. What else could Thorn have found that would tempt him away from his daughter, grandchildren, and a steady job?

She had some research to do.

CHAPTER FIVE

Morning whispered through the windows in soft purples and golds, the smell of trees and water and a few whiffs of food from vendors already up and at 'em drifting to LuAnn through the open window. She sat at her pretty antique desk in her sitting room on the fourth floor, facing the river to the south, where the beauty of the sunrise spilled onto the clouds.

A cup of coffee steamed beside her, fresh from the little fourth-floor kitchen she shared with Janice and Tess for their personal needs. Her Bible lay open before her, half-atop her notebook. She hadn't gone searching for references on treasure this morning, but there had been one in that familiar passage from Matthew 6, which she'd been working through.

"Do not store up for yourselves treasures on earth, where moths and vermin destroy, and where thieves break in and steal."

She picked up her pen and wrote the word *treasure* in her journal. So many images sprang to mind when she pondered the word. Pirates' hoards and crown jewels, chests full of pearls and coins…and bracelets glinting with emeralds and diamonds and gold.

In this modern age, where pirate hoards weren't so common, people had other forms of treasure though, didn't they? Gleaming cars and big houses, closets bursting with clothes, gadgets and gizmos. So many things sought—so many things so easily lost.

Moths, vermin, thieves. She wrote those words and then drew arrows across from each of them. *Depreciation, crashing markets, identity theft.* New, modern ways for things to lose value or be stolen.

But the old-fashioned ways still worked too. Though she never claimed to be much of an artist, she sketched the bracelet they'd found yesterday—now stored in the safe in Tess's office downstairs—and stared at it. It was beautiful, yes—and people stole plenty of things for plenty of reasons. But it wasn't in itself worth enough to inspire betrayal in a friend, was it?

Still, how had it ended up in the wall to begin with? Certainly not by accident. Had it been stolen? Hidden?

She let out a long breath and read the next verses. *"But store up for yourselves treasures in heaven, where moths and vermin do not destroy, and where thieves do not break in and steal. For where your treasure is, there your heart will be also."*

How many times had she read that? Countless. Just as countless times she'd heard it quoted and preached on, countless times she'd called it to mind.

Her gaze went around her sitting room—so prettily appointed, so carefully put together. Part of her treasure, she'd admit it. When it came to earthly things, this was where her heart was. This inn, and all it represented. The friends with whom she'd fashioned the dream, the ministry they wanted it to be.

But oh, how careful she had to be to make sure it wasn't her true treasure. That she remembered how quickly it could all vanish and guarded her heart against that. She had to keep a constant check on herself to guarantee that her focus remained not on the building or the furnishings or the soup or the prestige of owning such a historic place but on the hearts they could touch, the souls they could win, the love they could share for the Lord.

When they'd found Thorn camping out on this very floor before they'd bought the inn, homeless and hopeless, they'd seen him as the first of the people God sent here to be ministered to. They'd given him a place to live, and a job. Introduced him to a church family. They'd given him their understanding, their trust, their love.

No treasure in the world was worth sacrificing that.

Not in her mind, anyway. But far too many people disagreed with her, if the state of the world was any indication.

She read another section, journaled her thoughts, and spent the remainder of her cup of coffee praying over each guest in the inn, each vendor and booth and boat at the festival, and for Tory Thornton. When she opened her eyes again, the clock read only six fifteen. She still had a few minutes before she had to be downstairs setting up breakfast, so she pulled up her laptop and opened her browser.

How to even start searching for something like this? After gnawing on her lip for a moment, she tapped in *antebellum lost jewelry emerald gold Marietta*.

A few seconds later, search results showed her a YouTube video for a country singer—not helpful—a few links to jewelers, some real estate listings, and an article about a hidden waterfall discovered behind a cotton mill in Georgia, which may have tempted her to click on a different day.

Today, however, she scrolled down until another link caught her eye. "Missing Family Treasure Linked to Confederate Spy in Marietta, Ohio." Now *that* sounded promising. She followed the link to the page, and her eyes widened at the image in the article. "Janice! Tess! Get in here! I think I found our jewelry!"

Marietta, Ohio
May 1862

Prudence tucked the quilt around Moses's sleeping form and sat there beside him for a minute, just watching. The way his chest rose and fell, how his mouth slacked open, the precious sweep of his lashes over a round cheek. So long they'd prayed for this child. So long her arms had been empty. So full they felt now, with her little bundle of energy bouncing in them.

She smoothed a lock of dark hair from his brow and smiled as she stood. Nap times were precious too—the only time in the day when she could get her housework—and other work—done without that nearly-three-year-old bundle of energy underfoot. She was oft amazed at how rarely her son ever stopped when he was awake.

Treading lightly from his small room and along the hallway, she drew in a deep breath and tapped on the door at the end.

It swung inward, and Tilla smiled. "Mrs. Willard, hello. Can I be of help with anything? Have you gotten the message to the plantation like I asked?"

Prudence's smile felt as fragile as a goose egg. "May I come in?"

"Of course," Tilla's lips said. But her eyes shouted discomfort.

Such must be borne—heaven knew Prudence had felt little else since this woman arrived yesterday. She stepped inside and motioned for her guest to retake her seat on the crude wooden chair, though Tilla remained standing.

They didn't host escaped slaves in their home—not anymore. They were all supposed to arrive by river and be taken to the inn via the tunnel. But given how this young woman arrived, she and Jason had deemed it safest to keep the secrets of the inn hidden from her. And given that she could clearly pass for white, they would simply claim, if anyone asked, that she was visiting family.

Though that had required giving her one of Prudence's few spare dresses to wear, and the hat and cape that would mark her as a Friend, along with strict instruction to either not speak to anyone who saw her or to remember her *thees*.

"That is why I wanted to speak to thee. This plantation to which thee want the letter delivered—it is a slaveholding estate."

Tilla blinked beautiful gray eyes at her. "I'm aware."

Prudence's fragile smile wore thin. "I dare not ask most runaways for much information on where they have come from, but forgive me—thee are requesting we contact someone for thee in a slave state. If this is another slave who is to meet thee, then we can use the proper channels to—"

"Lewis isn't a slave." Tilla thrust her chin out, as if she were offended at the insinuation that he was, or proud that he wasn't.

A free black, perhaps? But on the Humphreys plantation? So far as Prudence had ever heard, the wealthy family who owned miles of land on the Virginia side of the river weren't fond of paying a free man for what they could compel a slave to do.

"So he is free, then, to meet thee? A relative perhaps?" Usually, she would never dream of prying into a refugee's life like this. But something about this one still settled uneasily upon her spirit. Something about the way Tilla arrived. The way she carried herself, with a strange degree of pride. Her claims that she had her own escape to Canada already planned and only needed a safe haven for a few days while awaiting this mysterious Lewis.

Tilla, whoever she was, was no normal slave. What if she were an enemy rather than a friend, out to infiltrate the Underground Railroad? Prudence would have to tread carefully. She had far too much at stake to be discovered.

The beautiful young woman sighed. "He *will* be family, as soon as we can be reunited. I met him two years ago, when my master's family visited his. We fell in love, Mrs. Willard."

Her smile was bright as the sun, and just as blinding. "I'm sure you can understand that. You and your husband are clearly in love as well."

Prudence inclined her head, but she wasn't about to be distracted. They must unravel the mystery around Tilla's romance, not dwell on Prudence's. "So thee have been to this area before."

With an exuberant nod, Tilla sat upon the narrow bed. Something about the way she bounced as she sat made her suddenly seem more girl than woman, which in turn made a bit of the wariness thaw from around Prudence's heart. "That's right, two years ago. We mostly stayed on the Humphreys' plantation, what with that being who we were visiting, but we came to Marietta one day too."

"And how did thee learn that we could be of help to thee?"

Tilla glanced toward the window, as if someone might be listening outside it. She leaned forward, and a dark curl fell over her shoulder. "Lewis—he has done a bit of work with the railroad himself. He didn't know your name, just that after he helped people to the river, they went to a farm. He didn't dare bring me near his plantation though—they'd have known me."

Yes, if they'd met her before, they certainly would. This young woman's face wasn't one easily forgotten. She had the sort of beauty that would be prized by any race—symmetrical features, full lips, unblemished skin... Whoever her Lewis was, his infatuation was no surprise.

Something niggled about that though. What had she said? *"He didn't dare bring me near his plantation..."* Well, that was surely just the way Tilla thought of it—the place where her love could be found.

Prudence renewed her smile. "You must have been close to your mistress, if you traveled with her."

Winter stole over Tilla's face, freezing it. "No. Not the mistress. She tolerated me only because her husband told her she must." Her lips pursed, and she held up her hands. "It's obvious that I'm more white than black. The master was my father."

Though no great surprise, Prudence gave a sad shake of her head. This was one of the great evils of slavery too—this betrayal of marriage vows it seemed to inspire far too often, and the poor children who were rejected by all as a result of it.

Not for the first time, Prudence said a prayer of thanksgiving that she had been born first into a community of Melungeons who gave her an identity apart from any one race—they who could claim African, Cherokee, and Portuguese blood in their veins in addition to English—and then adopted by Quakers who saw far beneath the skin.

"I imagine that made life difficult for thee in thy master's house."

"My *father's* house." Tilla's nostrils flared, and her eyes misted. "He loved me, and he never let me doubt it. Never failed to provide for my safety and comfort. He would have set me free, had he lived long enough. When he realized Lewis and I had fallen in love, he swore to help us get north so we could wed."

Prudence had begun nodding, but now she stopped. Had Tilla been granted that freedom, they wouldn't have *had* to go north to wed. Not unless… "Lewis is a white man."

Tilla twisted the corner of her borrowed apron in her fingers. "Lewis *Humphreys*."

Gripping the edge of the doorframe for support, Prudence sucked in a breath that did nothing to steady her. "Thee… thee are running away with the heir to the largest plantation in the area?"

Tilla opened her mouth to reply.

Prudence silenced her with a raised hand. "No. Even more, thee expect me to believe that Lewis Humphreys is a friend to the Cause? The heir to a slaveholding plantation in Virginia?"

Tilla's luminous eyes heated with passion. "*West* Virginia. And why do you think they separated? To remain a part of the Union, to—"

"To acquire the statehood they had sought without success for years." Her fingers bit into the doorframe. "Thee forget that I have long lived with but a river separating me from this *West* Virginia. I know well how many side with the Confederates. I know that the condition on which the president and congress granted its statehood was the *gradual* abolition of slavery."

"Which they agreed to! And besides, those men making the laws—they aren't Lewis. You don't know him."

"And you do?" Never in her life had Prudence ever thought so scoffing a laugh would come from her own throat.

Some quiet part of her whispered that she ought to button her lips and say no more, unless it be an apology. Before she could heed that part, more vicious words came spilling out. "You met him once, two years ago. Who is to say he can be trusted? With your life? With ours?"

With Moses's?

Gone was the bounce, gone the pride. Tilla lowered her eyes. "Your question and your caution are logical. But we have been writing to each other weekly these two years. Waiting for the war to be over so I could reach him in safety—but my father died, and I could wait no longer. My father's son was going to sell me. To appease his mother."

The fight leaked from Prudence, leaving her weak in its wake. "I am sorry. So sorry, Tilla. To be treated so by one's own brother..."

"He never acknowledged he was such. I never expected him to act like he was. Even so." She sniffled and wiped a tear that had gathered in the corner of her eye. "Lewis is all I have left, Mrs. Willard. I have to get to him. Or rather, tell him how to get to me. I promise you, he is trustworthy. He is not like his father and grandfather—he is no friend to slavery. If the law has not abolished it for him by the time he inherits, he will free them all of his own will. He is most passionate about this."

Perhaps he was. Perhaps Prudence was being too cynical, too full of doubt. She would give it to prayer... and in the meantime, endeavor to get Tilla's letter to him by some means that would not implicate her own family. "All right. I will do what I can to help thee. I think I know someone who can get thy letter safely into his hands."

"Thank you. A thousand times, thank you." Her bounce having returned, Tilla leaped to her feet, hands clasped with joy before her.

Prudence's smile felt a bit more authentic this time. At least until she turned to leave, and a glint of sunlight drew her eye.

There, half-hidden—and no doubt intended to be *entirely* hidden—behind the washstand was something shining gold. Tilla squeaked a protest as Prudence bent to retrieve it, expecting at first to find coins. That would be odd, but not impossible, if her father had doted on her.

Instead, her fingers closed around what were clearly links. Chains. Gems. With a gasp, she fished a hoard of jewelry out from under the stand.

Emeralds. Diamonds. Intricate goldwork she had no words to describe. A necklace, a bracelet, a brooch, earrings, a ring, even a sparkling diadem.

Her eyes flew to Tilla, whose face had washed pale, and the floor felt as though it would fall out from under her. "What have thee done, Tilla? What have thee brought upon us?"

Slaves were sought when they ran away, yes—but no slave was worth nearly as much as these jewels. She wouldn't just be *sought*—she'd be *hunted*.

And so then, would they all be.

CHAPTER SIX

The ladies all hovered around LuAnn's laptop as she scrolled slowly down the article. Her gaze, however, kept going to the photographs positioned after every few paragraphs. They were black and white, but a few had been colorized, and one was of an oil painting.

An oil painting of a woman in a green evening gown. Throat, ears, wrist, and head encircled with gold and emeralds. *The* gold and emeralds. It had to be.

Janice pulled a chair over. "Unbelievable."

"You can say that again." Tess nudged LuAnn to the side so she could share her seat.

"Belle Arbor Plantation," LuAnn murmured more to herself than her friends. "Still owned by the same family that had it during the Civil War—that has to be some kind of miracle."

"Owns it *again*." Janice pointed at a paragraph beneath the one LuAnn had been reading, the tip of her nail stopping just short of touching the screen. "Looks like the descendants of the original family bought it again in the 1950s. Isn't that something?"

"Can you just imagine if one of our great-great-grands had owned the inn?" LuAnn let the romance of it curl around her for a second and then blinked it away. It was Brad who had a family claim to the place, not any of them. Still. "That's pretty cool. I can only imagine how hard they had to have worked to buy it back and restore it."

"But the greatest family treasure was never recovered." Tess shook her head. "Wow. How many runaway slaves dared to make off with the family's most prized possessions?"

"None that I've heard of." LuAnn tapped the scroll button again. "Anybody see yet how this stuff ended up *here*?"

Janice shook her head. "Not yet. Keep scrolling. History of the jewelry...history of the family...vanished along with a slave girl in 1862..."

"Ah! There." LuAnn centered the paragraphs on the screen so they could all read them.

During this slave's flight toward Canada, she crossed over the Ohio River. After this, she vanished from history—but another figure sauntered onto the stage. The jewels were said to be in the possession of a man in Marietta, Ohio—a suspected spy for the Confederacy. A man who vanished, and the jewels with him. Did he take the jewels? Or perhaps the escaped slave reclaimed them and took them with her to Canada.

"Or perhaps she buried them in the walls of the Riverfront House." Tess let out a low whistle. "What do we do, girls? Contact this family? Tell them we think we've found one piece, at least?"

"It's rightfully theirs. Certainly not ours." LuAnn grinned. "But let's take some really nice photographs of it first. You know, so we can send them to the owner."

"And have them for our scrapbooks," Janice added with a chuckle. "If it keeps up at this rate, we're going to be able to have a display solely of artifacts discovered at the inn."

"Who knew all this history was sitting here so long, undiscovered?" Tess leaned her elbow on the desk, squinting at the screen.

"My love language. History." LuAnn put a dramatic hand over her heart and tapped on her mouse to verify they'd reached the end of the article. "It really is crazy. Why don't you two go take those photographs—I'll figure out how to contact the owners of Belle Arbor and start composing an email."

They both stood, but then Tess halted, her brows furrowed. "Should we wait a day or two, maybe? Until Thorn...?"

Until he showed up—or didn't—with answers about how he found that box. And if there had been anything else in it. LuAnn pursed her lips. "I don't know. Janice?"

Janice focused her gaze out the window for a moment. "It's our opening weekend—and the busiest three days all year in Marietta. If we send an email now, we're going to be thinking about it all day, when we need to be focusing on our guests—and on Thorn. I say we hold off on all of this until things quiet down."

Though part of LuAnn rebelled at the thought of letting a mystery languish away in the safe downstairs, she couldn't argue with the logic. "You're right. We'd better get a move on—those cinnamon rolls need to get into the oven pronto."

Still, while Tess and Janice headed back for their own rooms, she couldn't just click out of the site entirely. First she bookmarked it, then she gave in to the urge to scroll back up to that painting.

The eyes of the woman looked warm. They were green, to match the dress and the gems. Her hair was a deep brown, and the combination put LuAnn immediately in mind of Scarlett O'Hara, though the dress was from an era a few decades before Scarlett was making gowns out of curtains, if LuAnn's fashion memory served.

The profile of the skirt was much smaller than the hoop or bell shape of the Civil War days, closer to what one would expect from a Jane Austen heroine. The cloth boasted a gorgeous pattern in gold against the green that must have cost a fortune. The perfect little poof of sleeve on each ivory shoulder was more gold than green. Pretty, costly, and perfectly complementing the jewels.

She gave herself ten more seconds to lean in and look at the depiction of those gems. Which ones would have the emeralds the size of the loose one Brad had found? The necklace? It had two huge ones as the central pendant, but then smaller ones marching up and around. Could be about right. Or the ones in the tiara—who had a tiara?—might be the right size.

Perhaps, if they found them all, she could convince the girls to play dress up just once before they gave them back to their rightful owners. Just for a little photo shoot.

Shaking her head at herself, LuAnn closed her laptop and hustled down the stairs to the kitchen. That would have to be enough thinking about gold and jewels for the morning. Time to move on to those more attainable, more delicious things: butter and cinnamon.

Perspiration was trickling down LuAnn's back—which ached more than she cared to admit—by the time the last customer cleared out of the café that afternoon. One of their servers had called in sick, so she'd spent the last two hours taking orders and shuttling trays of food out of the hot kitchen, after spending all morning on her feet, chatting with the guests over their coffee and baked goods.

The chairs at the kitchen table beckoned her. Unable to resist their siren song, she plopped down with a bit of a groan and fanned herself with her hand. "Why don't we have the air on?"

From her place at the stove, where she was working on tomorrow's batch of navy beans, Winnie chuckled. "We do, Miss Lu. You've just been running around too much today. Have you eaten?"

"Of course I have. I had a cinnamon roll this morning." Of course, that was at six forty-five. And she hadn't taken a break to eat anything since then.

"Now, tasty as they are, you know they aren't enough to keep a body going all day. Here." Bustling toward the fridge with far too much energy, Winnie soon had a salad and a roll positioned before LuAnn. "You eat that up."

LuAnn blinked. "How did you make that so fast?"

Winnie laughed and sauntered back to the stove. "Magic. Or maybe I made up an extra one by mistake during that last rush and just stashed it in the fridge. I knew one of you ladies would have forgotten to get your lunch. Always do."

"Because there's so much to do. But don't worry. We make up for it at dinner." LuAnn rallied herself enough to grab a fork and knife and sat again to pour the homemade vinaigrette over the mixed greens. "This looks fabulous, Winnie. Thank you."

"Sure thing."

LuAnn said a blessing over her meal and dug in, allowing her mind to let loose all the strands of thought she'd been clasping tight that day. The guests, the festival, the jewelry, the missing handyman. She and the others had exchanged countless glances that day, every time they expected to see Thorn come striding in and he didn't.

Her cell phone squawked, making her jump. Gracious, but she hated that walkie-talkie app! She tugged it out of her pocket and silenced its second squawk with a swipe of her thumb. "Yeah?"

"Laura just called." Tess. Of course. Janice never used the walkie app. "She wanted to let us know that she called around to all the hospitals and medical facilities. Nada."

"Well that's good. I guess. I mean, good that he's not hurt enough to have checked in. But not so good that we've crossed off one of the best leads."

"Yeah. She sounded pretty upset. Said she and Jake cancelled their plans for dinner with the Prescotts and said to let them know if we hear anything."

"Poor thing." LuAnn's gaze swept the kitchen, snagging on the to-go containers stacked on the counter. "Maybe I'll run some dinner over to them. I don't imagine she feels like cooking."

"That sounds like a great idea. Oh, phone's ringing. Bye."

"I got some chicken noodle ready that her kids should like. What do you think for the grown-ups? Cheddar broccoli? Loaded potato?" Winnie was already reaching for the lidded bowls.

"You're a saint, Winnie Washington." LuAnn shoved the last couple of bites of lettuce into her mouth and moved to help. "Whatever we have most of. I'll pack up some rolls too."

"I'll remind you of my sainthood when I'm ready for a vacation." Grinning, Winnie motioned toward the container of cookies they'd baked Thursday night. "Take some of those too. Can't bring dinner without dessert."

Five minutes later, LuAnn was armed with a bag full of food in one hand and her car keys in the other, heading out the door. She made it all the way to the parking lot before she was stopped by someone calling her name.

Someone masculine and, at the moment, grating. She turned to face Brad but couldn't quite conjure up a smile. Not knowing what he thought of Thorn's disappearance. All she could manage was a lift of her chin.

He smiled without any effort though as he jogged up to her. "Hey there. Wanted to stop by and see if Thorn is back."

"Nope." She turned back to her car and opened the rear door so she could slide the to-go bag onto the floor. "Are you going to gloat about that?"

She spun back around, hackles raised.

Brad's look stopped her. Hurt gleamed bright and biting in his clear blue eyes. "Why would you think that? I told you my *fears* about it, not my *hopes*."

With a sigh, LuAnn's shoulders sagged. "Sorry. We're all a little on edge. And worried. I was just about to run some dinner over to his daughter and her family."

"Wait—his daughter?"

She brought him quickly up-to-date on Laura and Jake Getty. "She's understandably upset, so I'm taking some soup. Want to ride along?"

The half-hearted movement of one corner of his mouth didn't quite attain the title of *smile* again, but it at least seemed to be an acceptance of her peace offering. He nodded and opened her door for her, then moved to the other side of the car.

LuAnn took a moment while he was walking around to breathe a prayer. For answers. For patience. For peace, as her heart filled more and more with worry.

Brad slid into the passenger's side on her silent *amen*.

Neither said anything until she'd nosed her way into traffic. Trying to drive in Marietta this weekend might not have been the smartest choice. But walking with a bag full of soup wasn't exactly practical either.

"So . . ." Brad said with obvious caution once they were on Front Street and moving at a steady snail's pace. "Is the jewelry a safe enough topic? I did some research last night."

Part of her wanted to snap that it wasn't his mystery to research. Or perhaps that they'd done some of their own, thank you very much, and didn't need his help.

But that would be her irritation over his thoughts of Thorn surfacing, not her actual feelings on the subject. Why wouldn't she take any help she could get? She forced her voice to come out upbeat and easy. "Yeah? We did a little bit this morning but didn't have much time to devote to it. What did you find?"

"Well, I remembered seeing something at the mansion that kept niggling me, so I paid a visit to the aunts last night." He angled himself on the seat so he was facing her. "Irene has a rather extensive jewelry collection."

Remembering seeing her toddle into Antoinette's Closet with old clothes and jewelry sprouting from her arms like leaves, LuAnn grinned. "I can only imagine."

"She had something that reminded me of that bracelet. It was white gold and sapphires, not emeralds, but the styles were very similar."

LuAnn lifted a brow and slowed for a gaggle of pedestrians crossing Second Street. "You must have quite a memory for jewelry."

He chuckled, but there was a sad note to it. "Steph wore the set on our wedding day. For our twenty-fifth, we had this giant close-up portrait made from one of our wedding photos—it's hanging in the hallway, where I see it every time I come out of my room. Guess I've looked at it a million or two times. I'd forgotten what colors the pieces were—we had the photo done in black and white—hence the visit to the mansion last night."

"Ah." She didn't know whether to smile over the sweetness or sorrow with him over the loss. She settled for sticking to the topic at hand. "So what do you make of the similarity?"

"Well, that was my question. It could be nothing, but I asked Irene what she knew of that set. She went through an old scrapbook she had from her grandfather and discovered that it was a piece created in the 1860s, modeled after a famous set that had recently gone missing—here in Marietta."

LuAnn sucked in a breath. "From the Belle Arbor plantation in South Carolina, perchance?"

She glanced over in time to see his crestfallen look. "How'd you know that?"

She laughed. "We looked it up this morning and found an article about the missing treasure of Belle Arbor." Her brows suddenly knit. "Wait, so jewelers started copying it? How would we know, then, if we have the real thing or a copy?"

Brad shrugged. "Got me. Though why anyone would hide a copy in the wall..."

"Well, there's that, I guess. Unless they didn't know. We have no idea when it was put there, after all. It could have been when the elevator was installed, in the twenties. Maybe someone had stolen it and stashed it there, thinking to come back for it later." One of those gangsters dining with Al Capone on the *Rufus B II*, maybe. She could imagine one sneaking off the sternwheeler under cover of dark and moonlight, slipping back to the hotel where he was staying…stealing down into the basement in search of a likely hiding place. Maybe the wall had just been built over the bricks, to enclose the elevator, and he took a panel off and…

"Isn't this the Gettys' street?"

"Huh? Oh!" She flipped on her blinker and was grateful for traffic so slow she still had plenty of time to make the right onto Washington Street. "How'd you know where they live?"

He snorted a laugh. "Who do you think sold them the place? I didn't realize she was Thorn's daughter, of course, but they were sure motivated buyers. Great neighborhood, classic Victorian but with modern updates, office and room for a gym for Jake, and priced in the mid two-hundreds."

LuAnn grinned. "What exactly does Jake do, anyway?"

"Um. Something on the computer. Runs some sort of online academy."

She was a bit surprised to realize they'd bought a house here—a not-cheap house, apparently—given Laura and Jake's conversation last night about the agreement being to only spend a year in Marietta. He must be a fairly successful online guy. Or not mind debt. Or have something against renting.

"But apparently, moving from California, they were pleasantly shocked by our real estate prices." He chuckled.

Or that. She scanned the row of tidy Victorians. They were gorgeous, though not necessarily what she would have expected for a young couple used to California style. Then again, maybe they were enchanted by the charm. "Which one?"

"The yellow one with the colorful trim."

"Really." Her brows lifted. If she were to pick out a favorite on the street, that would be it. Something about the touches of green and coral along with the yellow brought posts and railings to life. "It's beautiful."

"It's one of the houses I was going to show you if you ladies hadn't decided on the inn." He flashed his Realtor's smile.

LuAnn parked along the street and cut the engine. "I have a feeling I would have been charmed. But I'm glad we got the inn."

"As are we all." He hopped out while she was stowing her keys and jogged around to get her door for her. She let him help her out and even handed over the bag of soup in deference to his gentlemanly instincts.

But he let her lead the way to the door and ring the bell. She wasn't sure if he was just letting her be in control of her own errand, or if he didn't want to be the one to talk to whichever Getty opened the door.

It was Laura, with an adorable cherub of a baby on her hip. She looked as lovely and put-together as she had last night but with the same crease of worry between her brows. "Ms. Sherill, hi. And Mr. Grimes. Good to see you again."

LuAnn indicated the bag. "Brad's helping me carry—we brought you guys some dinner. I didn't know if you were the type to cook out your worries or the type who didn't want to step foot in the kitchen after a stressful day, but I figured after being on the phone all afternoon…"

"Oh wow. That's so nice. Come in, come in." She held the door wide for them. "Guess you haven't heard from Dad in the last fifteen minutes since I talked to Ms. Wallace, huh?"

"No, I'm afraid not." LuAnn stepped into the foyer and nearly gawked at the gleaming woodwork. "Wow. What a gorgeous home!"

"Oh, thanks. It was in great shape, already restored and updated. Not quite used to all the stairs yet, and there's still a whole room upstairs filled with boxes I haven't unpacked, but I love it." As soon as the door was shut, Laura set the baby down on her feet. The tot immediately folded to her knees and, with a happy squeal, scooted off toward the living room. Laura reached for the bag Brad held out. "This was really so sweet of you. You didn't have to do that."

"Well, we have no shortage of soup and rolls."

"Still." After glancing after her little one, Laura led the way along the short hallway to the kitchen. Aside from papers and a notebook strewn over the table—a phone atop them—the place was pristine. Either Laura had a tendency toward admirable neatness, or they hadn't used the kitchen much in the two weeks since they moved in. Though the assortment of gleaming appliances—mixer, scales, a french press—made LuAnn lean toward the first.

Laura no more than got the bag put into the fridge than that happy squeal accompanied the sound of palms slapping quickly on the floor behind them. LuAnn moved to the side to let the little one by. She couldn't help but grin at the sweet girl. "I think someone followed you, Mama."

Laura chuckled and bent down to scoop her daughter up once more. "She doesn't often let me out of her sight, especially when Noah's not in the room to distract her. Do you, Paisley-poo?"

Paisley's answer was to clap a hand to Laura's cheek and exclaim, "Mumumum. Ma!"

Laura caught the chubby little fingers, kissed them, and then met LuAnn's gaze again. The baby-inspired grin faded back into worry. "I don't know where else to check, Ms. Sherrill."

"You can call me LuAnn, you know." *Ms. Sherrill* felt a bit formal when they were talking about fears for her father. "Where all have you checked already?"

Laura nodded toward the table and its helter-skelter paper collection. "You're welcome to look at my list—and add any place I missed. I haven't been in town long enough to know where all he might go."

"I don't know that I have either." And even though Thorn had done a lot of opening up over the last few months, he also kept a lot locked away. Tory Thornton was a private man—perhaps by nature or perhaps inspired by the judgment he'd endured for the years he chose to live on the street.

When you'd seen people's worst, you didn't often want to show them anything of your own.

LuAnn stepped to the table and looked down at the list written in sure, beautiful pen strokes. The kind of handwriting that would have made grading her in-class papers a dream.

The things she still thought of.

"Looks pretty thorough." She scanned the list again but couldn't think of anything she would added.

Laura pulled out a chair and plopped down onto it, handing Paisley a ring of plastic keys to chew on. "Wish I could take the credit for that, but most of the places were Kip's suggestion." Something flickered across her face as she said it.

LuAnn sent a look to Brad and eased into the chair adjacent to Laura's. "He's a nice kid."

"Yeah. Dad thinks of him as a son, I know." Laura gave a rueful smile. "Stupid to be jealous. But it seems like my life is one long example of coming in second with him."

"I can't think that's true. These last two weeks—we didn't know what was going on, but we'd never seen him so happy." LuAnn reached out to brush Laura's hand with her own. A quiet touch that she prayed would tell this hurting young woman that she wasn't alone.

"It is true." A quiet statement that told LuAnn she couldn't undo three decades of hurt with one touch. "He could have come and seen me any time through the years. My mom never tried to keep me from him. But he never did. Not once. By the time I was old enough to ask, he'd stopped offering excuses. Stopped talking to my mom at all. He just...moved on. Remarried, had another little girl." She squeezed her eyes shut and shook her head. "I never even met my little sister, but for so long I hated her. Hated that she had my dad while I had nothing but this gaping hole and a mother too gun-shy to ever even *try* to find someone else."

Oh, the hurts, old and new, rolling off her. LuAnn leaned a little closer and stroked a hand over Paisley's baby-soft head because it seemed like the best way to reach the heart of the mother. "I know exactly how you feel."

Though Laura's lips didn't say, *"Yeah, right,"* her snort did.

LuAnn offered a crooked, sad smile. "No, really. When I was six, my mom packed us up and left. I never saw my father again. I always wondered why we left, where he was, what he'd done. I remembered this loving, kind man...but if that was true, why did he just vanish from my life?"

Perhaps the memories were old, but they'd clobbered her when she moved back to Marietta. She shook her head. "I didn't learn until just a few months ago what really happened—he'd testified against a union boss with mob ties, and our lives were in danger. He ended up in witness protection. Where he remarried, had another family. I never saw him again and didn't know the truth until this past spring. So yeah—I get it."

Laura sniffed and met her gaze for a fleeting instant. "You seriously went all those years without knowing anything?"

"I did."

Paisley tossed the keys to the ground and lunged for a pen on the table. Laura intercepted her and handed her a spoon instead. "I don't even remember him from before. I was only Paisley's age when he left for Desert Storm. But I don't remember my mom ever once saying anything bad about him in my hearing. She didn't try to poison me against him or anything. But she said, when I was a teenager and asked if maybe it was PTSD or something...she said my dad had a wanderer's heart, that he always had." She looked up, her gaze crashing into LuAnn's. "What if Jake's right? What if this is just him following that pattern, going off in search of something new, something more, something... *better*?"

If that were true, then Tory Thornton wasn't just a wanderer—he was a thief. LuAnn made it a point *not* to look over Laura's head at where Brad leaned against the counter. Instead, she lifted her chin. "There is nothing better, Laura. Nothing better than finding family when you thought you'd lost all your ties to it. Your dad knows that. You, your kids—you're the best thing."

"So why's he gone again?"

"I don't know." The words, whispered, sounded like defeat. But they couldn't be so easily beaten after a mere twenty-four hours of questions. Especially when they had access to the One who had all the answers. "Do you mind if we pray?"

"Oh." Laura shifted on her chair, not meeting LuAnn's gaze. "I, uh. I guess. Can't hurt."

LuAnn smiled a bit as she closed her eyes. "Heavenly Father, we thank You so much for friends and family—for those who gather around us when we need them most, who act as Your hands and feet in our lives. We come before You now on behalf of Thorn. We don't know where he is or what happened or what's going on. We don't know, but we can trust that You have him in Your capable hand. Please minister to him, wherever he is and whatever he needs. We ask for Your guidance, Father, as we look for him. Help us to find him, and give us Your peace in the meantime. It's so hard for us to sit back and not know. To just trust. And so often You ask us to act— show us how we should, and in what ways. Please show us too, Lord, what You want us to learn through this situation." *And use it, somehow, to draw this precious young woman to You,* she added silently. "Amen."

"Amen." The echo came from Brad.

Laura sniffled and was wiping at her eyes when LuAnn opened her own. "Thanks," she said. "I haven't done much praying since at bedtime when I was eight, but that was nice."

"Prayer is nice. More, it works." LuAnn patted Laura's shoulder as she stood. "You'll hear from your dad soon, Laura. I know it."

"I sure hope so."

"You will." There was no way he'd abandon the only family he had left without so much as a word. No possible way. "We'll get out of your hair, but let me know if I can do anything else to help, okay?"

"I will. Thanks, LuAnn."

"Of course." She couldn't resist trying to tuck down a stray wisp of the baby's pale hair. Paisley rewarded her with a four-toothed grin. "Bye-bye, Paisley."

"B-bye," the little one answered, waving at herself rather than LuAnn.

She chuckled and motioned for Brad to precede her toward the door. "We'll show ourselves out."

Laura followed them anyway, waving from the door.

LuAnn and Brad stepped off the porch just as another voice from within reached them. "What were they doing here?" Jake. The door shut before any more of his irritated words could make it out to them, but his displeasure was clear.

Why? Just because he thought of her as Thorn's friend? Because she'd called him on his lie yesterday evening? LuAnn frowned. "I wish I knew why her husband is so set against Thorn."

Brad's hum didn't sound exactly baffled as he walked to the driver's side to open her door. "Well, from where he's standing, LuAnn, Thorn's just someone who keeps hurting Laura. Guess that would sour me if I were him too."

"Then why agree to move here? That's a pretty big step for someone who's so reserved about his wife's father." She folded herself into her seat.

"Not if he really loves his wife and wants to be proven wrong." Brad shrugged and shut the door.

LuAnn sighed while he walked around. Maybe he was right, that Jake's reaction was reasonable. But it still struck her as strange. How set was he, really, against Thorn? Did he regret the move? Want to go back to California? Enough, perhaps, to try to sabotage Laura's blossoming relationship with her father?

But he surely didn't dislike Thorn enough to hurt him. That would require some serious bitterness.

Or… She started the car while Brad climbed in, careful to keep her expression neutral while her mind spun through the possibilities. Or maybe he disliked him just enough to hunt him down for a conversation yesterday. Maybe things got heated, something happened, and Thorn got hurt. Maybe Jake panicked and…

What? She shook that thought away. So far as she knew, Thorn wasn't in any grave danger. She couldn't exactly go around accusing anyone of anything when she had nothing but a bloody rag and a fingerprint to hint at anything having gone wrong.

They were halfway through their five-minute drive before Brad broke the silence with a clearing of his throat. "LuAnn . . . I know you don't want to admit this as a possibility. But if he didn't seek medical help anywhere, we have to assume Thorn isn't all that badly injured. So his disappearance has to be willful. And he obviously left with at least one emerald in his hand, to have dropped it outside. Maybe it's time to face facts and call the police. Report missing jewelry and let them know you think it was Thorn who took it."

"No." Her hands gripped the wheel until she thought she'd leave dents in it. "If we report this, it'll be as a missing person." But that wasn't really hers to do, was it? It seemed like a move Laura ought to make, if anyone were going to.

Because there was another option, even further from what she wanted to believe—that Thorn was simply unable to seek help.

Chapter Seven

LuAnn took in all the color, the noise, the scents of the festival and tried to let it form a good working backdrop for her thoughts. Tried to let the something sizzling through her turn itself into productivity. Tried to think not of the worry, not of the frustration with Brad and Jake, but of where else they could look for Thorn.

Upon arriving back at the inn, she'd announced she was taking a short walk to clear her head, not expecting Brad to follow her into the crowds of festival-goers. He didn't say anything as they walked, and she couldn't decide if that was a mark for or against him just now. He wasn't trying to actively convince her of his theory, she'd grant him that. But he also wasn't asking her to explain her thoughts. He was just there, beside her, occasionally touching a hand to her elbow to steer her through the crowd, but otherwise as silent as her own hope.

When she got back, she'd sit down with Janice and Tess—maybe in the office downstairs, so they could be there if anyone needed them—and insist they contact the current owners of the Belle Arbor Plantation. That, at least, was something they could do. Something they could affect. She had no idea if finding out more about the jewelry could shed any light on the current situation, but at this point something felt a whole lot better to focus on than the nothing they'd found out about Thorn.

"Lulu? Is that you?"

She froze, the voice halting her more than the nickname that she hadn't heard spoken by a man in thirty-odd years. It rang all sorts of long-dormant bells—most of them alarms and sirens and screaming warnings to get far away, as fast as she could.

Her feet obeyed, pivoting around—where she ran smack into Brad. "Yeow!" Slapping a hand over her smarting nose that had become far too violently acquainted with his shoulder, she lost those crucial three seconds of getaway time.

Maybe it didn't matter. Maybe it wasn't the voice she thought it was, and some stranger was just calling to some other Lulu.

"LuAnn Sherrill!"

Or maybe not. Maybe it was just a weekend for nightmares. She squeezed her eyes shut and prayed that if she didn't answer, he would just go away. She stepped to the side of Brad, eyes scanning for the best escape route.

"You okay, LuAnn?"

She ignored Brad and latched her gaze onto an empty stretch of pavement.

Empty until *he* stepped into it, grinning like a snake. "It is you! I thought it must be. Wow, you look great!"

LuAnn lowered her hand from her aching nose and forced a smile. She wasn't coward enough to turn and run after he'd cornered her so effectively. And why should she? He was nothing but a blip from her past.

A particularly painful blip, granted, but that pain had helped shape her into the woman she was. A woman she was proud to be.

Still, she had to swallow before she could force anything past her lips. "Phillip." She wasn't going to lie and say it was good to see him. Nor was she going to dwell at all on how he looked—it was that handsome face, paired with a too-charming tongue, that had taught her those hard lessons to begin with. "How have you been?"

"Good, good." He stepped closer, though he didn't do anything as stupid as try to hug her. He'd always been smart too. "Enjoying retirement. Jill and I have been traveling, exploring." He motioned toward a blonde who had to be fifteen years younger than him, if not more. And who was definitely *not* the wife he'd still had at home while he was charming LuAnn and telling her he was single thirty years ago.

But maybe he'd changed—it had been a long time, after all. Heaven knew *she* had changed plenty. She made a concerted effort to relax a degree. "Your wife?"

"Nah. Girlfriend. Three times is enough for me, thanks."

Or maybe he hadn't changed as much as one would hope.

With a used-car-salesman smile that could have given Bart Sandman a run for his money, Phillip held out a hand to Brad. "You must be Lulu's husband. Phillip Whitman. Lu's old flame."

Brad shook his hand. "Brad Grimes." No correction of their relationship—he must have sensed her unease and decided to leave all that up to her.

He was making it difficult to stay mad at him. But she wasn't going to lie—that would feel like saying she needed a man, when she didn't. "Brad's my Realtor. And my friend. We were just taking a walk before the crowds get any crazier."

"Yeah, it's some festival, huh?" Phillip angled to take it in, showing off a trim profile and hair that still blew just enough in the breeze to look dashing. But it couldn't really still be so dark, could it? Maybe he dyed it. Had to look young for Jill, after all.

She took a breath and said a silent prayer. *Lord, purge me of these thoughts. I don't need to put him down to make myself feel better. He's the past, nothing more.*

Just the man she'd given her heart to so disastrously, before she'd met Jesse.

"We're proud of it," Brad said. It took her a minute to realize he was answering Phillip's observation about the festival. "Have you ever been before?"

"Once, about fifteen years ago. You're actually part of the inspiration for us coming this year, Lu." He grinned while she tried not to gawk. "Saw an article in the Clarksburg paper about how you and the girls bought an old inn and it was opening this weekend. Jill tried to get a room, but they were all booked by the time she got online."

Thank You, Lord, for that! She made sure her smile reflected only normal amounts of joy. "We were full within twenty-four hours of opening reservations."

"I bet. Pretty place—we walked by a couple of hours ago. Do you do tours or anything? Jill said there's a bunch of Underground Railroad connections and junk."

The last thing she wanted was this man meandering through her house, insinuating himself into her present. But he was nothing to her now. And she was a businesswoman. "We will be, but we haven't launched them yet. Tell Jill to keep an eye on our website for the schedule. It should be posted sometime this week."

He nodded, a corner of his mouth turning up in a grin. "Somehow I wasn't surprised to learn you'd bought a place packed with history. How'd you talk Tess and Janice into it?"

"It was Tess's idea, actually," Brad said. His grin didn't look nearly so superior. Just comfortable, friendly.

"Yeah?" The information didn't seem to mean anything to Phillip, who was chuckling. He rapped a knuckle against Brad's arm and leaned in, as if they were part of the same conspiracy. "Anything history or literature and it hooks our girl Lu, right? I always said she only looked twice at me because my last name was Whitman. Had my first name been Walt, she never would have let me get away."

Let him? Did he just say she'd *let him* get away? LuAnn was pretty sure steam was whistling from her ears like an old cartoon. "Phil, even had you been the real Walt Whitman, and acted as you'd done, the only difference would have been that I'd have gotten you to sign a few books before I kicked your sorry behind to the curb." Chin up, she turned away. "I'd better get back to the inn. Enjoy the festival."

Not caring whether Brad followed or not, so long as Phillip didn't, she spun on her heel and marched away, back toward the safe comfort of home. Friends. Something she'd built, that they'd built together, something unstained by memories of her biggest mistake.

"I take it that guy isn't really a good friend?" Brad had, apparently, followed.

LuAnn didn't slow her pace any to accommodate him. He was in fine shape, he could keep up. "No."

"I didn't know what you'd want me to do about the whole husband comment. I hope I didn't—"

"You did fine, Brad." She conjured up a smile and looked at him, where he'd fallen in at her side. "Thanks."

"I don't mean to pry..."

"Smart of you."

He chuckled. "Come on—I'll answer any of your questions about *my* past that you want to know. I'm just asking for a little illumination here. Were you really involved with that guy?"

LuAnn sighed. "A long time ago—I was only a few years out of college. Thought I was in love"—*was* in love, however disastrously that turned out—"and then discovered he was married. The end. But since you're offering your own history—I don't think you ever told me how you and Stephanie met."

He sent her a look that said he knew very well she was trying to change the subject. Still, he played along. Earning himself another point on the LuAnn-o-meter. "Pretty cute story, I think. It was the first really warm day of summer—you know the type, when everyone's outside. Well, I'd decided to walk to my showing that day—one of my first ever. On the way back to the office, I see this woman chasing after a squirrel."

"Chasing a squirrel?" That was enough to make LuAnn grin.

He chuckled at the memory. "I know. I thought at first she must be crazy. Then I heard her yelling, 'Give it back!' The thing had stolen one of her chess pieces. So being the heroic guy I am—and she being quite lovely, as I quickly saw—I offered to help. Never did find the pawn, but we ended up having dinner. I knew by the end of the evening that I couldn't let her get away."

The way his voice softened when he spoke of his late wife, the obvious, bone-deep love he had for her...it was enough to make LuAnn's chest fill. Mostly with respect for this new friend of hers but with a little bit of jealousy too, she had to admit. Not because she wanted him to love her like that but because no one did. Phillip didn't really love anyone but himself. And Jesse, the love of her life, had died two weeks before their wedding, taking with him all her hopes of growing old with someone.

She still missed him. And yes, she missed what never was— those days and months and years spent at his side, shaping their lives into contours that would fit together. Developing a language of inside jokes and memories all their own. Knowing that when he said her name, like when Brad said Stephanie's, everyone could just tell how much he loved her.

"It's one of the great mysteries, isn't it?" She turned her face into the afternoon sunlight, let it warm her and soothe her and remind her of how bright God's love was in a world of shadows and regrets. "How God always leads us exactly where we need to be. Even when we end up taking detours, He guides us back to the right paths. The right people. We might not always recognize those moments at the time, but looking back, His fingerprints are always there. Even the threads we would have avoided on our own end up in His tapestry for our lives."

Brad smiled, soft and comfortable. "You're a smart woman, LuAnn Sherrill."

"Some of the time." With a few notable exceptions. But this, the right-now, the adventure the Inn Crowd was on—this wouldn't be one of them.

"Are we all good with it?" LuAnn lifted her fingers from the keyboard of Tess's laptop and looked over her shoulder at her friends.

Tess gave a decisive nod, even smiling. "I think it hits just the right note. Says we've found information, not that we have the whole set sitting here. Friendly and inquisitive, nothing more."

Janice's eyes were still going over the email LuAnn had composed to Belle Arbor Plantation. "Is it maybe *too* vague? I mean, they might not think it's a serious enough request to even answer right away. Maybe we should say we found *something*."

"If we don't hear back from someone in a reasonable time, we can always call or send a more pointed email." Riffling her fingers through her hair, Tess shrugged. "And it won't break my heart if they don't get back to us until next week. Our points from this morning still stand, you know. This is *not* the weekend to be distracted with this stuff."

As if to prove her point, the bell on the reception desk chimed, pulling her from the room with magnetic force. Her cheery, "Hi, Theresa, what can I help you with?" came through the door well before she could have actually reached the carved bar.

Janice grinned. "I don't know how she does that. It used to take me *weeks* to remember my students' names every year."

LuAnn leaned back in Tess's comfy desk chair and chuckled. "That was the whole point of assigned seats, right? But I guess this is similar—assigned rooms."

"True. Plus she's had plenty of time to learn their names for this weekend. We'll see how she does in a few months, when it isn't so new anymore." Janice pursed her lips and looked back at the email. "I guess it's okay. Tess is right that we can always follow up. Maybe after things quiet down on Monday, we could even call."

"Yep. So we're good then? Send?"

"Send."

LuAnn hit the button and let out a sigh that must have sounded a bit too blustery, given the brows Janice arched.

"You okay, Lu?"

Were it not redundant, she would have sighed again. It had been that kind of weekend thus far. "Phillip's here."

"*What?*" Janice pulled over a straight-backed chair and plunked herself onto it, eyes wide. "Here as in ... "

"In town for the festival, with his girlfriend. Who tried to book a room *here*, but we were filled already."

"Praise God for that." Janice shook her head, eyes still as round as the gorgeous antique doorknobs they'd found for Lilac and Sage. "Did he know this is our place? Yours?"

Nodding, LuAnn closed her eyes. It had been two hours since she'd spun away from him, but she could still feel him there, looking over her shoulder. He'd always made her so annoyingly aware of herself. She'd loved that at first—that just being around him or even thinking about him heightened her senses, made her conscious of everything. But now it made her shudder. It felt more like a ghost story than a romance. Someone always watching, even when no one was there.

"He was all casual, as if this hadn't been the first time we'd seen in each other in over thirty years." Well, not true. She'd seen him in Clarksburg a time or two, but she'd always been able to duck out of sight before he saw her. "And I guess it doesn't matter. Because it has been that long."

"Still. It takes some nerve, showing up out of the blue at a business you know your ex owns, not even bothering to send a warning first. I mean, how hard would it have been to send an email asking if you *minded* if they booked, before trying to? Common courtesy, if you ask me."

Good ol' Janice. Her friend's gusto over the right thing to do brought a smile back to LuAnn's lips. "Phillip was never much for common courtesy, I guess. You know, like telling your girlfriend that you're married."

Janice snorted. "I hope he was fat and bald and wrinkled."

A hoot of laughter slipped from LuAnn's lips before she could stop it. "Janice! I've been praying *not* to think such things!"

"Well, was he?"

"No."

"More's the pity. And I'm sorry, but I'm not sorry. I'm Team Lu here, all the way." No doubt she could say such things without any real venom or bitterness invading her spirit. Unlike LuAnn.

Her smile faded.

Janice scooted closer and reached over to rest her hand on LuAnn's arm. "You okay, sweetie? It can't have been easy, seeing him again, even after all these years."

"It's not that." Not really. She covered Janice's fingers and let her gaze lift to the wall. Painted a soft, butter-yellow, it provided the perfect backdrop to the painting Tess had hung there. The viewer had a perspective from the ground, looking up at a field of wildflowers that were all lifting their faces to the sun.

A reminder that she should do the same—lift her face always toward the Son, like she'd done on the walk home. She had to keep reminding herself of that this evening.

Janice squeezed her arm. "So what is it then? Thorn?"

"Partly. Maybe. Yeah, I guess it is." She let out a long breath and focused on the splash of unmitigated red in the painting—a poppy that stretched up, just to the left of the middle of the painting. "It's just...how do we ever know if we really *know* someone. You know?"

Janice breathed a laugh. "That's a lot of knowing, Miss English Teacher."

She almost said, *You know what I mean*, but stopped herself, and smiled. "Think about it though. I can't believe Thorn would run off with a treasure. And yet... I couldn't believe that Phillip would be cheating on his wife, either. I knew him. I loved him. Six months we were together, and never once did I think, 'Hey, this guy's hiding something.' He fooled me. For half a year, he fooled me."

"All of us." Janice stroked a thumb along LuAnn's forearm. "Which is your point. We've only known Tory Thornton a few months, really. My acquaintance with him before was eight years out of date, and not that deep to begin with. So how do we *know* that we know him?"

"Exactly. It's like all that scandal always in the news—a prominent pastor or leader suddenly found out to have had affairs or harassed women or worse. And no one ever thought he would."

Janice, who would no doubt always be a pastor's wife in her outlook even though she was no longer actively in the role, winced. "Hearing those news stories always hurt my heart. I never wanted them to be true. And surely some weren't."

"But others were—we know that, because they admitted to it."

"Who admitted to what?" Tess said, coming back into the room.

Janice brought her up to speed on their conversation.

LuAnn pushed to her feet and gestured Tess into her chair. She sat without taking her eyes from LuAnn as the story was completed. "Are you okay?"

She waved that off. "I'm fine. Seriously—Phillip is nothing. It's just that it brings up the question of how reliable our judgment ever is." She leaned against the desk and looked toward the door. Not too long ago, Thorn had stood right there, screwing in hinges and testing the strike plate. And now... "I told Laura her dad wouldn't have left her again. And I sure believed it when I said it. But I could be wrong. I could be wrong about him like I was wrong about Phil."

Saying it out loud, hearing her words spoken into the air, solidified them somehow. Made them more likely, less impossible.

And neither of her friends said anything in the wake of them, to chase them away. They just let the words bounce around, shake up their memories, and soak in.

It felt like a long time before Tess looked up again, her brows drawn together. "When Laura checked with the hospital—did she just check for Tory Thornton, or did she give them his description?"

"I don't know. Do you think it matters?" Even as she asked, LuAnn drew her phone out of her pocket.

"It could. I mean, if he's injured, he might not have been able to give them his name. I'd think he'd still have his ID on him, but who knows, right?"

"Right." She pulled up a text and jotted off a quick message.

Janice blew a breath out through her lips, vibrating them. "I sure hope we're wrong. Or that we're not wrong. Wrong to question, not wrong to believe in him. And I sure hope all this comes to nothing. Phillip the Jerk goes home, Thorn shows up with a perfectly reasonable explanation, and we can happily reunite some old jewelry with a family who..."

LuAnn lifted her eyes and lowered her phone, message sent. "Who...?"

Janice tapped a manicured-especially-for-opening-weekend nail on the desk. "What about the journal? Prudence's, I mean. If the jewelry was hidden here, it could have been during her tenure. Maybe we should check and see if she says anything about it."

"It's possible." Tess rolled her chair toward her desk. "I don't recall seeing anything about it offhand—I think I'd remember mention of jewelry—but who knows? Maybe if we read it with this in mind, we'll find something. Let me pull out the pages we copied." Tess bent over and opened a deep file drawer.

Da-la-ling, sang LuAnn's phone. The text message chime. She swiped the screen and saw that Laura had answered her already—no doubt her phone wasn't far from her hand right now. "Laura says, 'I asked by name and also if a man in his late fifties with a gray ponytail had been seen. All said no to both questions.' Well, then."

"Well, then indeed." Janice stood. "I'm going to go play. Clear my head."

"Have at it." LuAnn loved listening to her friend play any of the many instruments she knew—and loved the endless hours of listening pleasure they'd had since Christ Fellowship had donated the baby grand to them. Janice had been so thrilled that the beautiful old piece wasn't just being sold or scrapped, and they all benefited from her joy.

A minute later, the beautifully embellished strains of a familiar hymn wove their way through the air.

"Here we go." Tess pulled a stack of papers from the drawer.

LuAnn drifted out of the office, into the parlor, lured by the music. She still loved walking in here this time of day, when the southern-facing windows let in golden evening light. Her gaze skimmed over each piece of furniture they'd collected—the couches and chairs clustered around the fireplace, the Victorian urns with big leafy plants in them, the wall-to-wall bookcases and reading nook in the back, which also hosted the piano.

Janice hadn't bothered with a book of music—how she memorized such intricate pieces but supposedly couldn't memorize students' names was a bit of a mystery—but played without a falter.

At the start of the third verse, LuAnn came in with the alto line. "'And when I think of God, His Son not sparing, sent him to die, I scarce can take it in...'"

Within a few words, Janice had picked up with the soprano line, and LuAnn wasn't surprised when Tess abandoned her printing and joined them in time for the second line, filling out their little trio. It wasn't exactly the performance they'd talked about starting on Friday or Saturday nights at the inn, but it felt good. Right. To be spontaneous, to praise their Lord even now, to lift up their voices in worship of Him.

How great Thou art. Even when she couldn't trust her own judgment, she could know that He was great. So much greater than their worries, their cares. Her soul lifted as they sang, her chest expanding with the joy of making harmony with these friends—friends that she knew, who had sung with her through years of both good and bad.

Then sings my soul. Yes, her soul sang, and in singing, some of those worries eased. Just by focusing on God, the other stuff shifted in perspective and didn't look quite so terrible.

They were halfway through the last chorus when an enormous crash from the basement silenced them all.

CHAPTER EIGHT

They took the steps to the basement at a pace that probably wasn't all that safe. But LuAnn's thoughts were far from the risks of falling, and fully set on getting to the basement before whoever was down there had a chance to escape.

The lights actually came on when they flipped the switch, giving credence to the theory of faulty wiring somewhere. But then they shut off again when LuAnn was halfway down the steps.

The sudden fall of darkness brought a screech from Janice. Okay, to be honest, they all screeched. Janice just screeched a little longer than LuAnn or Tess, who had taken the lead.

Not that a little thing like complete darkness could stop them for long—especially on steps they'd climbed up and down so many times with their arms full of boxes. With something that sounded like a growl, Tess moved downward again. LuAnn was right behind her, on flat ground when Tess switched the work lights on.

Janice had remained firmly in place on the stairs. Once a bit of light reached her, though, she drew in a deep breath and followed, despite being none too fond of the basement in general. And well beyond none too fond when there were crashes and darkness, LuAnn knew.

"Well, no wondering what the noise was." Tess, from by the still-gaping wall beside the elevator, pointed to Thorn's toolbox. It rested on its side, spilling tools a fair distance onto the floor. Some had even made it as far as the elevator gate, which had no doubt produced that reverberating bang.

Janice backed up a step. "Wait, so...someone was obviously down here."

"Uh-huh." LuAnn stared at the box. It was heavy—she knew, she'd tried to lift it before. Really heavy. It would have taken a lot of force to knock it over like that.

"So why are *we* down here? With an intruder?"

"We don't know it was an intruder," Tess said, pacing toward the exterior door. "It could have been..."

Apparently her imagination ran out of options. LuAnn looked up, keeping her face in what she hoped was a casual expression. "Robin. It could have been Robin, trying to make herself useful. You know how she is. I mean, she startled me and Tess down here just last night, but it was perfectly innocent."

"Right. Robin." Janice still gripped the railing of the stairs. "So...where is she?"

"She must have..." Appearing at a loss for words, Tess motioned to the door. "You know. Gone outside. The door isn't quite latched."

Right. Because after making a racket that she knew would scare the socks off all of them, Robin would just run away rather than rushing up to assure them all was well. Even LuAnn's active imagination couldn't picture that one. She walked over to stand beside Tess, where she could see the door cracked open, and tried to tell her scalp not to prickle.

But someone had been down here. Someone who didn't belong, or they wouldn't have run off like that.

Then the questions started hammering at her brain as her gaze drifted back to those scattered tools. "What if it was Thorn?" She didn't want to say the words, and so they came out quiet and hesitant. "What if...what if he realized he'd left the bracelet and came back looking for it?"

Silence answered her, louder than any reprimands could have. She wished her friends would declare the possibility absurd and point out something far more logical. But they said nothing. And in that awful silence, dread found a place in her stomach and rooted there.

It couldn't be true, that fear she'd spoken. But...what if it was?

Sleep had been as elusive as answers. Eventually, an hour earlier than usual, LuAnn gave up and rose, deciding it was a good morning for a cup of steaming tea, a blanket, and a soft chair. After breakfast she and Tess would head to church while Janice manned the inn—to be traded off on other Sundays. But for now, she'd soak in some quiet time. Maybe read a chapter or two of a good book after her devotions. Something to take her far from the inn for an hour, in thought if not in actuality.

Cup of Pomegranate Delight in hand, she opened her sitting room window to let in the autumn-tinged air and snuggled into the chair with a blanket. The temperature didn't demand it, though there was a blessed touch of coolness to the air. But her heart did.

Journal and pen resting on one wide arm of the chair, she balanced her Bible on the other and opened it to where she'd left off yesterday. Matthew 7.

"Do not judge, or you too will be judged."

She drew in a breath. She wasn't judging. She was wondering, and she was fearing, and she was hoping. But then, *judge* here didn't mean that she wasn't to see things clearly—in the Epistles, Paul was pretty clear that the church needed to be wise, and to know people by their fruits. If Tory Thornton wasn't the man they thought he was, then they needed to know that. To know, but not to judge. *Judge* here, she was pretty sure, meant something more like *condemn*. Sentence, perhaps, in a legal sense. That wasn't hers to do. She had to recognize right from wrong, but who was she to punish someone for it?

She jotted down her reflections on that section, only to pause again in verse seven. Such familiar words. *"Ask and it will be given to you; seek and you will find; knock and the door will be opened to you."*

She held her pen over the lines on her notebook. These verses certainly didn't mean that every answer to every question under the sun would be given to every person who asked. So what would be given?

She took another sip of her fragrant tea and let the words swim through her mind while the hot liquid swam over her tongue. Sometimes it was so easy to just accept the pat, easy answers to these verses she'd been hearing and seeing and memorizing since she was a kid. To hum the melody to the song they'd been put to.

The key, I think, she wrote, *is in what we're asking for and seeking. Are we looking for Him? For His truth? His understanding, His wisdom? God won't withhold those from us. I want to say too that He won't withhold what we need . . . but I guess that depends a lot on the definition of "need." There are people in the world who starve to death. Who are killed by persecution. Who never learn to read or have any basic schooling. These are things that our culture would deem necessary—food, safety, education. But if God doesn't always grant those, they must not be the things Jesus means here.*

But nothing touches me more than hearing about the faith of martyrs or how loudly people praise Him when He is literally all they have. They've sought Him, and they've found Him. They've knocked, and a door to peace is opened before them despite physical lacks.

Lord, please give me that. Give me that confidence in You, no mater how not confident I am in the things of this world and the people around me.

She finished the chapter and sat for a moment, warm cup cradled in her hands and gaze focused on the sky and rooftops visible from her window. It was still early—the sky was just beginning to turn pink with dawn. Plenty of time for a chapter of a novel. She got up and slid her Bible and notebook onto her desk. She selected a book from the small shelf against the wall and then, after a moment's indecision, grabbed her laptop as well. She'd check her email, maybe see if she could unearth anything else about the jewelry. Then read a bit.

Her personal email yielded nothing but the usual newsletters she'd subscribed to and a note from a former student letting her know he'd had an article accepted in a major magazine, and it was all thanks to her—the sort of letter that always made her smile.

Then she clicked into her business email—the one she had listed on the inn's website—and her smile froze.

From: Phillip Whitman
Subject: Good to See You

For a moment she just stared at that name, her finger hovering over the Delete button. Getting rid of it without even looking at it might be the safer thing, but then, it was a little bit cowardly too, wasn't it? And for goodness' sake, she was a grown woman of a certain age. She was perfectly capable of reading an email from an old boyfriend without letting it get to her.

She double-clicked on it before she could change her mind.

I'm glad I ran into you this afternoon, Lulu. Sorry if I put my foot in my mouth with that "letting me get away" comment. Some things never change, and my propensity for tasting shoe is apparently one of them. Obviously, looking back, I don't blame you for ending things—I was the one in the wrong there, and though it probably doesn't mean anything to you now, I did take your advice back then. I focused on making my marriage work. We lasted another ten years before she left me because I couldn't give her children. Not exactly something I could help.

I know, I know, you didn't ask for my life story. But your opinion always mattered to me, and I guess I wanted you to know that I saw my mistake and tried to fix it. I tried to be a better man. Doubt I ever achieved the level you expected of me, but I tried.

I hope life has treated you well. You certainly look great. I was pretty impressed when Jill told me about the inn, and I realized it was you and the girls. I don't know too many people who are still best friends with their group from college. But then, you were always loyal to a fault, and certainly easy to be friends with. The article we read said a little about how Janice's husband just passed away last year, and Tess's a while ago. Tell them I said I'm sorry. I know that has to hurt.

Well, I won't ramble any longer. I just wanted to apologize if I was a jerk this afternoon and assure you that I'm proud of you. Not that you asked for my opinion, but there you have it. My unsolicited approval. You're doing an impressive thing. Be well, Lulu, and good luck with your inn. I hope it exceeds all your expectations.

LuAnn let out the breath she'd been holding and blinked a few times to be sure she was seeing the words clearly. But there they were. A surprisingly human letter from someone she'd come to think of as lower than human. Nothing rude, nothing too charming. Just...honesty. And a bit of humility. And...well, and proof that she really was bad at judging a person. Though she wasn't sure how many times she could mess up in her thinking about the *same* person.

She debated for a moment, gnawing on her lip as she rested her fingers on the keys and then withdrew them again. Then, with a cluck of rebuke at herself for putting too much thought into what should simply be politeness, she hit Reply. She wouldn't write much. Short and sweet. Well, not too sweet. But short and polite.

Thanks, Phil. For the apology and the well-wishes. I guess I was just surprised to see you like that, so I didn't exactly behave with all the good manners I should have. I'm sorry for that. I hope you and Jill enjoy the rest of the festival and all your retirement travels.

There. She mentioned Jill, which surely was a clear statement that she wasn't trying to strike up anything more personal with the reply. She didn't start rambling on about their goals for the inn, as she too often did to friends who made the mistake of mentioning it. Just a polite reply. She typed her name—LuAnn, not Lulu—and hit Send.

Satisfied, she stood to slide her laptop back on her desk and had just settled again to crack open her book when a light tap sounded on her open door. She looked up to see Tess, *her* laptop in hand and her eyes glued to the screen. "Lu...you're not going to believe this."

LuAnn slid a bookmark into page one. "What is it?"

"We heard back from the owner of Belle Arbor."

"Already? That was quick." She motioned Tess over and made room in the wide chair.

Still in her bathrobe, her hair a mess that Fully Awake Tess would never tolerate, she perched on the arm of LuAnn's chair and held the laptop so the screen was visible. "McKenna Garrison is apparently her name—and she's coming here."

"She's *what?*" Thinking maybe Tess's eyes were still too bleary from not having coffee yet, LuAnn angled the screen down a bit more.

"Coming. Here. To talk to us in person."

I happen to be coming through your area this week, the email said.

LuAnn let out a sound that was half snort, half laugh. "Just *happens* to be coming through? Who ever just *happens* to be coming through Marietta from South Carolina? She does know this is Marietta, *Ohio* and not Georgia, right?"

"She says she's on her way to Cleveland. Quite a coincidence isn't it?" Still looking more than a little shocked, Tess ran a hand through her wayward hair.

"Hmm." The question in her mind was whether this was God ordering it all perfectly...or whether Ms. McKenna Garrison was perhaps going out of her way to see them and glossing that over. Though why? "Our email was so vague though. She couldn't know we have the jewelry here."

"We don't—not much of it." Tess's fingers dropped to squeeze at the bridge of her nose. "If she realizes we have the bracelet and that Thorn is missing, she could jump to the same conclusion as Brad about him taking the rest. And as the rightful owner, she could get the law involved."

LuAnn's stomach tightened. Laura had likely reported him missing by now . . . but the police looking for a missing person was a bit different from them hunting one suspected in a crime. "Oh dear."

"You can say that again." Tess stood once more, balancing the laptop in her arms. "It seems she's going to show up on Tuesday though—there was no question in that email other than what time would work best for us to meet with her. So we'd better just figure out how much we're ready to tell her."

LuAnn sighed. "Why are discoveries in this place never just simple and fun?"

Tess followed her own snort of laughter out the door. "Now *that's* the question! I'm getting in the shower. Then I'll help in the kitchen however you need me."

"'Kay." Only after LuAnn yelled her reply did it occur to her that maybe Janice was still in bed and wouldn't appreciate their volume on this Sunday morning. She rose to go and check and, if necessary, apologize . . . or else to let her know about the emails that had come in that morning.

But when she peeked into Janice's sitting room, she found her wrapped in her favorite sweater, standing by the window and staring blankly out. From the partial-profile view she had of her face, LuAnn could see that tears had left a glistening track down her cheeks.

"Hey. What's wrong?" Speaking in a hush that early-morning tears always demanded, LuAnn bustled in to put an arm around her.

Janice sniffled and leaned into her. "Just a bad dream. Or a dream that should have been good. Lawrence preaching, me at the keys of the baby grand, ready to play the recessional. But then when he should have been saying an amen to the closing prayer, it was silent. And I looked over, and there was his coffin, and..."

"Oh, sweetie." LuAnn tugged her closer. There weren't words to make something like that better, to make the taunting images of a dream just disappear. So she held Janice and said a silent prayer that the Lord's comfort would be poured out like a balm on her spirit.

"I'm glad I'm the one who has to stay here this morning. I don't think I could stand to go in there right now and see all the changes Pastor Ben and Paige have made. I couldn't do it." She sniffled again and splayed a hand over her heart. "Most of the time I'm okay. You know I am. But then there are moments when it's just like...like there's a hole here."

"Of course there is. And there's supposed to be." LuAnn rubbed a hand up and down Janice's arm. "We're supposed to hurt when we lose people we love. Wasn't it Lawrence who said that sin is like a nail through us? That when we repent, the nail is taken out, but the hole is still there? I think grief is the same way. We're left with holes. We miss them, and that doesn't just stop or go away."

Janice's lips trembled. "But God's supposed to fill the holes, isn't he? I'm pretty sure Lawrence said *that* too."

"Maybe. With sin, certainly. But the grief...I don't know. Jesus himself wept in grief at the loss of a friend. It's natural. And maybe it's beautiful." She touched a finger to the intricate design in Janice's favorite sweater. "Like this. Lacework. It's the holes that make it special. That make it a work of art. Maybe we're the same way. God's lacework."

Those trembling lips tugged up, and a small chuckle even escaped. Janice wiped her face. "Look at you, speaking my language. Lacework." She drew in a deep breath, straightened her shoulders, and nodded. "I like that. God's lacework. Making us into the people He wants us to be, not *despite* those holes in our hearts, but *because* of them."

"Exactly." LuAnn gave Janice one more squeeze and stepped away. "You need coffee. Let me go put a pot on, and when you're ready to come out, I'll tell you about the email Tess just showed me."

Janice nodded again. "Thanks, Lu."

"Another day, you'll no doubt do the same for me." With a little smile, LuAnn turned and left Janice's sitting room.

She headed for their shared kitchen and went about putting a pot of coffee together without really needing to think about it, which let her mind wander back to her friends and emails and unexpected visitors.

Maybe this McKenna person's coming would be a good thing and not just another question mark. Maybe it was God bringing order from this new chaos.

But if so, why did the thought of meeting her leave LuAnn with a sick feeling in her stomach?

CHAPTER NINE

LuAnn wasn't sure if it was the short auburn pixie cut, the Minnie Mouse bow, or the double stroller that caught her eye first, but when she realized that the two young women on the sidewalk were Laura Getty and Emma from Antoinette's Closet, she zipped her car into the nearest parking spot.

Tess all but screeched her protest. "What are you doing? We have to get back! The lunch crowd will be in full swing, and you *know* how nervous Janice was over checking everybody out today. I need to make sure—"

"It's Laura and Emma." LuAnn waved a hand in the general direction of the sidewalk and put the car in park.

Tess didn't look particularly appeased. "You have a phone. Just call her when we get home. I have to—"

"This will only take a minute. And we're practically home anyway." She unbuckled her seat belt and opened the door.

"In which case, you won't mind if I just drive the last thirty seconds and check on Janice, and you can walk the last few feet." Tess unbuckled too, and opened her door.

It was more than a few feet, but LuAnn was wearing sensible flats in which she'd probably walked miles in the school hallways. She left the keys in the ignition. "Go for it. I'll only be a few minutes behind you, O Impatient One."

"Take your time, O Distracted One." Looking more than a little gleeful over abandoning her, Tess scurried in behind the wheel and promptly pulled out of the parallel parking spot.

LuAnn rolled her eyes and turned to go after Laura and Emma. Only when she saw them leaning in, exchanging words they apparently didn't want to say at normal volume, did she stop to think that this might be an intrusive way of touching base. Laura and Emma looked oblivious to the world around them as they continued toward her, Laura pushing the stroller.

Had she ever heard how they knew each other? If so, she couldn't recall. Thorn had mentioned at one point that Emma was his only real link to Laura, but now that she paused to think about it, it was a little odd. So far as she knew, Emma had grown up here in Marietta. And Laura's mom had moved them to California when she was just a baby.

Going for the casual approach, LuAnn started walking toward them. Maybe they'd look up as she neared. If not, she could just say hello and see if they paused. If they only waved and kept going, she wouldn't keep them. She'd just duck into Jeremiah's Coffee House, grab a pick-me-up for herself, Tess, and Janice, and then walk to the inn. Then text or call Laura later. Not a big deal.

But the women did in fact look up as she neared, and they both smiled. Laura brought her stroller to a halt—both of her kids were asleep in it—and said, "Hey, LuAnn. Have you met my cousin?"

Cousin. That made sense, then, as to why the girls had kept in touch when living across the country. LuAnn nodded and smiled at Emma. "Sure have. Her store was one of the first places we went shopping when I moved back. How have you been, Emma? I didn't realize you guys were cousins."

"Distantly. Our moms are." Emma's smile looked strained. "And I was great until I heard about Thorn vanishing. He wouldn't just do that. You can't think he would."

LuAnn held up her hands. "I don't think so either." Much. Or didn't *want* to think so. She transferred her gaze to Laura. "No word from him since yesterday, I take it?"

Laura shook her head. The two women certainly didn't look like they were related, though that was thanks to their very-different styles as much as to the contrast between their hair colors and hairdos. "I filed a missing person report this morning. I didn't know what else to do."

LuAnn's chest ached for her. And for Thorn. And a bit for herself, and everyone else who was left wondering. "I think that was probably smart."

Emma pursed her red lips. "I've been trying to convince her that she should tell her mom what's going on."

"I *will*." Laura didn't exactly sound eager to do it. She heaved a sigh and brushed her bangs to the side. "I just...I don't want to give her any reason to think he's falling into the same old patterns if this is something else. You know? She was leery enough of us moving out here to be near him. I mean, she wanted me to get to know him, but she was afraid I'd just get hurt. And so now…" Laura focused her watery eyes on the sidewalk.

LuAnn rested a hand on her shoulder. "It sounds like your mom's a fair lady with a pretty open mind. And I know she'd want to be there for you."

"Yeah." Laura's shoulders sagged. "I'll give her a call." She tilted her head and made a show of taking in LuAnn's dress and shoes. "I guess you were coming from church, huh? You go the same place Dad does?"

"Right on both counts." Though Thorn, of course, hadn't been sitting in his usual seat—and more than one person had come up to ask them where he was this weekend, claiming Thorn had promised he'd call or help or…

She hadn't known what to say. Even now, she kept replaying her answers, trying to come up with what she *should* have said. Something that would have been better than *I don't know. We've been wondering the same thing.*

She was still coming up blank.

Movement behind Laura and Emma caught LuAnn's eye, bringing her gaze up just in time to see a sliver of someone disappearing beyond the row of buildings. She wouldn't have thought anything of it, except that there was something familiar about this person.

Thorn? That's who sprang to mind. But of course, that was ridiculous—wasn't it? No doubt it was just inspired by the conversation. Far more likely that it was some other man in boots and jeans—no shortage of those around—ducking through the alley as a shortcut.

Even so, she couldn't fight the urge to go take a quick peek. She smiled again. "I won't hold you up. Let me know if you need anything, okay, Laura?"

"Yeah." Sounding more than a little down, Laura offered a faded smile of her own and pushed the stroller forward. "Your soup was delicious, by the way—and when we met Emily and Scott for breakfast, they said the inn was amazing."

"Thanks." On a normal day, that praise would have made the sun shine a little brighter. Just now, LuAnn filed it away for later and set off down the sidewalk as if she'd been headed this way for some purpose other than talking to Laura.

And she did have another purpose, now. Striding forward at a brisk pace, she was soon at the mouth of the alley beside Mahone Tire Service, looking around for that familiar figure.

For a Sunday, there were an awful lot of people out— the festival was winding down, but with the car show and boat race still going, it was far from over. And filled with people who fit the same basic description as Thorn. She saw no fewer than seven men who could have been responsible for the movement that caught her eye. Boots, jeans, a flash of a dark shirt. And none of them looking suspicious, as they surveyed and laughed over a few vintage cars parked along the street. Even the alley itself was bursting with people using it as a way to get from Front Street to Post Street.

LuAnn drew in a deep breath and came to a halt at the corner. *Lord, open my eyes to anything You want me to see.* She stilled, let her senses soak in all the movement like her skin soaked in the sun beating down.

She heard the coo of pigeons as they scrambled about for the crumbs and popcorn dropped by lunching tourists. Smelled the kettle corn from the festival mingling with the heavenly scent of pizza from Over the Moon, just behind her. Ignored the corresponding growl of her stomach. Let the ebb and flow of the crowd swim across her vision.

It reminded her, in a way, of the high school where she'd taught for so long. How many times had she stood beside her door and watched all those kids push through the halls? So set on beating everyone else to that prime real estate of space in the hallways, even though getting to their next class was never top priority. It was about seeing and being seen, flirting and taunting, avoiding or finding that friend or enemy sure to be lurking around the lockers.

And now, like then, homing in on one particular pair of jeans to find one particular person in the crowd was part skill and part the work of her subconscious.

There, emerging again onto Front Street, heading back in the direction he'd been going before the duck into the alley.

LuAnn swallowed and let out a breath. Not Thorn. But there *was* something similar in the way this man held himself, the way he moved. A rigidness to his spine. The posture he maintained while he carried himself. It was something she'd noticed about Thorn as he gained confidence over the summer—the hunch of the homeless man disappeared, replaced by the confidence that always reminded her he'd been in the military.

Maybe this man had been too. That could account for it.

She angled back toward Jeremiah's Coffee House, keeping the stranger in her sights. He looked familiar from more than what he had in common with Thorn. Wasn't he one of their guests at the inn? The man who'd shown up on Friday when his reservation hadn't started until last night?

"What is his name?" she murmured to herself as she fell in behind him. Bitner? Bishop? *Bricker.*

No wonder he'd looked familiar. She'd poured him a cup of coffee this morning in the café before she and Tess left for church.

Mr. Bricker wasn't ambling along like most of the visitors filling the streets, though. He was walking with purpose, striding, obviously in a hurry. Maybe he was just realizing that the boat race began in five minutes, and he didn't have much time to get there. Or that a band he wanted to hear would be going on. Maybe—

He stopped again, abruptly, and turned toward the glass windows of the store beside him. The Moose Lodge. Not exactly a shop or restaurant to claim his attention so fully. LuAnn ambled along behind him, skimming the crowd with her gaze. Her breath caught when she realized that Emma and Laura were still in view—and that *they* had stopped to peer into Twisted Sisters Boutique.

As she watched, they moved on, turning left onto Butler Street. And Mr. Bricker started walking again.

LuAnn kept her own pace even. Was he following them? But that made no sense. Why would a stranger in town for the festival be following two young women?

But he'd said he was a friend of Thorn's. Maybe he knew Laura was his daughter. Or thought she might be and was trying to figure it out without coming right out and asking her. She couldn't exactly accost him and interrogate him just for being on the same street, so she pushed into Jeremiah's.

The line was ridiculous, but her heart was now set on a caramel latte, so she took her place at the end and pulled out her phone. She couldn't accost a guest for being on the street, but she *could* tip Laura to his presence, just in case it wasn't entirely aboveboard.

Hey, just remembered. One of our guests this weekend mentioned being an old friend of your dad's. Marshall Bricker. I doubt he could be any help, but I thought I'd mention it. Just saw him on Front Street.

Satisfied that she'd done what she could there, LuAnn settled down to the serious business of waiting for coffee.

Half their guest rooms were empty again. Janice had apparently managed the checkouts without too much trouble, and Tess seemed happy as a clam with how their system was working. LuAnn stripped the sheets from the bed in Sunshine and Daisies and tossed them onto the floor, glad she hadn't returned to any chaos or catastrophes. They'd enjoyed their coffee and a light lunch together, and now they were each going about their daily tasks.

She snapped the set of fresh sheets out and wondered how long it would take her to regret accepting laundry as her daily task. Not that she minded yet, but carrying all the sheets and towels up and down those stairs would likely get old pretty fast. And at the moment, she wasn't even going to think about the elevator.

Humming as she worked, she'd soon gathered all the linens from this floor and carried them down the multiple flights of stairs to the laundry machines in the basement.

She did a fair job, she thought, of keeping her focus on the task at hand as long as said task demanded it. Laundry separated, lights in, correct amount of detergent, and so on. But once she closed the lid on the water streaming into the washer, she turned around and let the basement command her attention.

They'd picked up the tools that had been scattered last night, all of them uneasy the entire time. They'd dead bolted the door to the outside. But then, rather than try to discover anything more, they'd let Janice hurry them back up the stairs.

Now though, LuAnn looked around with more care, walking slowly back and forth across the floor, eyes scanning every inch of the floor. Someone was down here last night, that was obvious. And she would like to know who. Because while she couldn't dismiss the possibility that it had been Thorn—which raised one question but at least made her pretty certain they weren't in any physical danger—she also couldn't deny the possibility that it was someone else.

It could be something innocent. A guest who was curious about that hidden door that they kept open and wanted to see the basement—one, perhaps, even interested in renting it when it was ready for events in a few months. Someone could have just been meandering around, kicked the toolbox, and then panicked at the loud noise.

It could have been someone snooping around looking for the hidden tunnel—a history buff who got a thrill from poking around places where they didn't belong. Harmless.

It could have been that ghost who had tried so hard to scare them away from buying the place. Lips twitching up, LuAnn nudged the toolbox with her toe. It didn't budge. No way could Brad's ancient great-aunt—aka the ghost—have managed to move that thing. So she could safely cross off any faux-supernatural apparitions.

She stepped over to the open elevator, and frowned. There, caught in the bottom of the grate on the outside was something small, roundish, brown, and very much out of place. She bent down and picked it up.

A pinecone. Why in the world would there be a pinecone down here? They didn't have any pine trees by the inn. Certainly not any that had tiny little cones like this—she'd have noticed, because this itsy bitsy thing was adorable. It in fact reminded her of...

Dragging in a breath, she bounded up the stairs.

She found Tess in the café, laughing with Winnie as they wrapped silverware—something the servers usually did, but they'd been shorthanded today just as they had been yesterday.

"Hey. What does this look like to you?" LuAnn approached her friends with the tiny pinecone held between two fingers.

Winnie arched her brows, her lips in a teasing smile. "That's what we in these parts call a pinecone, Miss Lu."

LuAnn stuck her tongue out at Winnie.

Tess took it from her fingers and examined it more closely. "It's not just a normal pinecone. It has a clearcoat and glitter on it. It's one of the ones we used for decoration in Woodsmoke and Pine."

"That's what I thought!" LuAnn motioned toward the stairs. "It was in the basement. Caught in the elevator door."

"How would it have gotten there?" Frowning, Tess angled toward the basement door, as if staring at it would make the answer appear. "Maybe stuck in the sheets or towels when you took the laundry down?"

"Maybe." LuAnn hadn't honestly thought of that. "But I didn't see it down there when we were looking for more of the jewelry."

"We could have missed it." Tess set it on the table beside the silverware.

"Or..." LuAnn lifted her brows, waiting for one of them to make the connection.

Winnie rolled another knife and spoon together in a napkin.

Tess reached for another set. "Or?"

"Or whoever was down there last night could have dropped it. Who's staying in that room?"

"That'd be me."

At the masculine voice, they all spun toward the front, where Marshall Bricker stood, holding a baseball cap in his hands and looking half apologetic and half determined. Janice edged into view behind him.

He cleared his throat. "I'm sorry I frightened you ladies last night with that crash. I heard Laura Thornton saying on Friday that her father was working down there and then took off, and I...well, I just wanted to take a look. When I knocked over the toolbox, I panicked."

She'd had *that* much right in her thoughts, anyway. Still. She had no trouble putting her English Teacher face on and staring down this giant of a man, hands on her hips. "Now why in the world would you leave us to wonder if we had an intruder?"

"And what did you expect to find?" Tess had her teacher face on too.

"I don't rightly know." He looked sheepish, but it melted away into an expression far closer to sorrow, undermined in steel. "But seeing how it looks like Thorn has skipped town, I felt I ought to come forward. And tell you...well, tell you there are some things about him you likely don't know. Things that might make you as unsettled about having him in your basement as having a stranger down there."

Janice took another step into the café, a thundercloud over her face. "I highly doubt that, Mr. Bricker. We know Thorn's history."

Mr. Bricker turned a bit to include Janice, his eyes as hard as flint. "So you know, then, about the larceny charges that nearly landed him in Leavenworth?"

Tess groped for a chair. Janice washed pale. And LuAnn held her breath, already wishing unsaid whatever Marshall Bricker was about to divulge.

CHAPTER TEN

Marietta, Ohio
May 1862

She didn't trust him. Prudence tried to chalk it up to her frustration with Tilla, but it was more than that. As she slid a slice of pie onto the crude wooden table before the elegant man, she knew it was more than that.

He was white, he was rich, he was heir to a slaveholding plantation, and the whispers she'd heard around town when she eased his name into conversation had brought questions and doubts. And those had been from lips she trusted.

Lewis Humphreys was handsome, and he gazed at Tilla with moon eyes, to be sure. But Prudence wasn't entirely sure which side of the war he was on. And she wasn't exactly pleased that Jason had invited him into their home.

But then, Tilla had left them little choice.

"Tell them, Lewis," Tilla said, reaching for his hand rather than for her fork. "Tell them what my father said. You were there."

Prudence felt stiff as a board as she passed a piece of pie to Jason, now that their guests had theirs. He sent her a glance that said more than his lips could. He was wary too. And glad that they'd sent Moses to spend the night with Friends. He would have fun, playing with the little boys near his own age that he usually only saw at Meeting on the Sabbath.

And he'd be safe, if this was a trap.

Prudence sat at the table in her plain kitchen, rhubarb pie before her but with no appetite whatsoever. Still, she dolloped a bit of cream onto it and passed the dish to Tilla. She would pretend that all was well.

Lewis Humphreys nodded and wove the fingers of his left hand through Tilla's. "I was. He promised the jewels to her, ma'am. Sir. Said that he couldn't give her much else, as it would be needed to run Belle Arbor, but that those should go to her. They always went to the daughter of the family when she married—he only had them because his only sister died in infancy. And he had no other daughter to vie for them."

Tilla beamed at Prudence and Jason. Hopeful and young and seemingly innocent. But was she? "You see? I didn't steal them. I promise you I didn't—I wouldn't. They were mine."

Jason chewed his pie, slow and thoughtful, then took a sip of his coffee before looking at their guests. "And thy father's will, Tilla? What did it say about the jewels?"

The night was heavy and dark, hotter than it should be on the first of May. Thunder rumbled in the distance—not surprising given the green tinge to the twilight that had just passed. Her lamps cast the room in a cheerful glow, but

Prudence felt the electricity of the approaching storm in her veins more than the peace of her kitchen.

Lord, give us Thy wisdom, she prayed silently.

Tilla pursed her lips and dropped her gaze to the table. "I don't know. They wouldn't let me in for the reading—they wouldn't let any of the slaves hear. He could have freed us all, and we'd never know it."

"His lawyer would know." Lewis cut off a generous bite of pie and let the cream drip onto his plate. "I can contact him."

Tilla shook her head. "His lawyer is a young man—the new master's oldest friend—and a fervent Confederate. He is only back at home because of an injury. I have no doubt that even if my father had made allowances for us, Mr. Mullins would say nothing if the family wished him to be silent."

Prudence rested a hand on the table. A plea, silent but firm, if they cared to see it as such. "I mean no disrespect, Tilla. Nor am I saying I question that thee did not steal the jewelry." Though she did—she must. "But the question is irrelevant. Even if thee are innocent, even if thee can prove with a will they are thine, that will not help thee now. If the family thee escaped know thee took the jewels, they will pursue. Far more enthusiastically than if it were only thee thyself gone missing. They will enlist the help of law enforcement, and no one will ask them to prove the jewels are theirs. Thy word would never be believed above theirs."

She watched Lewis's face as closely as she did Tilla's. More so. Because his was the motivation she must sound out. And she thought she saw a bit of frustration behind his pleasant mask.

But frustration with whom or what?

He offered Prudence a smile. "This pie is delicious, Mrs. Willard."

She forced herself to cut off a small taste of her own. "I thank thee, Mr. Humphreys."

He then leaned a bit closer to Tilla. "Our hostess has a point, sweetheart. Those jewels increase the danger too much. You oughtn't to have taken them."

Tilla's eyes flared. "If I hadn't, we'd have *nothing* with which to start a new life! You said you'd take nothing from your father. How, then, would we buy land? Start the farm we've dreamed of in Canada?"

His eyes flickered at the mention of his father. His larynx bobbed at the mention of their shared dreams. "We'd make a way, Till. We *will* make a way. But not with the jewels. They'll get too much attention wherever we try to sell them. They're too distinctive."

She shook her head. "I'll not be destitute, like every other slave fleeing the South. I'm more white than black. No one will know to look at me. No one will wonder where we got them. I won't be reduced to nothing, like my mother. I *won't*."

"Darling." Lewis covered her hand with both of his, abandoning his fork. "Calm down. It wouldn't be as bad as that."

Prudence forced the bite of pie past her lips. She'd been a slave. Not for long, and not as miserably as some. But she'd lost her parents to the institution. Her hatred for it ran down to the very marrow of her bones. She had learned to use her indeterminate skin color to blend in with any society.

But she bore no shame for the Negro blood in her veins. She cherished the white heritage no more strongly. She had never wanted to be something other than what God had made her.

Tilla, much like Prudence's old Melungeon friend who had hidden her heritage behind white features, seemed determined to deny the truth of who she was.

Prudence lifted her chin. "Tilla. Slavery is an evil thing. And it does not, cannot define who we are before the Almighty. I believe this with every fiber of my being. But thee cannot escape the past that shaped thee. The family that bore thee. Thee must find thy contentment and worth in more than the trappings of this earth and the view in which men hold thee."

Tilla's beautiful face contorted into a mask of pain and hatred. "You don't know! You don't know what—"

"She does." Jason let his hand fall to the table with a thud. His countenance was even, strong. Like his voice, brooking no histrionics. "And thee will not throw our hospitality in my wife's face by reminding her of those days, or questioning them."

Love for this gentle warrior of hers filled her chest anew.

"I apologize." But it was Lewis who said it, not Tilla. "She is overwrought. But we will not impose on your hospitality much longer, I assure you. I have made what arrangements I can. We will be fine, darling, and happy. We'll not want." This he directed to Tilla, ducking his head to catch her eye. "Trust me. I'll take care of you."

With a sniff, Tilla nodded.

"Good. So we'll return the jewelry then. It is the safest way."

Tilla's eyes slid shut, and she shook her head. "How? How can we return them? If we try to send a package, it will likely be seized and stolen. Not to mention that the post is not exactly reliable just now between here and the Carolinas."

"Perhaps, Mr. Humphreys, there is someone you trust to act as courier?" Jason suggested.

Again, a hitch in Lewis's movement, and his eyes clouded. "I...I will find someone. Or deliver them myself."

That brought Tilla's shoulders back to square, her chin up. "No! You're going to Canada with me, not—"

"I will do what needs done, my love." He looked sincere as he said it. Determined. Kind. "To ensure your safety. To guarantee you will never have to go back to them. You will not serve your brother and his vengeful matron."

The young man lifted the hand he held and kissed Tilla's knuckles, then looked up toward Jason. "It is no secret that fleeing slaves seek to cross the Ohio—and will make sense to the family, or whomever they hire to seek her, that she would come to the one part of Ohio she has visited before. I can craft a story to make this believable. Claim I saw her, tried to detain her and send her home. That she slipped away, but I managed to grab her bag, which had the jewels in it. Of course, I would know to whom they belonged. My seeking to return them would be deemed a favor to the family, don't you think? Nothing suspicious."

Prudence gave up all pretense of eating her pie and set her fork down upon the table.

Jason made no immediate response. Instead he considered it as he took another sip of his coffee, the thoughts ticking steadily through his soft brown eyes. After a moment, he looked at Tilla. "How long since thee left Belle Arbor?"

Tilla looked up to the ceiling, lips moving silently as she calculated. "I guess... ten days. No, eleven."

"They are likely hot on thy trail already." He encompassed Lewis with his gaze. "Whatever arrangement thee plans to make to get to Canada, it ought to be enacted as soon as possible. Given that Tilla can pass for white, I would recommend an overt route—put her on a train wearing fine enough clothes that she will garner no undue notice. And then try to contact Belle Arbor by wire. Feed them false information about which direction she has gone." He paused and swallowed.

Prudence envied him the ability. Her own throat had closed off at the thought of slave hunters seeking Tilla here, at their house. The home they'd gone to such lengths to protect from her work.

Tilla had paled. "Alone? You want me to go to Canada *alone?*"

"Not all the way to Canada." Lewis offered a smile no doubt meant to soothe her. "I've a friend from school who lives in Cleveland. He is in the war, of course, but his wife will welcome you. You can stay there and await me. They've a shipping company we will use to cross Lake Erie."

"Meanwhile, convince them you think she headed for Toledo." Jason nodded his approval of the plan.

Lewis pushed his chair back a few inches. "I'll purchase the ticket tomorrow for the following day. As soon as you've gone, darling, I'll contact them." He sent his gaze, blue and unfamiliar, to Prudence. "Can you help with her clothing, perchance? I can get you what money you need for it, but it would look odd for me to do so."

Prudence hesitated only a moment before nodding. She still occasionally helped her friends at the hotel—she could claim to be running an errand for a guest. "I will see to it."

"Good. And now I had better hasten home before the storm breaks." In proof, he stood, drawing Tilla up with him by the hand. "See me out?"

The girl dimpled and nodded, no doubt meaning to let him steal a kiss as she bade him farewell outside.

Prudence made no effort to stop them, as it would likely fail. She simply stood and began gathering pie plates and coffee cups.

Jason helped her, silent for a moment. Once they'd scraped the remains into the slop pail and put the dishes in the sink, he looked up. There was a twinkle in his eye. "That's long enough, don't thou think? I had better remind him that the storm will soon break."

Prudence managed a grin for her husband, wishing it were a normal courting couple he was prodding along. Wishing this war was over, the prisoners all set free, and this part of her life a footnote.

Wishing she knew how Lewis Humphreys had learned of their involvement with the railroad so she could go back in time and prevent the learning.

She clasped her elbows with her hands while Jason was outside, staring at the dishes rather than washing them. She couldn't shake this dread that had possessed her since the moment she saw Tilla in their barn. Bad was going to come of all this. She felt it in her marrow.

A moment later Tilla came humming back inside, sparing Prudence only a smile before disappearing up the stairs to her room. No offer to help tidy up, to inquire as to whether there was anything else she could do.

It shouldn't grate as it did—she was a young woman in love, her eyes filled with stars. And usually the surety that Prudence had been called to serve those fleeing subjugation made her happy to do whatever she could for the poor souls who found her.

But *poor soul* was not a phrase that seemed to describe Tilla. *Proud soul* would suit her better. Hence the grating upon Prudence's raw nerves.

It was another two minutes before Jason returned, lines of worry in his face and something in his hand.

Prudence lifted a brow. "What troubles thee, Husband?"

In answer, he unfolded the sheet of paper he held along with a few paper dollars. "This was folded with the money

Humphreys gave me for clothing. I suspect he didn't mean to give it to me—it was stuck between two bills."

"What is it?"

"I have not looked yet. Perhaps nothing. A shopping list, a note to himself. Except he had it, and the money, in a pocket hidden inside his boot." Looking over his shoulder—no doubt to be sure Tilla was nowhere around—he set the paper on the table.

Prudence came near to read it along with him. Her tight throat burned as she saw the collection of numbers and words. "Is that...?"

Jason drew in a long breath. Another man may have let it out in an oath. He let it out in a prayer. "God above, help us. Troop movements."

Union troop movements. Prudence gripped her husband's arm, neither of them needing to give voice to the undeniable conclusion the evidence suggested.

Lewis Humphreys was a Confederate spy.

CHAPTER ELEVEN

LuAnn clicked the mouse and watched the image from the microfilm pop up on the wide flat-screen monitor. The computerized experience was different from the last time she used microfilm. Which, granted, had been twenty years ago. She scanned the headlines, but she was already clicking the mouse. Again. Again.

She had only an approximate date to go on—1862. Which left a whole lot of newspapers to sift through.

And it was more than a little hard to focus when her thoughts kept reverting back to the café last night, when Marshall Bricker had dropped his bombshell.

Larceny charges. Leavenworth. Trial.

Even as the words had swirled through the air, her walls of denial had risen. That couldn't be Tory Thornton—not the Thorn they knew. There was simply no way that the man who was so conscientious about every aspect of his job, the man who'd loved his family so fully that he gave up after losing them, could willfully harm someone else.

And yet Thorn was gone. And jewels were missing. And Marshall Bricker painted a picture of a far different man than the one they knew—or thought they knew.

LuAnn clicked the mouse again, sitting up straighter when the front page headline for May 4, 1862, jumped out at her.

"Emerald Treasure Still Missing"

Even more than the headline, though, was the image that went along with the story. A sketch of a necklace, a bracelet, and a tiara—rather familiar-looking ones.

The article didn't give her much information. It simply stated that a set of priceless emerald jewelry went missing during the capture of a fugitive and had yet to be recovered. Anyone with information leading to the jewels would be rewarded by the family and should come forward....

She pursed her lips. Surely there was an article about the fugitive. The capture. Some mention, perhaps, of the Riverfront House that would give her a glimpse into why, over a century and a half later, the missing pieces had turned up in a panel in the elevator shaft.

She sent the film back in the other direction, backward in time, but she hadn't just been so distracted she missed it. There was no mention of an arrest or anything of that sort.

Maybe one of the other papers they had in the archives would help. But if so, she'd have to find it another day. LuAnn closed the program, stood with a sigh, and took her leave. She still had a lot to do today, and no more time to spend in the Local History and Genealogy Archives of the public library.

She smiled and waved at the clerk manning the front desk, glad he didn't ask her if she found what she was looking for. Defeat was never fun to admit.

Outside, the September sun was baking the ground but the air had a cool note to it, prompting her to draw in a deep breath. She cast an appreciative look over her shoulder at the building—lovely with its Grecian columns in white against the red brick. It wouldn't be a hardship, on the one hand, to come back another day. Something in her always thrilled at the excuse to go to any sort of library.

But still, she wished she'd found what she was looking for *this* day. They could have used the encouragement after the silence in which they'd all sat around last night, after they'd exhausted their arguments in Thorn's defense.

Marshall Bricker had answered every one of them. Then he'd simply offered an apology for being the one to share the information, tipped his hat, and retired to his room.

This morning, he'd checked out without a word.

But had not, apparently, immediately left town. LuAnn paused when she caught sight of him down the street, his tall form combined with his distinctive gait. And this time, she didn't have any illusions that it was Thorn.

There was one thing none of them had thought to ask him last night. Charging after him, she determined she'd put it to him now. "Mr. Bricker!"

He paused and turned, something in his face going from shuttered to open when he spotted her. He even carved out a smile from the stone that was his face. "Mrs.... I'm sorry. I don't recall your last name."

"Sherrill. And it's Miss." Hand still clutching her purse strap from her jog down the street, she planted her feet in front of him. "I have a question, if you don't mind."

He inclined his head. "Ask away, ma'am."

She lifted her brows. "If Tory Thornton is such a shady character, then why did you come to visit him?"

It gave him only a second's pause, and then he tilted his head toward the river. "I didn't, ma'am. I came to the festival. Then just thought I'd get in touch. We may not have parted on the best of terms, but Thorn and I were buddies once. Before things went sour for him in the service. I guess...I guess I hoped to find he'd changed. Heaven knows *I* have over the last twenty-some years."

The heat of her anger cooled. That made sense, she supposed. "Right. Sorry to have run at you like that."

"You're trying to make sense of things. Can't say I blame you—makes you a good friend." He gave her a nod and then stepped around her and continued on his path.

Tension wracking her shoulders and neck, LuAnn continued on hers as well.

"You are a freak of nature."

LuAnn sent Tess an upside-down smile and held her position for another ten seconds, straightened, and reached for the sky. "Just keep reading."

Tess was lounging on the sofa in their upstairs living room, head propped on one arm and feet on the other, looking utterly relaxed. "How am I supposed to focus on Quakers from the Civil War when you're tying yourself into knots?"

"I am *untying* the knots." Just to give her friend a chuckle, she moved next into a stretch that did curl her up into a ball that could resemble a knot from a certain vantage point. And which helped release the tension in her lower back from all the bending and raising that changing sheets had inspired.

From the kitchen side of the common room, Janice laughed. "Can you still do that headstand thing?"

"But of course." LuAnn obligingly planted her hands and head and raised herself up. Granted, not as smoothly as she'd once been able to do, and she didn't often attempt lowering into arm balances anymore. But it earned her some applause and hoots from her friends. "Inversions are awesome. Totally change your perspective. You ladies should try one some-time."

Tess's answer was to shift slightly on the couch so her head dangled off the side. "There. I'm inverted. Which is great fun until all the blood rushes to my head."

Janice laughed. "Doing that always reminded me of the upside-down house of Mrs. Piggle-Wiggle. Did you read that to your kids, Tess? Stacy loved it."

"I think so. That's the one about the funny little woman who solved the problems children had with ridiculous reme-dies, right?"

"Yep." Janice tapped a spoon to the side of a pan. "Another ten minutes or so, and it'll be ready. Anything relevant in the journal, Tess?"

"I'm really not sure." She righted herself and settled once more on the pillows, printouts held above her head. "There are a few that are vague enough that they *could* have something to do with something. But nothing I've found yet comes right out and says anything about jewels or jewelry or treasure or anything like that."

LuAnn lowered her feet back to the floor, did a few push-ups, and held the high position for a minute. Having sucked up her stomach, her voice came out a bit funny when she said, "What about a fugitive in connection to valuables?"

"Nothing yet. What month did you say that was?"

"May."

"Of 1862… Let's see, here's a February entry…then a March…" Pages rustled from the couch. "Well, this is the right time period anyway. I'll see what it may or may not mention."

Deciding some cardio was in order, LuAnn lifted her back a little higher and started pulling her legs up and then back, basically running with her hands on the ground.

"You are insane," was Janice's proclamation from the kitchen.

"Mountain climbers," LuAnn panted back. "Good…for you."

"You know what's good for me? A decadent dark chocolate."

"Antioxidants," Tess put in from behind the journal. "Flavonoids. It's a true superfood."

"No argument here." Still, LuAnn pushed herself through another thirty seconds of the killer climbers, and then was more than happy to lean back for a rest. "How long until dinner?"

"Ten, she said." Tess turned another page.

Janice opened then shut the oven door. "Might be more like fifteen."

"Then I'm going to hit the shower." LuAnn uncurled until she was standing and stretching up, then relaxed. "Unless you need a hand with anything, Janice."

"Nope, I'm good."

Fifteen minutes later, LuAnn emerged, clean and comfortable in shorts and a T-shirt, into the fragrant kitchen. There was nothing in the world like the smell of a good red sauce and garlic bread, and her stomach rumbled its agreement.

Though it was a bit warm in the common room now. "Anyone mind if I open a window? I think the air outside is cooling off." And the air conditioner up here never quite managed to cool the place when they cooked. No doubt the extra warmth would be lovely in the winter, but with summer still holding on, not so much.

"Please," Janice said, her hands in mitts as she pulled a pan from the oven.

LuAnn opened the windows and smiled at the cool evening breeze that wafted in.

Abandoning her journal printouts, Tess joined them in the kitchen to set the table. A few minutes later they'd said grace and were digging in.

"It's weird," Janice said as she tore off a piece of garlic bread. "All those months of prep. A few mad-dash days of playing hostess. And now we're empty again. No one in any of the rooms downstairs."

"But only for tonight." Tess grinned and brandished her pasta-loaded fork. "We'll be half-full again tomorrow. Totally full over the weekend. Ebb and flow."

"Did you guys see we had our first online reviews?" LuAnn asked.

Now they looked at her with wide eyes, all but bouncing in their chairs.

"No! Who left them?" Janice leaned closer.

Tess clapped her hands. "Where?"

LuAnn set her phone on the table and swiped to the pages. "Three on Yelp, four on Google, and even two on TripAdvisor. I mean, those are repeated, it's not like there are nine unique reviews, but still! Those cards you put in the rooms were obviously a great idea, Tess."

Tess grinned and took the phone. "Five stars, even! 'The proprietors couldn't have been more hospitable and conscientious. They've created a gorgeous inn that has all the comforts of home with all the style and service of a first-class hotel.' Oh heavens, I love that Emily. I'm going to send her a card."

"Lemme read the next one." Janice wiggled her fingers until Tess handed over the phone. "Let's see...okay, here we go. Another five stars from the Kellys. 'We had the joy of staying at Wayfarers Inn on their opening weekend and were so, so impressed! The inn is gorgeous, the staff helpful, and we especially appreciated the little touches that made staying with kids extra easy, like the complimentary snacks in the rooms. We'll be staying here again for sure our next time in town.' Awwww."

"They're all like that. Pretty cool, huh?" LuAnn sopped up some sauce with her bread. "I know they won't always be great, but I'm so glad these first ones are. Thank You, Jesus."

"Amen to that. And this definitely calls for some chocolate for dessert," Tess declared.

Janice set the phone back on the table. "I'll read the rest on the computer later. And I got some berries and whipped cream for dessert."

"Add a drizzle of chocolate syrup, and I'm sold." Tess grinned and then looked past them, toward the window. "It'll get old eventually. I know it will. The guests, the chores, the reviews."

LuAnn held up her water glass in salute. "But not yet."

"No. Not yet." Tess lifted her glass too.

Janice added hers for a three-sided *clink*. "To us, and a successful opening weekend."

"Cheers." LuAnn happily drank to that. She didn't mind the quiet night, either, truth be told. Time to process those first days as official innkeepers, to unwind and relax and regroup for tomorrow, when new guests would arrive.

The sun's setting painted the horizon in gold, scarlet, and vermillion while they finished eating, chatting happily about everything and nothing. By the time they took their plates to the dishwasher, dusk had settled outside the window in shades of purple and gray.

The beauty of which was shattered by the clear sound of shattering glass from outside. They all dashed to the window overlooking the parking lot.

They'd put in a dusk-to-dawn light out there, but it wasn't on. It should have been, but it wasn't. And its lack left the strange shadows of pre-night to steal over the ground. Still, LuAnn could just make out a figure at the rear of the lot.

At Thorn's ancient blue pickup.

"Hey!" Tess screamed out the window. "Get away from there! We're calling the cops!"

That was all it took for the figure to dash away.

"Should we?" Janice asked as they all rushed to the stairs.

"Let's see what glass broke first." Though she figured it was a window in Thorn's truck. In which case, they would definitely have to call the police, though they'd hopefully scared the vandal off before he could turn into a thief.

Why, though, would someone break into that old thing? It didn't scream, *I have valuables inside.* Her car, or Tess's or Janice's, would have been more likely targets for a robbery, wouldn't they?

They reached the main floor in record time and burst outside into the settling night.

"Why isn't the light on?" Janice stuck close between LuAnn and Tess as they moved farther away from the porch light.

"Good question." Tess pulled her cell phone out and switched on the flashlight. A few seconds, a few feet, and it glinted on broken glass.

Not from the truck, or any other car in the lot. From the dusk-to-dawn light.

LuAnn knew her frown matched the ones on her friends' faces. "Someone took out the light? And then went to Thorn's truck?"

"Why?" Janice clasped her arms and turned toward the unassuming pickup.

"Good question." LuAnn steered them wide around the radius of broken glass and headed for the truck in the corner.

"Could either of you make out anything about the guy trying to get into it? I only have an impression of denim and a man-sized figure." Tess flashed her phone this way and that as if expecting whoever it had been to reappear.

LuAnn was glad no faces popped up over the fence. "No. A hat, I think? Baseball cap style?"

"Dark shirt. Long sleeve, maybe." Janice shook her head. "Couldn't see anything else."

They arrived at the truck and stopped. LuAnn pursed her lips. "It couldn't have been Thorn, right? He wouldn't have smashed the light. If he wanted something from his truck—or the truck itself—he would have just waited until we were asleep and gotten it. I mean, assuming he wanted to be sneaky. Though it's his truck, so he wouldn't need to be sneaky."

"Agreed." Not that it was any surprise that Janice agreed—she would defend him to kingdom come and back again.

LuAnn wanted to as well. Still, things weren't looking great for him, and this was just one more bizarre thing she couldn't account for.

Tess stepped forward. "Let's see what someone might have been after, shall we?" She shone her light into the cab of the truck.

LuAnn sighed and rolled her eyes. "If we're going to snoop, we might as well do it without a glare. We all know he never bothered to fix the broken lock." Just in case the intruder had already touched something, though, LuAnn used the bottom of her T-shirt to push in the button and then tugged on the handle.

The door felt like it weighed a ton—far more than the more modern door on her own car. It squeaked on its hinges as she pulled it open, ignoring the gasp of protest from Janice. If Thorn had done nothing wrong, then he wouldn't mind them checking his truck for clues. And if he had done something wrong, then she didn't much care what he thought about them snooping.

"Well there's certainly nothing that would have gained someone's attention from outside," Tess observed, illuminating every surface of the cab in turn. The seats—clean if worn—the dash—dusty but its trays empty—the floor, with nothing but a shop rag on it.

"Wait. The shop rag." It was on the driver's side floor—not where Thorn was likely to toss it if he'd been wiping off his hands one day when he got in. That would have landed it on the passenger's side floor, wouldn't it? But there it was, directly below the steering wheel. More like where he'd have dropped it if he were leaning in the open door for something.

And it was stained. Dark. She reached for it by a corner and hoped, as she had just a few days ago when she saw a similar rag on the basement floor, that it was just oil. "Oh gracious." Janice pressed a hand to her mouth. "More blood."

"More blood." LuAnn dropped it back down to its place on the floor, brows knit again. "But that means he came out here to the truck after he was injured. But he didn't get in and drive away."

"But he came out here." Tess leaned against the seat, the shadows deepening the lines of consideration on her face. "Why? To get something out? To put something in?"

"If it was to get something out, we won't be able to tell what," Janice said from a step back.

LuAnn granted that with lifted brows. "But if it was to put something *in*…" She leaned down, wishing she'd grabbed her phone off the table so she had her own light. But Tess held hers out, illuminating a few rocks from the parking lot trapped in the mats, a stray receipt for the nearby gas station dated a month ago, and, when she reached under the seat, something cool, rubbery, and rectangular.

She pulled it out to a collective gasp.

Thorn's phone, with its industrial-style, can't-possibly-break-me gray case. She looked over to meet the gazes of her friends.

Tess was the first to put words to the question they were surely all asking. "Why in the world would Thorn, injured, come out here and hide his phone under the seat?"

CHAPTER TWELVE

The phone sat on the table, staring up at them with its gaping face, nothing to display but the green battery symbol, slowly growing from the zero percent it had been at before. A charger stretched from the connector to the outlet like an IV, slowly pumping life back into the device.

In the light of their upstairs kitchen, they could make out faint marks on the case that may have been blood. Though if so, it had been wiped off enough that it was hard to say.

The kettle whistled on the stove, and LuAnn moved to pour the steaming water into four mugs. The occasion had seemed to call for something soothing. Something to occupy their hands while they sat or stood around the table, just staring at the phone and watching it charge.

Da-la-ling.

LuAnn set the kettle down and pulled her own phone out. "Laura's here."

Tess was already on her feet, headed for the stairs. "I'll bring her up."

In debating what to do with Thorn's phone, they'd decided that it made the most sense to call his daughter. If anyone had a right to go snooping through the device, it was her. Similarly, she should be the one to decide what, if anything, to do with it then.

Of course, they'd caught her just as she was getting her kids down for bed. It was now nearly eight thirty, but that just meant that the phone was no longer completely dead and could be turned on. They'd let Laura do those honors.

Janice accepted the mug LuAnn handed her, the tag of her favorite tea dangling over the side. If she was true to form, she'd add two heaping spoonfuls of sugar to the mug, and maybe a dollop of milk.

LuAnn wasn't in the mood for sweet, which was why she'd ignored the berries and whipped cream still in the fridge and opted for tea. Not that Janice or Tess had made mention of their forgotten dessert either.

Janice turned toward the counter and the sugar bowl. She added the expected two scoops to her own, and half a teaspoon to Tess's mug—*her* usual.

There was something comforting in realizing that no matter the upheaval, some things didn't change. Tess would always want half a spoonful of sugar in her tea. Janice would always want two. LuAnn would always drink hers straight, unless it was chai, which got a dab of milk. The steady, constant, silly things of life—and the fact that they knew each other's habits so well—soothed LuAnn's nerves as much as the mint-scented steam rising from her cup.

Footsteps sounded from the stairs, steadily growing louder as the two sets of feet hurried up. Another half a minute and Tess appeared, Laura right behind her. The poor woman looked frazzled. Purple smudges shadowed her eyes, her hair had the distinct look of having had toddler hands in it, and she had a smear of something orange beneath her ear, all betraying her rush from dinner to bedtime to the inn without taking the time to look in the mirror.

"Hey." LuAnn offered her a warm smile and a cup of tea. "We made you some red rooibos. Hope that's okay."

Laura blinked rapidly and nodded. "That's great. Thanks." She managed a wobbly smile as she accepted the warm cup and added one level teaspoon of sugar to it.

Another person. Another preference. Another steady fact to keep a day marching on.

As they all sat at the small circular table, Laura looked around. "I love what you guys did with this space. Not as formal as the downstairs, and so homey." She took her purse off her shoulder and removed a notebook, pen, and phone from it before setting it on the floor.

LuAnn had just grabbed her own notebook and pen from the counter. "We haven't turned it on yet. Thought we'd wait for you."

"Thanks." Laura drew in a deep breath, blew it back out, and reached for Thorn's phone. With a push of the button, the screen shifted and it sang out its power-on song.

Janice reached for LuAnn's and Tess's hands. "Let's pray before we see whatever's on there." Not waiting for any objections—though their guest didn't object so much as shift in her chair and hesitantly join hands—Janice began. "Father God, we thank You and praise You for positioning us here at home tonight so we could hear that ruckus outside, and for leading LuAnn's hand to this cell phone under the seat. We ask now that You guide us as we see what we can find on it, and that You lead us to whatever information You want us to have. And we beg You, Lord, please keep Your hand on Thorn wherever he is. Touch him, whisper Your love into his heart. Thank You for already working here, in ways we can't see as well as in ones we can. Thank You for loving him so much more than we ever could. In Jesus's name, amen."

"Amen," LuAnn pronounced in unison with Tess. She squeezed the hands that held hers and then turned to Laura.

She used her newly freed hands to wipe tears from her eyes. "Thanks, guys. It means so much that…that…"

"Aw, sweetie. He's our friend. We're hurting and hoping right along with you." Janice reached across the table and, though she couldn't quite reach Laura, spread her hand out in a clear show of support.

Laura reached out to bridge the gap, rested her fingers on Janice's for a moment with a soft smile, and then looked back to the phone when it started buzzing and popping with alerts and messages. "Okay, wow. This thing has obviously been off for days."

LuAnn scooted her chair and notebook over a bit so she could see the screen. Given that Laura was holding it out for them all to see, she didn't figure that was too nosy.

Laura sucked in a breath. "Okay. Let's start with missed calls and voice mails."

"You scroll. I'll make the list." LuAnn took the cap off her pen and got down to business.

It seemed like half of Marietta had tried to call Thorn over the weekend—more people than she even thought he knew.

With the voice mail on speaker, they listened to neighbor after neighbor first calling to ask a question or arrange a get-together and then calling back in concern when a meeting was missed. Most of them were from people at church.

LuAnn jotted down every caller, every missed appointment that was mentioned, every invitation still outstanding.

Once they had heard every voice mail, Laura navigated to his text messages. "All right. Quite a few just from us, several that are reiterations of the voice mails. One from an unknown number. It says, 'Hey, Thorn. I'm in Marietta. Thought we could catch up. Brick.' Brick?" Laura screwed up her face.

"Marshall Bricker, I'd bet." LuAnn jotted the message down, word for word. "Time on that? Friday night, I guess?"

"No, earlier. Three minutes after noon."

"So *before* he tried to check in and said he'd give his buddy a call." LuAnn made a note of that as well. "Got it. Next?"

"Next was yours, then mine. Kip, with details on where to meet at the festival. Kip again, wondering if he got the previous message. Pastor Ben saying thanks for the help setting up the booth the night before. Kip again, saying he just talked to you, LuAnn, and he was getting worried."

They kept going, noting messages from several different men from church, one from Janice's daughter who rented him the apartment above her garage. Nothing out of the ordinary that LuAnn could see.

"Moving on. Let's check his calendar."

Janice twirled her empty cup in a circle on the table. "He actually uses that thing? I never could figure it out."

"I showed him how he could add things verbally and then just check it to see what was on the schedule for a given day." Laura tapped into Thursday. "Thursday he had men's Bible study and breakfast at seven in the morning. Meet Joe at eleven."

"Building inspector," Tess put in. "That was for us, with a question about the basement."

"Okay. Meet Ben at six thirty that evening."

"Our pastor. Booth setup, I guess, given that message on Friday thanking him for his help," LuAnn said as she made a note.

"Right. That's all for Thursday. Friday." Laura tapped the screen. "Eight o'clock. Jeremy." She paused, brows lifted.

LuAnn shook her head, as did Tess and Janice.

"Maybe a friend of his, but that one wasn't for us," Janice said.

Laura nodded. "There's nothing else noted on Friday until the evening, when he was supposed to meet Kip. Saturday he was volunteering at the church booth from ten till two. Meeting Kevin and Sam for dinner. Kevin and Sam?"

"Kevin is one of his friends from church," Janice supplied. "I don't know about Sam."

"Sunday he has 'greeter' marked down at eleven."

"Church again. He's a greeter all month." Tess rubbed her shoulders.

"And helping with the booth from one till four. At six, he has a note to sand the bookcase."

"Must be one of his carpentry projects." LuAnn finished that list and looked over at Laura. "Should we go on, do you think?"

Laura scrolled through the screen. "The rest of the week just has notes for different projects—sanding, varnishing, sanding, cutting boards. Another men's breakfast and Bible study. A few lunches with Kip, Kevin, Sam. Looks pretty normal to me."

"Yeah." Though what had they expected? Something that said, *Scare all my friends by vanishing* or, worse, *Get fake ID and flee the country?* LuAnn set her pen down and leaned back in her chair.

Laura glanced up at the clock on the stove. "I'd better get home. Is it okay if I take this with me? I'll go through the rest of his calendar and see if anything jumps out. Check his social media—though he never posted anything, just liked other people's."

"Of course that's fine." Tess stood, her face soft and encouraging. "It's your dad's phone, not ours. You have every right to it."

"Thanks." Laura stood too, though she made no other move. Instead she just stood there, looking down at the phone on the table. "Can I come by tomorrow, in the daylight? Go through the truck?"

"Of course!" the three of them answered at the same time.

"Thanks," Laura said again, her smile small but sweet. Still, she hesitated, not grabbing the phone or her purse. "Can I... I mean..." She paused and blew out a breath. "Could you guys pray again before I go? I feel like I should be doing that more, but honestly, I don't really know how. Not like you guys do."

"We'd be honored." Janice nodded to Tess. "Your turn, I think."

They all drew together around Laura, settled hands on her shoulders or gripped her hands, and Tess led them in prayer. The words weren't all that different from what they'd prayed before, with Laura or on their own. The sort of words that LuAnn had prayed thousands of times over the years. Comfortable words, familiar words.

This time, she listened to them as Laura must be doing, with ears unaccustomed to the turns of phrase and the familiarity with their Lord. Tears stung LuAnn's eyes. How amazing it was that the God of the universe bent His ear and heard them. How great was He, how small were they, and how utterly beautiful that Jesus stretched Himself out as a bridge between them.

Not for the first time, she marveled at how different it was to go through each day knowing that, trusting that, rather than to think one was set out on this sea of life all alone. And as Tess prayed for Thorn and the rest of them looking for him, LuAnn again offered a silent prayer that the Lord would tug on the heart of this young woman and her husband. That He'd use this, somehow, to grow His family by adding theirs.

After Tess said *amen*, they all took turns hugging Laura, who held them tight and made no attempt to wipe the tears from her eyes as she did so. As she pulled away from LuAnn, she said, "I did call my mom. I have a feeling she'll be showing up at my door in a day or two."

LuAnn smiled. "Good. Did you tell Emma she won that argument?"

That earned a bit of a laugh. Laura sniffled and wiped her face. "She was there when I did it. And then tried to convince me to dye my hair purple. Said it would brighten my whole outlook."

They all got a chuckle out of that one.

"I'll walk you back down," Tess said as Laura reached for her things.

"Thanks. Bye, guys." She wiggled her fingers at the rest of them, slid her dad's phone into her purse, and fell in with Tess.

LuAnn sighed and leaned against the counter as they started down the stairs. "Is there a way to look into the things Marshall Bricker said about him, do you think? To find out if Thorn really was up on larceny charges when he was in the military? What happened?"

Janice gathered the tea mugs and carried them to the dishwasher. "I'm really not sure. I don't even know if military trials—if he really went on trial for that—are open to the public. Stu might know, though. He's a fount of random information." She glanced at the clock and then pulled out her phone. "He'll still be up. Let me ask."

LuAnn held her position while Janice wandered toward the living room section of the common space. She wished, sometimes, that she had family she could just ring up at nearly ten at night. Siblings or kids or . . . all these years, and still it bit at random moments. The longing for what should have been. The wonder at how things might have been different if Jesse hadn't died before their wedding.

She'd never have a second chance at that. She couldn't just change one thing and suddenly have a grown son or daughter in her life.

Not like Thorn.

The window was still open, and a gust of air wafted in, chilling her arms. She rubbed her hands over them but made no move to close the window. The room could use some airing out. As could her mind.

Thorn...he'd known about Laura. LuAnn didn't know what had made him reluctant to reach out to her until recently, but she knew the light that had entered his eyes when he said she was moving home to Marietta.

He wouldn't throw all that away for some jewelry, would he?

She hugged her arms to her middle. For the most part, she was happy with the life God had given her. The fact that she had students rather than kids of her own to nurture and teach. That she had these friends rather than sisters or brothers. That she was free, now, for this new adventure.

She was content with the paths God had led her down. But she couldn't begin to understand someone turning his or her back on everything she once dreamed of. Not for any reason, but especially not for mere things.

Had Thorn done that? Now? Back then, when his first wife left him?

The *back then* shouldn't really matter—not if he'd changed.

But if he hadn't...

"Would you?" Janice said brightly from the living room. When LuAnn glanced over, she saw a smile on her friend's face as she spoke into her phone. "Oh, that would be great, honey. Thanks. I'm sure there's nothing to learn, really, but I sure appreciate you asking him to check." She turned to face LuAnn and gave her a thumbs-up. "Wonderful. I'll let you go then. Night night, sweet boy."

She grinned and snickered as she disconnected, Stuart's exasperated *Mom* still sounding. "He doesn't really mind that anymore—the 'sweet boy' thing. It's just tradition to object to it."

LuAnn smiled. And she ached. And she reminded herself that she shouldn't mourn what she never had. She shouldn't resent those who had it and walked away from it. She *shouldn't*.

But if they learned that Thorn really had made off with the jewels…well, it wouldn't be the stealing that most disappointed her. It would be that he had the thing she'd most wanted from life, and he'd not appreciated it.

Chapter Thirteen

Since there were no guests to prepare breakfast for on Tuesday morning, LuAnn, Tess, and Janice took the opportunity to slip out for a brisk walk when they'd normally have been rushing cinnamon rolls into and out of the oven alongside Winnie, and offering warm smiles and friendly banter with the guests dining in the café.

After a mere three days of that bustle, she wasn't exactly tired of it. But this was to be enjoyed too. "You know what, girls? I say that any morning we don't have guests, we come out and do this. Rain or shine or snow."

"With the exception of ice," Janice put in.

"And thunder," Tess added.

LuAnn laughed and looped her arms through each of theirs. "Fine, deal. Aside from ice and electrical storms, any guest-less morning will find us taking a walk along the river." She tilted her head to the side. "And subzero. I don't do sub-zero. But aside from ice, lightning, and sub-zero—"

Laughter cut her off, and she let the words fade without any great need to cling to them. Another something she appreciated about these friends of hers. The silences were every bit as meaningful as the conversations.

They kept their pace high as they followed the Ohio toward where it met the Muskingum, then of one accord they slowed, then stopped. The sun was warm on their heads and arms, the morning one of those quiet, gorgeous types that painted the world in pastels.

"This is quite the place God has put us, isn't it?" Tess drew in a long breath and kept her gaze steady at the confluence of the waters.

"Mm." LuAnn smiled. How many people had stood here before them? She could imagine herself positioned in this exact spot a hundred and fifty years before. She'd be in a hoop skirt—or if she were a poor farmer's wife, rather than a society girl, perhaps the skirt would be a little narrower. Expensive silk satin or humble calico?

Likely both had stood here, looking out over this water. Maybe the humble farmer's wife had stood here looking over into West Virginia and wondering what desperate souls might be trying to sneak across to freedom that night. Out of the slave state, into the free territory of Ohio. Perhaps Prudence Willard had even stood in this spot, where she was to meet escaped slaves and ferry them to safety in the inn.

What an odd, wonderful thought. So much changed over the course of the decades, but the rivers still flowed, and people still stood looking at them, knowing that with a river came life.

"Coming, Lu?"

"Hmm? Oh." She jogged to catch up with Janice and Tess, who had apparently continued the walk while she was debating between fabrics for her frock.

Tess was laughing at her. Not out loud, but she was laughing. "What was it this time, Walter Mitty?"

"Just a little abolitionist intrigue." She grinned and caught up with them. They walked a little ways farther along the Muskingum and then turned back toward home, opting to take Front Street for the return walk.

When they were a few blocks from home, the barber stepped outside and flipped his sign to Open, lifting a hand at them in greeting as they passed. "Morning, ladies."

"Hey, Jeremy." Janice lifted a hand too, and slowed her pace. "Stacy said she made an appointment for Larry. Good luck with that."

Jeremy laughed, hand on his door handle. "I'm an expert with the kids, don't you worry. No way he can be as wiggly as some of the others I've had."

"Yeah, we'll see what tune you're singing next week after you've met the little explorer." Still chuckling, Janice led them on.

LuAnn made it three steps past the shop when it hit her. *Jeremy.* "Jeremy!"

Her shout made her friends jump, and apparently also halted the barber halfway through his door. "Yeah? Need a haircut, LuAnn?"

She spun to face him with wide eyes. "No—but Thorn. Did he get one here? Last Friday?"

Jeremy's mouth moved back into a grin. "Oh yeah—I kinda forgot with all the festival stuff going on, but I was wondering what everyone was going to say about that. Couldn't believe he wanted it all cut off! What did you think? He asked for a crew cut, but I convinced him to go for something a *little* softer. Didn't want it to be too big a shock."

She could feel Janice and Tess beside her, staring at him every bit as intently as she was. "So, wait. He cut *all* his hair off?" LuAnn gaped at him. "Like, short?"

Jeremy's brows drew together. "Didn't you see it?"

LuAnn looked to Janice. "Did you see when he came in?"

Janice shook her head, her eyes still wide as the delta. "I only talked to him on the phone. He said he'd just go straight down, in through the basement. He texted me when he got there, but…"

"So none of us had actually *seen* him Friday." LuAnn lifted a hand and pressed it to her temple. "Oh, man. So his hair is *short*."

Jeremy's smile had faded to a concerned frown. "Yeah. About like mine. Is everything okay?"

"Thorn has been missing since Friday," Tess answered. "No one's seen him."

"And his daughter was describing him to everyone as having a long gray ponytail." LuAnn had her cell phone out and was already dialing Laura's number. It was still early, but she had two young kids—surely she was already up.

She answered on the second ring. "LuAnn, hi. What's up?"

"He got his hair cut!"

"What?"

LuAnn took a deep breath and forced herself to calm down and speak intelligibly. "Friday morning. The appointment that just said 'Jeremy.' It was the barber. We're standing here talking to him, and he said your dad got his hair cut. As in, *short*. No more ponytail."

"Okay." She sounded a bit unsure as to what that had to do with anything. "That's—I mean, I didn't know he was going to. But…"

"The hospitals! You said you described him by his hair."

"Oh!" The light bulb going on was audible. "Man, I haven't had my coffee yet. You're right. Why didn't I describe his tattoo or something?"

"The hair was an easy marker. We had no way of knowing it wasn't right anymore."

"Yeah, but—oh, I hope this changes things. I think I hope so."

High-pitched screaming covered anything else Laura might try to say, along with a not-quite-as-high voice yelling, "Give it *back*, Paisley! It's *mine*!"

"Noah! Sorry, I have to go referee. I'll make some calls as soon as I can."

"Absolutely. You do that, and let us know if you learn anything. Or if you need us to do anything."

"Will do. Thanks, LuAnn."

"Sure thing. Talk to you later." She disconnected, heaving another sigh as she did.

Jeremy was still standing half in his shop. "Hospitals? Thorn's really missing? Wow."

"Yeah." Tess squeezed LuAnn's elbow. "Good thinking, Lu. I don't know when I might have drawn that connection, if ever."

She shook her head and slid her phone back into her pocket. "We'll call that a God-thing and pray it was for a purpose. Thanks, Jeremy."

"I didn't do anything. But if I can, let me know."

"Thanks." Another reason she loved living in a small town. Neighbors still cared about neighbors.

They started back for the inn, their pace once again brisk. The rest of the town had come to life around them while they were out, cars rumbling by, joggers finishing up their morning runs, businesses all flipping their signs over or lighting them up. LuAnn spotted Winnie's car in the lot beside theirs—she hadn't had to get here quite so early today, but lunch prep still needed to be done.

There was another car in the lot too. An unfamiliar luxury car. Janice looked to Tess. "What time did the woman from Belle Arbor say she was coming?"

"All she said was 'morning,'" Tess answered.

LuAnn's eyes tracked from the silver car to the front door of the inn. It was locked—Winnie would have come in the kitchen door, to which she had a key—but the porch wasn't empty.

"Oh, boy," LuAnn said under her breath. The woman who stood there tapping a foot had the look of an executive. Crisp blouse, tailored slacks, shoes with heels high enough to serve as ice picks in a crunch. Her dark hair was pulled up in a severe style that accentuated the bone structure of her flawless face. She looked to be caught somewhere between thirty and forty—and was probably none too happy about it.

When she saw them approaching, she started toward them, one hand on the strap of her portfolio bag and the other outstretched. Her face set in determination, she thrust the hand toward Tess. "You must be Tess Wallace, the business mastermind behind the inn. McKenna Garrison—we spoke via email."

"Right. I—"

McKenna had already reclaimed her hand and held it out toward LuAnn. "And you're LuAnn Sherrill, the history lover and soup maestro." She flashed a smile full of blindingly white teeth.

LuAnn didn't even have time to formulate a response beyond a nod before McKenna was shifting her attention to Janice.

"And Janice Eastman, the artistic visionary of the trio." Obviously proud of herself, McKenna reclaimed her french tips from Janice's hand and smiled again. "I do my research."

And could quote directly from their website. Bully for her. *Calm down, Lu. She doesn't know how bad her timing is.* LuAnn drew in a deep breath and forced her lips to hold a welcoming smile. "So good to meet you, Ms. Garrison."

The woman waved her hand in the air. "Just McKenna, please. I'm sorry for coming so early. My appointment in Cleveland was moved up a few hours, so I had to adjust my arrival accordingly. I hope it isn't a bad time. I assumed, being a bed-and-breakfast, that you'd all be up and about early."

Janice's smile may have been a bit strained around the edges, but she brightened it and even added a chuckle. "Up, about, and out even, as you can see. Won't you come in?" As the one who'd been assigned to carry the keys on their walk, Janice fished them from her pocket.

Tess shifted into hospitality mode. "Would you like some coffee? Or one of our famous cinnamon rolls?"

"They're to die for," LuAnn added. No need to tell her they were left over from yesterday.

McKenna laughed and followed Janice through the front door. "I'm sure they're delicious, but my waistline would have a fit if I agreed. Though I'd love a cup of coffee, if it isn't too much trouble."

"No trouble at all." Tess motioned toward the sitting room. "You ladies have a seat while I bring in the coffee service."

LuAnn nodded, trying to suppress a twitching smile. Tess had been dying for an excuse to bring out the silver coffee service that had been left to them, along with a bunch of furniture originally from the inn. So far, it had only served as decoration.

Janice led the way into the parlor, McKenna striding in behind her. LuAnn brought up the rear and decided that she might as well be amused by their guest, since resenting her presence wouldn't do any good.

And really, she could almost like her when McKenna tilted her head back and gasped. "Those ceilings! They're *divine!*"

LuAnn chuckled. "Aren't they amazing? One of the things we fell in love with the moment the Realtor showed us the place."

It was hard for LuAnn to continue thinking of McKenna as a stiff-with-style snob when the woman stood there with her head back and her mouth still agape with delight. "I love it! I wanted to do a pressed-tin ceiling in one of the rooms at Belle

Arbor, but there were none originally. And my grandfather's will only gives me leave to restore things to their original condition, aside from what's necessary to meet modern building codes." Her head came back down and revealed a glint of sad resentment in her eyes. "He considered the restoration phrase 'better than original' to be an oxymoron. But," she added with a little sigh and a renewed smile, "he's the one who invested his fortune in re-buying the place, so I intend to honor his wishes."

"It must be rewarding, though, to know you're seeing the house as your ancestors did all those years ago." LuAnn ran a hand over the brocade of one of the wingback chairs. They'd gone for a style that fit the era of the building, but they certainly had no way of knowing what *original* would even mean.

"It stifles the creativity a bit, but it is rewarding, yes. Do you mind if I look around? This is a gorgeous room." She set her bag down on one of the sofas and motioned toward the length of the room, taking in the fireplace, the piano, the bookshelves.

Janice smiled. "Go right ahead." As their guest wandered a few steps away, Janice stepped close to LuAnn's side. "If you can entertain her for a minute, I need to run to the restroom."

"Sure. Go on." From the looks of it, McKenna wouldn't require much entertainment just now. She was studying the mantel as if it contained a long-lost Shakespeare manuscript.

LuAnn left her to it and headed to the shelves to tidy up the books the guests had left out over the weekend. She'd put a discreet little sign up asking them to leave any books they took out on the empty shelf reserved for that purpose. Because, yes, she was a little bit obsessive compulsive when it came to the organization of the books, and the thought of someone filing Hemmingway before Hawthorne was enough to make her break out in hives.

"Is this period?"

LuAnn looked around to see McKenna not quite touching a finger to the base of the oil lamp on the end of the mantel. She slid the book in her hands into its proper spot and turned. "Circa 1850s, I believe. We found it at this wonderful antique mall in town."

"It's perfect. Very *Gone with the Wind,* with that etched globe. I don't suppose they have anything else similar at the antique mall? I've been searching for a tall oil lamp for the formal parlor at the plantation. There's a painting of the room that shows one."

LuAnn had to smile at the way McKenna leaned in to better see the details of the painted ceramic base. "It's possible. We haven't been in for several weeks, but I think Harry's been actively hunting for things that would work for the inn—we may have become his best customer in years," she admitted, laughing.

McKenna grinned. "I can imagine, if he found things like this."

"There are a couple of families in town who have been here since the city was founded, more or less, and they've been cleaning out their garages and attics with renewed fervor since they realized there was a new market for it. I can give you the address of the antique store, if you like."

"Oh, I would *love* that!"

LuAnn turned back to the books. "It's a great place. We found everything from light-switch plates to bed frames. And the best part was that he had a few things that had come from the inn. His buddy had managed this place when it was a warehouse and sent anything that looked promising to Harry rather than trashing it."

McKenna turned wide hazel eyes on her. "That's like finding buried treasure! I've hunted through all the local shops near Belle Arbor, praying the previous owners had done the same with some of the original things from the plantation, but no such luck so far. We have nearly complete catalogues of everything in the house in 1860, but most of the items have long since been lost." She offered a sheepish smile. "That's why I was so excited by Tess's email. I've made it my mission to find everything I can from the original house, and if I could recover the family jewelry, that would be amazing. My grandfather left a trust for that purpose, so if you guys find anything here, know that I come armed with a checkbook."

LuAnn's first impressions of this woman were getting all knotted up. She didn't appreciate the way in which she'd come, but she could certainly understand her enthusiasm. And she knew Tess and Janice would agree with her in saying there was no way they could charge the rightful heir for the return of her property. "Oh, we—"

"Coffee!" Tess entered the room pushing an ornate vintage cart that perfectly suited the elegant silver coffee urn she'd been so eager to use. "We have cream and sugar, of course, and some flavored creamer as well."

McKenna was descending on the cart like a locust. Though, not surprisingly at this point, it was the coffee set she was inspecting rather than the coffee itself. "Perfect! You must have worked for hours to get this pot back to such a shine! What did you use to polish it, if you don't mind my asking? I've tried the baking soda and foil method for some of our silverware, but I don't suppose that would work so well for something this size."

LuAnn chuckled and slid the last book back into its place while Tess waxed philosophical about the virtues of homemade polishes versus store-bought varieties.

By the time LuAnn approached the cart, Janice was reentering the room. Surmising in a moment the state of affairs, she sent LuAnn an amused look and reached for the coffeepot. "I'll pour, shall I?"

Otherwise they might be standing here until the coffee was cold, still debating ketchup and lemon-lime soda as polishing agents. LuAnn grinned. "Please."

Janice handed the first cup to their guest. "What do you take in it, McKenna?"

"Oh, just black. Thanks." She took the cup with a distracted smile, keeping her gaze riveted on Tess.

LuAnn couldn't help but note the rings that flashed on her left hand as she steadied the cup and saucer. An engagement ring that had to be close to a carat and a half, along with a wedding band heavy with diamonds too. Mister McKenna Garrison must be a successful guy.

Janice doctored each of their cups to their tastes and passed them out. They moved toward the sofas and chairs, McKenna taking a seat beside her abandoned bag. LuAnn chose the chair adjacent while Tess sat beside her and Janice in the other chair flanking the sofa.

"Well." With a smile that looked more genuine than trying-to-impress, McKenna set her cup and saucer on the end table and reached for her bag. "Let me show you ladies what I've learned thus far about the link between Belle Arbor and Riverfront House. I just finished up this research a week ago, so it seemed like providence when you emailed."

Somehow, LuAnn hadn't expected this woman to come ready to give any information. She'd been expecting demands. And from the surprise she read in Tess's eyes, she wasn't alone in that assumption.

She scooted to the edge of her seat, ready to look at whatever the mistress of Belle Arbor pulled out of her stylish leather bag.

CHAPTER FOURTEEN

McKenna Garrison had further tarnished the image of herself as a stiff-and-stylish snob by sprawling on the floor, a ream of papers spread out before her. She sat cross-legged, proving her tailored slacks were stretchier than they looked, and had kicked off her ice-pick heels at about minute two.

The Inn Crowd had joined her on the floor, each of them having grabbed a different section of the documentation she'd pulled out of her portfolio. The one currently in LuAnn's hands seemed to be a list of slaves held by Belle Arbor in 1862, along with their ages. It was a color photocopy, the original handwriting faded in some places and blotchy in others, but mostly legible. The page was filled, the columns tight.

Isaac	*52*
Jess	*35*
~~*Solomon*~~	~~*27*~~
~~*Melchizedek*~~	~~*22*~~
Sophia	*13*
Sally	*60*
Tilla	*17*
~~*Henry*~~	~~*19*~~

LuAnn scanned about sixty names on the page, looking for a note as to why some of them were crossed out. They couldn't be deaths—deaths were marked with a date of passing, some in the previous year, others in 1862, but written in a different hand. Still, there was something final about those brown lines through the names. At the bottom, she spotted an explanation, half cut-off by the copier. *Excluding males sent to dig trenches.*

Better than death. Maybe. From what she'd read on the subject, digging was often a death sentence in itself, given the diseases that ran rampant in the trenches in the South. She read through the names again more carefully, noting that every male over thirteen and under fifty appeared to have been recruited for the task.

She flipped the page and found what was either a letter or a journal entry, written in the same hand as the list. The color of the copy showed yellowed pages and words gone brown as the iron ink rusted with age.

Resentment for the Confederacy continues to mount. Yet more of our slaves have been conscripted, forced to leave the work that means life to us in order to dig trenches for the soldiers. Just as our sons have been conscripted to be those soldiers. Why, my neighbors have asked, and with which questions I must agree, did we secede, if not to secure the basic rights the government was denying us? The basic rights of which this new government has wasted no time in stripping us as well? We were promised no conscription. The right to retain our

*property. Our slaves. To be first South Carolinians or Virgin-
ians or Georgians.*

*Instead, our boys are sent to defend other states, other men's
property. Davis continues to demand more and still more for
this Confederation, while our plantations fall into ruin and
our sons spill their blood in Pennsylvania and Maryland and
Virginia.*

*And yet I cannot be glad that my own son has been sent
home. The lost arm that has made him unfit for soldiering has
made him a bitter man as well. I fear the resentment I see in
his eyes whenever the war is discussed. Even when peace is
eventually reached, whatever the outcome, he will never forgive the Yankees for what they did to him, and I fear he will
seek vengeance on any and all who oppose him, no matter
their birth.*

LuAnn hunted for a signature but found none. "I'm guessing these were written by the owner of Belle Arbor? Your great-
great-great-great-grandfather or so?"

McKenna leaned over to see which papers she had and
nodded. "Yes, those were written by Virgil Garrison not long
before he died. According to the family Bible, he passed away
in April of 1862. That list is from January. There's a new one
every year. Here's 1863, if you care to compare."

LuAnn accepted the second list of slaves and put it beside
the first. They were written in different scripts, though the lists
were largely the same. A few had dates of death written beside
them—including Solomon, who had been digging. There were

a few new names, with dates of birth listed from the previous year. She compared each column, noting very little that she'd consider a discrepancy.

Except for one name that simply vanished. She looked up. "Do we know what happened to Tilla?"

McKenna's eyes positively sparkled. "That's the million-dollar question. She's the one who ran away and stole the jewelry you asked about."

"Tilla." Frowning, Janice sorted through the stack of papers in front of her until she came up with another color copy of a watercolor painting. Several, actually, of different people. She set them side by side and pointed to the one on the right. "Is this her? But why would someone have done a portrait of a slave?"

LuAnn leaned over to get a glimpse and found the painting to be shockingly good—done either by a professional or a very skilled amateur, from her guess. It showed a girl on the cusp of womanhood, maybe fourteen or fifteen. Her clothes were superior to what one would expect of a slave, though certainly not so fine as those worn by the woman in the next painting. In the bottom corner *Tilla* was written, along with *1860*. The same date as the others, which were inscribed *Madeline* and *Oscar*.

"They were painted by Virgil." McKenna leaned over and tapped a french tip to the picture. "I don't know if you can make out his signature in the copy—the originals were larger and clearer. Tilla was his daughter with a slave woman named Silva. He doesn't mention them much in the writings I've found, but from where he does, it's clear that he was fond of

Tilla and treated her more as a daughter than a slave—not always the case. The others are his wife and son, of course."

"He was good." Janice looked from one portrait to the next, brows raised. "And she was beautiful."

"Yes and yes." McKenna's sigh sounded far more wistful than her tightly pulled hair had made her look capable of. "My grandfather shared what he'd found of her story with me when I was fifteen. I used to dream that I was born to the family then, and that I'd helped her escape. Of course, Granddad pointed out that I wouldn't have been raised to think slavery evil at that point in history, so it's unlikely I would have done that. But I like to think I'd have been forward-thinking enough. Brave enough."

"Don't we all?" LuAnn smiled and flipped to the next page in her stack. "But we're all born for our own 'such a time as this.' The Lord put us in the here and now for a reason, as my friends so often remind me as I'm dreaming of belonging to the past."

The mention of God didn't seem to faze McKenna a bit—though coming from the Bible belt, that may only have indicated a general familiarity rather than a personal one.

"Granddad always said that too. And that perhaps my reason for being in the here and now is rediscovering our family history." McKenna dug through her notes and came up with another piece of artwork. "Tilla seems to have inherited his skill. At least, I think this is by Tilla—that's what the signature looks like to me. What do you think?"

LuAnn accepted the paper. This one was a black-and-white sketch of a hill—no, not just a hill, a graveyard. There were a few tombstones and a fence. But the focus was on the young oak tree outside the fence, and a couple standing underneath it. Their faces weren't detailed, as they were too far away, but their postures indicated romance. It took her a moment to find the small signature hidden among the blades of grass by one of the grave markers. "Could be Tilla. It's a little blurred."

"Yeah. I like to think it was by her, though. Maybe even *of* her." She pulled out another page. "I've been trying—mostly unsuccessfully—to track the routes of the slaves that ran away from Belle Arbor. Some were caught and brought back, which is the only way I can guess at their paths. From what I've been able to glean, the search for her was focused on Toledo. But lately I've been thinking, what if that's wrong? What if she went through Cleveland instead?"

Tess leaned back against the sofa and stretched her legs out on the floor in front of her. "Cleveland was a pretty major stop on the Underground Railroad, from what I understand. Though finding any documentation on it is difficult, given the secretive nature, as I'm sure you know."

"Do I ever. But I've made contact with a lady who runs a museum up there. We can be pretty sure Tilla came through Marietta." She brandished another clipped-together passel of papers. "In which case, Cleveland would have been the logical next stop before Canada. It's a straight shot."

"And you're meeting her today?" Janice turned another page over.

"I am. In fact, I'd better get going soon, if I want to leave myself time to get lost." This time the smile she flashed was lopsided. "Even with GPS, I'm hopeless. I won't tell you how many times I missed the right turn even in little Marietta."

"You have to go so soon?" LuAnn looked from the papers spread on their floor to the woman already gathering them up, though they'd scarcely had time to scratch the surface of them.

She hadn't expected to be so sorry to see McKenna Garrison make a quick exit. She hadn't even asked them a thing about what they may or may not have found. LuAnn cast a glance at Tess, lifting her brows. *Should we show her?*

Tess cleared her throat. "Maybe you could stop back in on your way home again. We don't want to keep you from your appointment in Cleveland, of course, but we have some things we'd like to show you, when you have time."

McKenna's whole face lit up. "Oh, that would be great! I was afraid I'd be making a nuisance of myself, showing up basically uninvited as I've done. In fact... do you have any rooms available this week? I'd love to explore Marietta and do some digging on my own, and let you guys look through the rest of this."

Tess nodded, not even needing to reference the computer. "We sure do. We're booked over the weekend, but Woodbine and Roses—one of the third-floor rooms—is available all week. As is the honeymoon suite, if your husband wanted to join you."

"Oh. No husband." The light in her face eclipsed, McKenna fisted her left hand, covering the rings with her thumb. Perhaps because LuAnn had looked right at them at that pronouncement. Her smile was more self-deprecating than annoyed. "I need to work up the gumption to take these things off. The divorce will be final in a month."

"I'm so sorry." It wasn't a sentiment LuAnn could always offer in response to news of a divorce, given that all too often the concerned parties were not sorry. But McKenna clearly was.

She lifted her brows for a moment, as if to say, *What are you going to do?* "Me too. You think you know a person better than you know yourself, and then he informs you he's found someone younger and prettier."

"Prettier?" Janice sounded genuinely outraged. "Are you kidding? You're gorgeous! You look like a supermodel!"

McKenna laughed, sunshine edging back into her face. She leaned over and slung a companionable arm around Janice, looking to LuAnn and Tess as she said, "Allow me to introduce my new best friend, Janice Eastman."

Janice grinned. "I'm serious though. I can't argue that there aren't younger women out there—that's always true—but I can't imagine a prettier one."

"That's…a balm to my heart right now. Thank you." Reclaiming her arm, McKenna continued scooting papers back into a stack, keeping her gaze on them. "I was heavier when he left. He said I'd let myself go. Though apparently emotional turmoil is a pretty good diet in my case. Between the divorce and Granddad passing away…" She sighed and picked up the stack, tapping the pages against the floor to align the edges. "Sorry. Too much information."

"Not at all." Janice settled a hand on her shoulder. "Divorce is like death—the death of your marriage. It requires a grieving process, especially when it isn't something you sought or wanted. To have to deal with both that *and* the loss of your grandfather...I can only imagine how hard that must be."

McKenna sniffled and slid the papers into her bag. "It's been pretty miserable. My daughter says I've been throwing myself in to this research to the point of obsession to counteract it."

Janice's smile was that particular degree of warm that one mother gave to another when talking of their children. "You have a daughter? How old?"

"Fourteen." She pulled the bag into her lap and held it against her stomach. "She just started at this prep school. It's an amazing place, and I'm so proud of her for getting in. But it's fifty miles from Belle Arbor. She's staying with her grandparents—*his* parents—during the week and only coming home on weekends. At least for now, at the start of the year."

LuAnn splayed a hand across her chest. She didn't have to have watched a child of her own spread her wings to know the ache it would leave a mother. She'd experienced plenty of similar feelings over the years, always going home to an empty condo. "You must be so lonely. Is there anyone else at the plantation?"

McKenna shook her head. "No. My parents are in Florida, my little sister in Oregon. There are a couple of day staffers who come to give tours, a gardener twice a week." Shrugging, she pushed herself to her feet. "Another reason staying in Marietta for a few days sounds like heaven."

Tess was on her feet as well. "Well you just come with me, McKenna, and we'll get you booked in Woodbine and Roses for as long as you like. You can stay with us all week if you want and then get home for the weekend with your daughter."

"That sounds beyond perfect."

While those two headed for the front desk, LuAnn stood as well and gave Janice a hand up. After glancing over her shoulder to make sure they wouldn't be overheard, she murmured, "Well that sure went differently than I'd anticipated."

"I know!" Janice's exclamation was equally hushed. "Makes me rather excited to show her what we've found, when she comes back. We should really hit our own research hard today and see if we can find out anything more for her."

"We should." LuAnn nodded and picked up their discarded coffee cups, putting them back on the cart. "What all do we have to go through? More microfilm at the library."

"Prudence's journal—maybe now that we know what names we're looking for, something will jump out at us."

"I'll call Brad too, and see if Irene and Thelma perchance have anything in their house that could help us out."

"It's certainly a museum of local history." Janice nodded, sending her blonde curls bouncing and her eyes a-twinkling. "Yes, you call Brad. Go ahead and do that now. Maybe schedule a lunch to talk it over with him."

"Don't start with me, Janice Eastman." LuAnn leveled a finger at her friend's nose and narrowed her eyes. Not that she planned on going, yet again, into why she and Brad had no desire to be more than friends.

Not least of which was the very reason McKenna Garrison had just pointed out. *"You think you know a person better than you know yourself, and then..."*

She'd call him though. For the sake of the research. After wheeling the coffee cart back into the kitchen and promptly being shooed out by Winnie, who assured her she'd be happy to take care of it, LuAnn jogged up the stairs to her personal quarters.

Her notebooks were all up there, and if Brad had any recommendations or information, she needed to be able to write them down.

Safely ensconced in her sitting room, she hit the space bar on her laptop to bring it to life while she opened her notebook and queued up Brad's number on her phone. Once settled in her desk chair, she hit the green phone icon to connect and clicked her pen into position.

Her screen blinked to life as the phone rang. Her email was still up—and the only bold, unread message made her pulse catch in shock. *Phillip Whitman. Re:Re: Good to See You.*

He'd written her back? After her vague reply?

"Hey, LuAnn," came Brad's voice in her ear. "What's up?"

She blinked and pivoted away from the computer to get the email out of her line of sight. "Hey, Brad. Well..." She filled him in briefly on McKenna and their renewed determination to discover anything they could about the jewelry's tenure in and connection to Marietta, ending with, "Did you by chance mention it to the aunts? Do you think they might know anything?"

He chuckled. "Funny you should ask. As it happens, I was going to call you as soon as I finished this email and extend an invitation from them to come for supper tonight. They spent yesterday afternoon sorting through some old files and said they might have some information to help you."

"Really? That's wonderful. We'll be there."

"Great. I told them you'd bring Winnie's peanut soup. Irene's been craving it."

She laughed and leaned back in her chair—a mistake, as that put her computer screen in her view again, with those taunting words. She closed the laptop in self-defense. "So you invite me to a dinner that I must provide?"

"Hey, you open a soup café, you get volunteered to bring soup. If you don't like that reality..."

Her chuckle tapered off. "That's fine. Biscuits and soup for...five or six? Are you joining us?"

There was a moment's pause. Was it weighted, telling? Or was she just reading into it? "Not tonight, I'm afraid. I have a late showing with some out-of-town clients. Then I'm meeting Grant and Saffron and Wendy."

"That sounds like fun." She kept her voice light and told herself he wasn't being weird, he was likely just distracted. Probably by the email she'd apparently interrupted. "Well, I'll let you go. But thanks, Brad. I really appreciate you asking them about it."

"Hey, no problem. I'll check in tomorrow to see what they found, okay?"

"Sure." They said their goodbyes, and she disconnected. Then she just stared at the phone. He hadn't mentioned Thorn, hadn't asked if they had any updates, or she would have told him about the haircut news. Not that it was necessarily anything. But he hadn't asked.

Distraction? Or just a symptom of his not-so-generous assumptions?

Well, she wasn't going to let it bother her. With a deep breath, she opened the computer again, brought it back to life, and clicked into that email before she could wonder too long what it said.

Not much. Just chatting about some of the things he and Jill had planned for the autumn, and a mention of booking a room at the inn during the Christmas season, perhaps. As vague as her letter had been, really.

Then came the next line. *Assuming we're still together by then. Jill seems a little restless . . .*

LuAnn hissed out a breath and closed out the email. She wasn't going to respond to that and get sucked into wondering about his love life. She wasn't even going to *think* about his love life. She was just going to focus on the tasks needing to be done today and—

Her phone's ring interrupted her. Thank heavens. She picked it up, swiping to accept the call as she registered that it was Laura's name on the screen. "Hi, Laura."

"He's in the ICU. I'm on my way there now."

LuAnn sprang to her feet. "What? Why ICU? What happened?"

She could hear hurried steps and the slamming of a door. "Severe concussion, they said. He's in a coma and has been since someone brought him in on Friday." Laura's voice cracked. "He didn't have his wallet on him—could you check and see if it's stashed in his truck somewhere? If not, it was probably stolen. I don't know if he was attacked and robbed or if it was an accident or...or *what*. But if it's not there, then we need to cancel his cards and get him a new license and—"

"Slow down, honey. Take a deep breath." Fingers pressed to her lips, LuAnn took her own advice. "All of that can be worried about later if it's not in the truck. Right now, just focus on getting to your dad in one piece, okay? Do you have the kids with you?"

A car door opened and shut in the background. "Emma's here with them. Jake's driving me." The unmistakable sound of a stifled sob sounded across the airwaves. "He's been in there since Friday, LuAnn. All alone. A John Doe. Five days that I should have been with him!"

"Don't you start with the guilt, young lady. You've done all you could to find him."

"But if I had just asked about the tattoo instead of the hair—"

"Enough. I'm serious." She lowered her hand and pressed it to the desk. "There are always going to be should-have-dones in life, but you can't dwell on that. Just be glad the Lord led us past Jeremy this morning after we found the phone last night. Be glad you found him *now*."

Laura didn't sound exactly convinced, but she agreed and soon said her goodbyes, no doubt needing to make other calls during the short drive to the hospital.

LuAnn had some informing to do herself. But first she closed her eyes and focused on that part of her heart where the Lord dwelled. "Thank You, Father God. Thank You. And please. *Please.*" She didn't say any more.

But then, she didn't figure she had to.

CHAPTER FIFTEEN

LuAnn went so far as to lie back on the not-exactly-pristine floorboards of Thorn's truck to better look under the seat. But despite the daylight and the flashlight she had in hand, she found nothing else shoved under there but a forgotten chip bag and a first aid kit.

The irony wasn't lost on her. But it only made her heart heavier.

"Anything?"

Shaking her head, LuAnn sat up again, nearly thwacking her temple on the steering wheel, and pushed herself back to her feet. "No wallet."

Tess sighed. Janice had gone around the passenger door and opened it as well, checking the pockets in the door and the glove compartment. "Nothing over here either."

"I was hoping it would be there." Rubbing her neck, Tess sent her gaze to the street. "I hate to tell Laura she has one more thing to worry about. Do you think maybe he dropped it somewhere? Could someone have turned it in at the police station?"

"Given the report Laura filed, I daresay if the police had it, they would have let her know." LuAnn brushed off the dirt and pebbles she'd picked up from the floor mats.

"There were an awful lot of people in town this weekend." Janice leaned onto the seat, her face a mask of concern. "I guess it's too much to hope that one of them didn't find it and take it, if he *had* dropped it somewhere."

"But why stash the phone?" Much as she tried, LuAnn couldn't make sense of it.

Tess shrugged. "If he got the concussion in the basement, which the blood seems to indicate, he probably wasn't thinking very clearly. He must have stumbled out here, put it under the seat for whatever reason, and then fallen somewhere along the street. Do you think he was trying to walk to the hospital?"

"Maybe." According to the text Laura had sent a few minutes ago, he'd been found at the intersection of Ohio and 5th Streets, unconscious, by a Good Samaritan from Pennsylvania who was in town for the festival. "He was heading in the right direction. But why wouldn't he have come to us?"

Janice shut the passenger door and came around the front of the truck to rejoin LuAnn and Tess. "Who knows? If I were to guess, the injury brought back his instinct to fend for himself. He was alone for a lot of years."

It made LuAnn's chest ache still more to think of it. Their friend, bloody and in pain and on the brink of blacking out, stumbling along the street while they were blissfully unaware, arranging chocolates in bowls and oohing over flower arrangements.

It wasn't right. Why hadn't God nudged them? Whispered in their hearts that they ought to check on him? Recalling her advice to Laura made her put a halt to that line of thinking, but it did nothing to ease the ache.

"I guess we might as well head to the hospital," Tess said, "unless someone can think of somewhere else he might have put his wallet."

They'd already rechecked the basement before coming out here. Where else could he have been? LuAnn shook her head. "Unless he left it at his apartment that day."

Janice tilted her head to the side. "I'll send Stacy a message on the way, asking her to check. I know she won't want to snoop, but I think Laura will be grateful to have all the bases covered. And Thorn would say he had nothing to hide."

Unless he did. LuAnn shook that thought away as they headed for Tess's car. The fact that Thorn was seriously injured was surely proof that he hadn't been doing anything under-handed.

Wasn't it?

She relinquished the front seat to Janice, happy to sit in the back where she could gaze unfocused out the window. It would only take a few minutes to get to Marietta Memorial, anyway. Barely long enough to let her mind wander, which was proba-bly a blessing, given the shadows it seemed determined to wan-der into.

"So when is McKenna coming back?" she thought to ask as they turned onto 5th Street. "Tonight or tomorrow?"

"Tonight. She was guessing it would be eight or nine o'clock." Tess glanced at LuAnn in the rearview mirror. "I still can't quite believe she blew out of here before even asking if we'd found anything. But I figured if we'd tried to show it to her then, she would have gotten so excited she'd have forgotten her other appointment."

"It'll keep until tonight." Janice sighed. "I thought we'd spend the day doing some research. I hadn't imagined a trip to the ICU."

Neither had LuAnn. She looked out the window again and watched the familiar buildings zip by. So quickly this place had become home again. She recognized the houses, many of the cars, scores of the people. But it wasn't perfect—no place was. Plenty of people *hadn't* welcomed Thorn back into the land of the living after he'd chosen to skirt society and all but bury himself with his wife and daughter. What if someone carried a grudge? What if he hadn't just hit his head in the basement but had been... attacked?

What if he'd been making off with the jewels like they feared, and someone saw him, hit him, and stole them?

They could be lost forever. And their friend could have betrayed them. And Laura's heart could be broken, even having found him.

Don't be a fool, LuAnn. A well-deserved lecture, but it didn't stop the rampaging thoughts. She knew what would, though. *Lord, help me to dwell on You, not on these doubts. Help me to keep giving all this to You. Whatever happened, You're still in control. And I'm going to trust that it's for Your purpose. Please reveal it to us, Father. And please heal our friend.*

Soon Tess was pulling into a parking spot outside of Marietta Memorial, and they were trekking through the autumn sun toward the glass doors. LuAnn had never been a fan of hospitals, but the past year as her mom's health failed, she'd spent her fair share of time in them. The moment she walked inside, the smell hit her. Cafeteria food and latex and disinfectant.

No, not a fan of hospitals. Her apologies to all her friends in the medical professions. She was grateful to them for serving and working in places like this, but she couldn't do it.

Janice, far more familiar with this particular hospital than either LuAnn or Tess, led the way to the ICU. Outside the doors, she lifted the phone and asked in her perfect pastor's wife voice—all confidence and sympathy and trustworthiness—about visiting Tory Thornton. A few seconds later she replaced the handset. "Only two visitors at a time, and Laura and Jake are both in there right now. But they'll let them know we're here."

LuAnn obligingly settled on a chair near at hand and opened her purse. She hadn't thought to stash her book in here, but a few lists would help calm her mind. She drew out her notebook and pen and worked on jotting down what they'd learned from McKenna that morning, questions she still had and hoped to find answers to in the rest of the documents, and what she should look for in the microfilm.

The name Garrison, certainly. Tilla. Belle Arbor.

The door *whooshed* open, and Jake strolled out. He didn't bother with a smile. "If one of you wants to go back, I have a couple of calls to return." Without another word, he breezed past them down the hall.

Wow, LuAnn mouthed. Tess snorted her agreement. And Janice stared after him with disbelieving eyes. LuAnn reached over to touch her hand. "You go ahead, sweetie. You were his friend first."

Janice made no argument and soon disappeared behind the glass doors.

Tess took a seat beside LuAnn and leaned in close. "What's up with Laura's husband? Could he have been any more abrupt?"

LuAnn shook her head and kept her eyes trained on the hall. "I'd have thought he'd have lost the attitude when they realized he was here. I mean, it was understandable before— he doesn't want her dad to hurt her again—but..."

"But we were obviously wrong to entertain any doubts about Thorn." Tess sent LuAnn a probing, uncertain look. "Right?"

"Right."

"You sound about as convinced as I do."

She sighed and leaned back in her chair, tracing a fingertip over the binding of her notebook. "Hypothetically speaking, it could have been the theft of jewelry that led to the injury. A mugging, if he had it in his hands or something. But that's surely farfetched."

"Mm." Tess pursed her lips and stared down the hallway too. "If we're thinking he was attacked, there are other motives that could be entertained. Like malice."

LuAnn fought off a shiver. She didn't exactly like Jake, given the impression he'd made on her thus far, but it was a long leap from not liking someone to suspecting him of something as heinous as assaulting his father-in-law. Just like it was a long leap from not liking one's father-in-law to wanting to assault him.

Then she recalled that first phone call she'd made, when he'd answered Laura's phone. What was it he'd said? *I just walked in to find...*

Though he'd supposedly called Laura home to see to the baby so he could do an online class, it had sounded as though he'd been out. What if he'd been out before too? Or had arranged for Thorn to meet him somewhere before he was supposed to meet Laura? What if that somewhere was near the inn? Or on the corner of Ohio and 5th?

All this uncertainty was enough to drive her nuts. She needed answers to something.

They wouldn't be coming from Tory Thornton though. That truth hammered into her ten minutes later when she was taking her turn beside Laura, lowering into a squeaky pleather chair by the hospital bed.

She wouldn't have known him if she'd seen him lying in a ditch. The short hair, combined with the ghastly swelling and bruising of his face, would have seen to that. But knowing it was him, she could identify his jaw, his neck, the hands that fixed so many things around the inn over the summer. The familiar gothic cross tattoo.

LuAnn made no objection when Laura's hand found hers and squeezed. "What did the doctors say?" She spoke in a hush, because a normal volume seemed wrong in this dim room with its beeping monitors and dripping IV.

Laura didn't take her eyes off her dad. "I haven't spoken to the doctor yet, but the nurse said he's been like this since they brought him in on Friday. She said it's a bad concussion." She squeezed LuAnn's fingers. "People die from injuries like this. Sometimes they just never wake up and stay in a coma forever. What am I supposed to do if that happens to him, LuAnn? I just got him back."

Tears stung LuAnn's eyes. For her friend, for his daughter, for the clear memory of sitting beside a loved one's bed and asking that same question. *What am I supposed to do, Lord?* She'd asked it when Jesse died weeks before their wedding. She'd asked it when her best friends' husbands were lost to them. She'd even asked it as she watched her mother struggle for those last breaths, even though she'd known that one was coming, that it would be a mercy for Mom. It had still left LuAnn with that dreaded *What now?*

She drew in a careful breath and covered Laura's fingers with her other hand too. "I want to tell you it won't come to that, sweetie. That he'll be fine. He's fit, he's strong, he's healthy. All that is in his favor. And I pray with everything in me that he opens his eyes and comes back to you. But..." She looked over at the young woman still staring at the figure on the bed. The carefully arranged hair, the impeccable clothes, the mascara streaks on her cheeks, the hollows under her eyes.

This was a woman who loved her father. And LuAnn prayed that Thorn was aware of it even now. Laura sniffled. "But he could die."

"He could. We all could, any moment. And if that were to happen to him, then you would mourn and grieve and rant and rail. And ultimately, you'd be grateful. So, so grateful that you had the chance to get to know him again. To be a part of his life. That you could erase once and for all the question of whether he loved you, whether you were enough. You can know he did, and that you were."

Laura finally turned her brimming eyes toward LuAnn. "Do you think if I'd been better at praying...? If I'd gone to church last week when he asked me...?"

LuAnn squeezed the hand between hers and offered a gentle smile. "No. I don't think so. I think God knows your heart. He knows how you've longed for reconciliation. He knows how earnestly you've been searching since Friday, and how selflessly. And He knows how you've sought those prayers and His help now. Maybe He'll use this to get your attention—but I can't believe it happened as it did to punish you."

Laura tried on a tremulous smile and wiped her cheek. "I hope you're right. This morning I...Dad sent me a Bible for my birthday last month—which seemed like a pretty stupid gift at the time. But I opened it this morning. And didn't have a clue where to start."

"Well, I think I can help you there." LuAnn opened her purse and pulled out a small memo pad. One that was ragged at the edges and had the look of something that had been tossed around in her purse for years, because it had.

She'd kept it near her all through nursing her mom, jotting down any Scripture that was of particular comfort during those days. Sometimes she saw them on greeting cards or wall hangings, sometimes she found them in her own devotions, sometimes a friend slipped them to her. Always they'd been a balm on her ragged-edged soul.

After tearing a fresh sheet of paper from her larger notebook, she wrote the verses down for Laura, careful to put them in order so she'd have an easier time of finding them for herself. And she tacked on some references that would explain faith in Jesus and salvation too, from John and Romans.

When she was finished, she handed the page to Laura. "Here you go, sweetie. I hope these help." Figuring she'd outstayed her allotted time by that point, LuAnn stood, resting a hand on Laura's shoulder for a moment. "Hang in there. And call if you need us. Or if he wakes up."

"I will."

She took her leave, not sure if her heart was heavier or lighter as she walked back through the doors to the waiting room. But when she saw the impassable face of Jake as he finished on the phone and started back toward his wife, it settled on heavy. That guy couldn't look any less happy to be here.

Which begged the question—how in the world could she find out where he'd been last Friday?

Marietta, Ohio
May 1862

Prudence chewed her lip and kept to the shadows of the alley, under the guise of watching over little Moses while he and Hezekiah Williams played with rocks.

Hezekiah's mother, Mercy, gripped Prudence's hand. "Thee has done the right thing, Prudence. We cannot hope to win this war if we allow spies in our midst."

Much as the words were what she wanted to hear, they couldn't penetrate the wall of fear around Prudence's heart. Evidence said she'd been hosting a traitor to the Union at her table. She and Jason had prayed all night over what to do with the information. When they traveled to the Williamses' farm to fetch Moses that morning, they had talked it over with their trusted Friends.

This was the course all had agreed upon. That Jason would take the incriminating letter to the police in Marietta, saying he'd seen it fall from Lewis Humphreys's jacket and didn't know what else to do with it. No mention would be made of Tilla, who would be on the train to Cleveland this afternoon.

"Back, back, back!" Mercy's voice, hushed but insistent, pushed Prudence farther into the shadows as surely as the touch on her arm did.

Prudence obeyed but looked past the blonde hair of her friend to the street, to see what had earned the alarm.

Two men *clip-clopped* over the cobblestones on tired-looking horses. They wore hats pulled low over their brows, dust-covered jackets, and expressions upon their countenances that could freeze the Ohio and Muskingum Rivers in their paths.

A shudder overtook Prudence as warning whispered up her spine. One of them was familiar—he'd come through Marietta several times over the years, always for the same purpose. Hunting escaped slaves. Could he have been hired by Tilla's masters? There was no reason to assume so.

And no reason to hope not.

The second man was the one who really arrested Prudence's attention, however. Despite being certain she'd never seen him before, there was something familiar about the slope of his nose. Or maybe the shape of his eyes. Or the length of his face?

Perhaps it was her imagination. Regardless, she doubted one could look into that hard face and *not* shudder. The eyes he swept over the street looked as cold as failed dreams. He gripped his reins in one hand in a way that denoted comfort in the saddle and yet alertness.

His other arm was naught but a tucked-up sleeve. Another something all too familiar as the war dragged on and boys came home with missing limbs and shattered spirits.

The two horsemen were just past the alley when the stranger pulled up suddenly with his single hand. Prudence's breath caught, half afraid he'd spin back on them. It didn't matter if he did—she was well versed in playing the part of an ordinary farmer's wife, and Mercy would aid her in that.

"There's Humphreys."

Prudence wasn't certain which of the men growled the name, but it was obviously not spoken in welcome. Her fingers bit into the bricks of the building at her back. The men could have seen another Humphreys on the street, she supposed. But she had a feeling it was Lewis, in town to purchase Tilla's train ticket as he said he would do. She prayed that Jason would remain out of sight.

"Local planter's son, on the Virginia side. You know him?"

"Yeah. I know him."

Both men's vowels had a drawl to them that carried into the consonants. *Southern.* Not surprising for the slave hunter or his traveling companion, but it sent apprehension through Prudence's stomach. What if they *were* here on behalf of Belle Arbor? It was too soon, their plan wasn't in motion yet. They could be discovered. Stopped.

Betrayed.

"Should we follow him?"

"No." The original speaker let the word roll out like a banner of war. "I know where to find him. Let's get to the hotel."

Prudence couldn't breathe until the men had passed. And once she'd gathered air into her lungs, she could do nothing but let it out again in a prayer. "Help us, Jesus."

CHAPTER SIXTEEN

LuAnn slid her notebook onto the coffee table beside the cardboard box Irene and Thelma had apparently had Brad haul down earlier. She and Tess had spent two hours in the archives that afternoon, poring over the microfilm of the newspapers, while Janice had been organizing folks from church to relieve Laura in the hospital and provide meals for them.

"I haven't really looked through all of this since I was a little girl." Irene pulled a scrapbook from the box, a twinkle in her eye as she opened it. "I remember spending hours looking through it back then though. I just loved the idea of missing treasure right here in town!"

"I bet." LuAnn smiled and flipped her notebook open. "We found a few newspaper articles that mentioned it."

"Though the accounts were confusing. Inconsistent," Tess added. "First they were all about the runaway slave that had stolen goods in her possession."

"'One Tilla,'" Thelma read over Irene's shoulder. "'Of seventeen or eighteen years, slender of frame, of middling height, last seen in a blue dress.' I daresay that could have described half the women in town, slave or free—aside from the age."

Janice shook her head. "And yet it doesn't describe her well at all. We saw a picture of her this morning—she was beautiful. It doesn't mention that she could pass for a white woman or that her clothes weren't those of a normal slave. Assuming she still had better clothes, I guess. She certainly did in what we saw."

"I wonder if perhaps the newspaper wasn't exactly keen to help find her?" LuAnn's lips quirked up. She could well imagine a typesetter with an abolitionist's bent, conveniently forgetting to include specific characteristics that would actually lead to a slave's discovery. Some ruddy young man with ink stains on his fingers and white shirtsleeves always rolled up past his elbows.

The aunts both nodded. "Possibly," Irene said. "There were mixed feelings here just like everywhere else, but in general Ohio was proud to be a free state and not eager to help the cause of slavery."

Tess flipped a page in LuAnn's notes. "But the next article seems to have forgotten all about Tilla. It's about a *man* who stole the jewels. Lewis Humphreys, a suspected Confederate spy."

"I have a page here from a journal that speaks to that." Irene tapped a finger to a laminated page. "The writing's awfully faded—nearly as much as my eyes. Can one of you girls read it?"

LuAnn did love spending time with these ladies who thought of *them* as youngsters. She accepted the scrapbook and squinted at the page. "Let's see. Looks like, 'Something doesn't add up about this late business with Humphreys, the alleged missing jewelry, and those two slave hunters who showed up in town. They are without question from the South, so Confederate by birth if not by persuasion. And given their career, I must think their persuasion lies that way too. The newspapers decry our neighbor as a Confederate spy—something that could have seen him lynched by any number of outraged locals. But it would *not* have outraged those two strangers. Why, then, was it by their hands that he was..."" LuAnn looked up, frowning. "Humphreys was killed?"

"That wasn't clear in any of the newspaper articles." Tess flipped through the notebook and back again. "Which is *really* strange. If he was a local plantation owner, shouldn't his death have been big news?"

LuAnn scanned ahead in the journal entry, her brows lifting. "The writer of this suspected the stranger bought off the local police. Says had she not been at Riverfront House that day, she wouldn't have known that Humphreys was dead at all. Word around town was that he'd run off to join the Confederate Army, armed with information on Union troop movements."

"So the newspaper just shifted its attention to the treasure hunt?" Janice pulled the scrapbook partway onto her lap and lifted the next page halfway, her brows lifted. LuAnn motioned her to go on, so she let the page settle.

And there was an original clipping of the same newspaper article she'd been viewing on microfilm the other day, mentioning only a fugitive and jewelry lost during the hunt for him. "It was suspected that he buried the treasure somewhere around Marietta..." LuAnn drew in a long breath. Buried in their walls? But how?

"That treasure hunt was apparently quite the to-do for a few months." Irene scooted forward, her faded eyes twinkling. "There are more articles and journal entries in there talking about it, if I recall. People were coming from miles around, eager for a distraction from the war, I suspect. That's when a local jeweler decided to copy the design of the jewelry."

"Here's the one Howard Bickerton, or rather Stuart Dawson, had commissioned for his wife." Thelma produced an ancient velvet box with all the flourish of a magician. She must have had it hidden in her seat cushion, just waiting for the chance to present it.

When she cracked open the lid and the light hit the white gold and sapphires, LuAnn couldn't help but whistle. "Those are gorgeous."

"I wore them on my wedding day." Irene touched her throat and straightened her spine, as if imagining again the feel of bridal silk against her skin. "We were so pleased when Bradley's Stephanie requested to borrow them for hers. She was a beautiful bride, wasn't she, Thelma?"

"Utterly captivating. I'd never seen Bradley so agog." Thelma motioned to the scrapbook and passed the jewelry to Tess. "Flip to the end. We added a photograph of her wearing them. Part of the jewelry's story—for our family, anyway."

LuAnn and Janice obligingly flipped to the end of the scrapbook. The ladies hadn't, in fact, only added a photograph of the new Stephanie Grimes—they'd added another of the wedding couple together. Stephanie looking at the camera, her joy palpable—and Brad looking at Stephanie in total adoration.

LuAnn touched a finger to the protective film covering it. Perhaps this was just what her darling friends needed to see to be convinced to drop the whole "soul mate" thing they kept harping on every time Brad smiled her way. He sure didn't smile at her like *this*. And she didn't want or need him to. He'd married his true love already, and lost her. LuAnn had found and lost hers too. Enough said. "What stunning photographs. Brad was telling me they'd had one enlarged for their twenty-fifth anniversary. One of these?"

"I believe so. Or very similar." Thelma squinted at the scrapbook, though she probably couldn't make much out from her perch on her chair.

"You can borrow the scrapbook for a few days if you like." Irene smiled. "We know you'll take good care of it."

"That would be great, thank you," Tess said as she finally passed the jewelry set to LuAnn.

She angled them into the light to better see the intricacy of the goldwork. She would have loved to ask to borrow *these* too, to compare them to the bracelet in their safe before McKenna Garrison took it home with her, but she suspected that might be stretching the ladies' generosity a little too far. "Do you mind if we take a few pictures?"

"Not at all!"

"Go right ahead!"

Tess drew her good camera from its bag—they'd decided before coming not to rely on their cell phones' cameras for this—and started snapping pictures of the pieces.

"Here." Jumping up with more energy than one would expect of a ninety-something woman, Irene pranced over to them, withdrew the tiara from its place in the box, and positioned it on LuAnn's head. "Take one of it on. It loses something in the box."

Suddenly self-conscious, LuAnn laughed and reached up to touch the circlet of white gold. "This is a far cry from the plastic and rhinestones I've worn before."

"Pretty as a picture yourself." Thelma folded her hands in her lap and grinned. "These things should really be worn more often, Reenie. Do you think Wendy will want to wear them? She's sure to get married sometime in the next few years."

"Or Saffron." Irene cracked up at that one. "Can you just imagine her wedding day? She'll probably wear a sari or sarong or kimono and declare this set far too 'establishment.'"

Certain Tess had snapped enough pictures—given that her shutter had been clicking like mad—LuAnn carefully took the tiara off and put it back into its pillowed bed. "Yet again you ladies have been so helpful." A grin took possession of her mouth. "Now, if you want to meet someone who would go 'agog' at your collection, we'll introduce you to a woman named McKenna Garrison."

"Goodness gracious goat." Janice leaned back, laughing. "You'd never peel her away! She'd be asking you about every lamp pull and end table and what polish you use on your floor!"

The aunts' eyes lit. "Send her over!" Thelma said. "Who is she?"

They explained the connection, much to the aunts' delight, and promised to introduce McKenna at some point during the week. Then, boxed scrapbook tucked under Janice's arm and jewelry returned to Thelma's seat cushion, they took their leave.

They had to get back to the inn in time to welcome their history-obsessed guest, after all. And make her day by opening their own safe.

McKenna sat in the desk chair in Tess's office, a loupe in her hand and a look on her face of pure astonishment. LuAnn fully expected delight to eclipse it soon, but just now, their guest looked as though she'd been carved of stone, with a perfect *O* of astonishment on her lips.

"It's real," she whispered. "You've— you've found them. Where, again?"

"In a wall in the basement, it seems." Janice looked over McKenna's bent head, to Tess and LuAnn. "Though it's possible it's not what it seems, even though the gold and jewels are real."

Tess nodded. "Apparently images of the missing jewels were published in the Marietta paper. Treasure hunters came from all around, and a local jeweler copied the originals and sold them as a sort of keepsake. We know for a fact the original owner of Riverfront House commissioned a set in blue for his wife. The Bickertons still have them."

"Though granted," LuAnn added, "we don't know why anyone would hide copies. Unless they didn't know they were. Or perhaps because they were simply valuable."

Light was beginning to dance in McKenna's eyes. "Failing evidence to the contrary, I'm going to assume these are the originals. I can't imagine why someone would go to the trouble of hiding copies either. Which one of you found the bracelet? Was there no sign of the rest of the set?"

LuAnn exchanged another look with Tess and Janice. None of them opened their mouths to tell this part of the story. At length, she sighed. "It wasn't one of us. It was our handyman, Thorn. The elevator's broken, and when he went down to fix it, he opened the wrong side of the wall. Found that instead of the panel."

Twinkle fully established, McKenna scooted forward on her chair. "Can I talk to him?"

"I wish you could." Now Janice spoke up, her face crumpling. "He's been injured—we're not sure how. Probably an accident in the basement. He stumbled out without us knowing and lost consciousness. He's been in a coma since Friday—severe concussion."

"Oh my!" McKenna looked appropriately horrified. "I'm so sorry to hear that! Will he be okay?"

"The doctors aren't making any promises one way or the other." Janice dabbed at the corner of her eye. "I know his family would welcome your prayers."

"Of course." McKenna lowered her gaze back to the bracelet. "Are you sure it was an accident?"

LuAnn leaned against the wall, trying not to exchange yet another glance with Tess. "It seems the most likely explanation."

"The simplest, maybe. But I don't know if it's the most likely." McKenna reached down to where her portfolio bag rested at her feet. "We didn't have enough time to get into it all this morning. But I'm pretty sure Oscar—he would have been Tilla's half-brother—killed someone in search of the jewelry. He doesn't come right out and say it in his journals, but he hints at it."

"Lewis Humphreys, maybe?" Tess moved to the little table on which she'd set the scrapbook from the aunts. "We have a journal excerpt from someone at the hotel who says she thinks two slave hunters killed him."

Janice had straightened, fire in her eyes. "But that was an entirely different situation than ours. That was someone specifically looking for the jewelry, removing obstacles in their path. Which definitely does *not* apply to Thorn. No one was looking for these things here, no one would have hurt him to get at them."

"It could have been a crime of opportunity." LuAnn didn't want to say it. She didn't want to think it. She certainly didn't want it to be. Her gaze found its way to Tess again. "Or a crime of passion for a different reason, and the jewelry just got caught up in it. Coincidence."

"That's ridiculous." Janice folded her arms across her chest. "Thorn may have gone a lot of years without any friends to speak of, but he didn't have enemies either."

Until a couple of weeks ago, when Jake Getty came to town. Though that still didn't quite make sense. If Jake was so set against Thorn, why agree to move thousands of miles with his young family?

LuAnn reached out to take the stack of clipped papers that McKenna had drawn out of her bag. "So these are from Oscar's journal?"

McKenna nodded, the glance she sent between them saying she wasn't oblivious to the undercurrents running through the office. "If he kept one before he inherited Belle Arbor, they weren't preserved. But we have four in our library that begin on the day he became master of the plantation. And let me just tell you, he was not a nice guy. I'm kind of ashamed to have to claim him as an ancestor."

Tess chuckled. "I think we all have someone like that in our lineage—we just don't all have the journals to prove it."

McKenna granted that with a smile and a lift of her brows. "True. Oscar was apparently injured in the war—you probably gleaned that from the bit his father wrote about him that we read this morning—and it made him bitter. He speaks of everyone in his life as if they all owe him something." McKenna shuddered. "I pity his poor wife and kids. I suspect, given what he says about them, that he was abusive. Emotionally for sure, and likely physically as well. He's the one who lost Belle Arbor, during Reconstruction. It turned him from bitter to downright hateful."

LuAnn opened her mouth to comment, but the ring of the doorbell silenced her. Given that they were expecting no other guests, they'd locked up after McKenna came in. She set the stack of papers down and turned to the door, since she was closest. "I'll see who that is. If it's an unexpected guest, I'll call for you, Tess."

Scrapbook still in hand, Tess nodded.

LuAnn headed for the front door. In the porchlight, she could make out through the glass a female figure, which certainly didn't narrow down the possibilities. It could well be Robin, stopping by to try to sweet-talk some more work out of them. But when she glanced through the peep hole before unlocking the door, she didn't recognize the woman standing on the porch. All she could tell was that she was probably in her late forties, maybe early fifties. She had gorgeous red hair. And when LuAnn opened the door, worry shouted from her blue-green eyes.

"Are you LuAnn Sherrill?"

LuAnn held the door wide. There was something familiar about the woman's voice. And the shape of her face. "Yes. Won't you come in? Can I help you?"

"I was reading your messages to my daughter. Laura." The woman stepped in, reaching out a hand as she said, "Bev Thornton. Tell me he's gone."

LuAnn shook Bev's hand, trying to file everything into its proper spot in her mind. Laura's mom, which explained the familiarity of the voice and face. And, for that matter, the hair. Thorn's ex-wife—who still, apparently, went by her married name. That was a bit surprising, given the complete break. Or maybe she was just using the name with LuAnn so she'd draw the immediate connection.

But that last sentence remained a question mark in her mind. "*He* who? Thorn? He's in the hospital—"

"I know." Her voice nearly broke on that. She reclaimed her hand and wrapped her arms around her middle. "I just came from there. That's where Lar showed me what she knew about what happened, including the texts you guys had exchanged. Including one saying Marshall Bricker was in town. Please tell me he's gone."

Marshall Bricker? *He* was the one who lit such concern in this woman's eyes? LuAnn closed the door on the night air and motioned Bev farther inside. "I guess he is. He checked out on Monday."

That news didn't make the lines in Bev's face ease any. "But then Tory's truck was broken into. Did you see the guy? Could it have been Brick?"

Brick. She said it like someone familiar with the name, with the person . . . and so, likely familiar with the accusations Mr. Bricker had made against Thorn. Of course, that made sense. She'd been married to him at the time, or around then.

LuAnn motioned toward the sitting area. "We didn't see anything definitive. A ball cap, dark clothes, long sleeve shirt. It could have been anyone. A man, given the size, but otherwise . . . "

Bev rubbed her arms and meandered into the room, though she didn't appear to actually be seeing anything in it. "I'm sorry. I didn't mean to burst in here and interrogate you. It's just—that's man's bad news. I didn't even know he was out of Leavenworth."

"Wait—what?" LuAnn gripped the back of the nearest chair. "*He* was in Leavenworth? But he said . . . "

Bev lifted her red brows. "Let me guess. He said Tory should have been?"

"Something like that." It felt stupid to even admit it, and thereby admit the thought had entered her head. She held up a finger. "Let me go grab my friends. Can I get you anything? Something to drink? To eat?"

The woman shook her head. "I just had dinner with Lar and the kids."

And Jake? Had he been around? LuAnn nearly asked but decided that could wait. Especially if they had a more likely suspect. She hurried back to the office and poked her head in. "Hey. Could you excuse us for a few minutes, McKenna?" She glanced from Tess to Janice. "Laura's mom is here, and I think we'll want to hear what she has to say."

McKenna nodded, her eyes wide. "Of course! Go, go." As she spoke, a song began playing from the vicinity of her bag, and a smile bloomed on her face. "My daughter. See, I won't miss you at all. I'll just take this call."

Tess and Janice followed in LuAnn's wake, closing the office door behind them to give McKenna some privacy for her call, and back into the parlor. Bev had wandered to the window facing south and was looking out, toward the river and perhaps even across it into West Virginia.

Or maybe back twenty-five years, to when she lived here and watched her marriage fall apart. Given the stoop of her shoulders and the bend to her back, memories were no doubt bombarding her.

LuAnn cleared her throat to get their guest's attention. "Girls, this is Bev Thornton, Laura's mom. Bev, my friends and partners in the inn, Tess and Janice."

Bev had turned around and offered a tired smile, reaching out a hand to each of them. "Good to meet you. Hi."

Pleasantries exchanged, Tess indicated the couches and chairs. "Would you like to sit, Bev?"

That tired smile reappeared. "I'd rather stand, if that's okay. After five hours on a plane to Pittsburgh and another two and a half driving here from the airport, I need to stretch out."

"We totally understand," Janice said with that sympathetic smile of hers. It never failed to put everyone at ease.

LuAnn nodded. "Now that we're all here... What is it you wanted to tell us about Marshall Bricker?"

The very name made Bev shift from foot to foot and cast another apprehensive look out the window. "That man... If it weren't for him, I never would have left Tory. I wouldn't have had to." Her gaze came back to them, darting from one to another, sharp as an arrow. "How much do you know about Tory's military days?"

"Nothing." Janice answered for all of them.

LuAnn knew her friend well enough to know she was thinking of that call she'd placed to Stuart, seeing if he could ask his friend to find out anything he could about a larceny charge.

With a sigh, Bev half-turned back to the window. "I was proud of him when he enlisted for Desert Storm. He always had a bit of wanderlust, I think. Even when we met in college in Columbus, he was always talking about seeing the world, doing big things. I thought this could be what he needed to satiate that, and to do some good besides. You know? Serve his country."

"Sure." Tess sat back in her chair. "What branch did he join?"

"Marines." Her sad smile was flecked through with uncertain memories. "Man, I thought I was lucky, seeing him in his uniform. He shipped out when Laura was just a month old, and I stood there, waving him off, so sure it would be a good thing for us. Then, within a few weeks, his letters and calls starting filling up with all his new buddies, his brothers. Specifically this guy named Brick. They were inseparable. Went everywhere together. Had each other's back, I thought."

Bev paused to shake her head, nostrils flaring.

"Marshall Bricker," LuAnn put in, to clarify for her friends.

Questions lit their eyes.

Bev seemed oblivious to them, but she would no doubt answer them anyway. She rubbed one hand up the opposite arm. "Tory had never been what I'd call a follower, not in the years I'd known him. But it started sounding to me like he was just blindly following this guy into all sorts of crazy situations. *Dangerous* situations. Of course, if I said anything, it was *me* who was causing a problem." She breathed a laugh filled with sarcasm rather than amusement. "The fights we had. All he could talk about was the adventures they had—he painted this picture like war was just a-an obstacle course, or something. You dodge here, you jump there, you race through, and then you claim a prize."

At that, her gaze swung back to them. "That's what he started talking about in spring of '91. Desert Storm was officially over, but they were still there, of course. Looking for the next adventure." Her eyes hardened. "Have you ever seen that movie with George Clooney, about the military guys trying to steal gold from the Middle East?"

LuAnn sucked in a breath. "Yeah." The others nodded too.

"Could have been an exaggerated account of what Brick started planning." Bitterness all but dripped from her as she paced a few steps. "I thought at first that the little things Tory said were just stupid dreaming, you know. 'You should see all the gold these guys have, babe. Gold toilet seats. Gold this, gold that.' Nothing serious. Then..."

Janice took a step forward, war rampaging across her face. No doubt at trying to reconcile *this* Tory Thornton with the one she knew. "Then?"

"Then he got really quiet. Wouldn't say anything more about *anything*, really. That's when I knew something was wrong. I..." Bev paused, averted her face, and pressed her lips together for a moment, obviously struggling to regain her composure. "If I had it all to do over again, I'd do it differently. But at the time, all I could think was that here I was with a baby, and her father was slipping away from me for good. He'd been caught up in who-knew-what, and I was afraid I'd never see him again. I don't know how I knew, really, but it was like this dark cloud came between us. I couldn't talk to him without getting the feeling that he'd been swallowed up by that dark cloud."

LuAnn sank to a seat on the arm of a chair. "So what happened?"

"All that talk went quiet. And I knew. I knew it had gone from stupid daydreaming to a real plan."

Given the dots, LuAnn could pretty much connect them. "Stealing gold."

Bev gave a curt nod. "To this day, I can't imagine what came over him to even think about it. It wasn't the kind of man he was. Something had gotten hold of him, that's for sure. Maybe greed. Maybe the allure of adventure. Maybe just that brotherhood tugging on him."

LuAnn took a deep breath. "So he really did it?"

"No." Bev deflated, going so far as to wilt onto the wide windowsill. "I remember the day. I knew something was coming to a head. When he called, I told him..." She swallowed and lifted her chin. "I told him I was leaving. Going to nurse my grandmother in California. I told him that if he didn't know what in this world was greater than gold, then he didn't need to bother coming to find us. 'I'll have your treasure,' I said. I'll never forget that. He'd always called Lar his treasure. 'You decide if she's worth more than a gold toilet seat.'"

"And he did." Janice edged a bit nearer to Bev, eyes so wide they were imploring, begging her to confirm. "You said he didn't do it. He made his choice."

LuAnn nodded along with the question, but had to wonder. If he'd made the right choice, why had their marriage still ended? Why had Bev and Laura stayed in California all those years? Why had Thorn essentially hidden all hints of his earlier life behind doors he'd never let anyone through?

Bev's unfocused gaze tangled with the past. "I didn't go to the trial, so I still don't know all the details. But he backed out, and that resulted in them getting caught—Brick and two other guys. Tory testified against them in return for an honorable discharge." She blinked her eyes clear of those cobwebs and refocused on LuAnn, Tess, and Janice. "He made the right choice. But he couldn't forgive himself for turning on his brothers, as he saw it. And they couldn't, either. Brick swore revenge. Said he didn't care if it took fifty years, when he got out, he'd come after him. Come after us."

Janice's inhale was sharp. "But surely he'd softened over the years."

Bev snorted. "Leavenworth isn't exactly known for softening a man. And Brick—he should have been out ten years ago. But his sentence was prolonged for bad behavior. I'm not sure what he did—Tory never told me. He just kept me updated on his release date. Or I thought he had."

LuAnn pushed to her feet again. "I know this is prying, so don't feel like you have to answer, but—but he made the right choice. So why didn't you come back to him?"

There was no denying the tears that pooled in Bev's eyes. "I was so mad. Furious. Hurt that he'd ever even gotten caught up in such stupidity. And then, when Brick swore revenge on us—on me and my baby girl—I couldn't. I couldn't go back to a man who would put us in that position. I—I told him he could see his daughter whenever he wanted, but that I never wanted to set eyes on him again. And I didn't. Not until to-today." A sob broke free, and Bev covered her face with her hands.

Janice was there first, an arm going around her shoulders and soothing words that meant nothing spilling from her lips in that tone that could do what the syllables themselves couldn't. Impart peace. Promise surety somewhere, if one turned to the Father Who could grant it.

Bev got herself under control quickly and wiped her eyes. "Sorry. I just never expected that the first time I saw him in twenty-five years would be like that."

"Of course you didn't." Janice rubbed a circle on Bev's shoulder. "You don't need to apologize for your emotions."

True as that was, Bev still made an effort to wrestle the rest of her emotions under control with admirable results. A few deep breaths and rapid blinks and she was saying, "I clung to my anger too long. All through the divorce, through a few years afterward. Then, just as it had started to cool, when I finally started to see that I missed him so much—that's when he let me know he'd met someone. He was remarrying. Best to bury the past, he said. Move on." A few more rapid blinks. "I think he had to do that, just shut it all out of his mind entirely, to live with himself. In his eyes, he first betrayed his family by getting involved with that plot at all, and then betrayed his brothers by turning on them rather than rescuing them from themselves."

Janice gave a thoughtful shake of her head. "I always sensed troubled depths in him, even before the accident that took his wife and daughter—his second wife and daughter, though none of us in the school system even knew about you or Laura."

Bev's shrug looked exhausted. "That was his way, I guess. Compartmentalize. Block out anything that alluded to the past. I nearly came when I heard about the accident, but…" Another tired shrug. "I didn't think he could handle it. Seeing me and Lar. But maybe I should have. Maybe if I'd reminded him that he still had a daughter, he wouldn't have fallen into such a depression. He blamed himself. Sent me an email one day saying how he failed to protect them just like he'd failed to protect us, and he didn't deserve to keep living his life as if he were a good guy."

She swallowed and drew in a shaky breath. "I thought he was going to kill himself. Then when he didn't reply to any of my messages afterward, I panicked. Contacted my cousin who still lives in town. It took her a while to verify he was still here, just off the grid. Roaming around like a homeless man."

"Emma's mom? And Emma, later," LuAnn murmured.

Bev nodded. Then, as if getting a second wind, she stood straighter and stepped away from Janice's hand, toward LuAnn and Tess. "But if Marshall Bricker's here, we can't assume it's to make amends. He's had a lot of years to stew over what Tory did to him and hasn't shown any signs of repentance for his crimes, from what I've been told."

Janice shuddered. "And we had him here, under our roof. I don't suppose we can run background checks on everyone who makes a reservation, can we, Tess?"

Tess clutched her elbows with her hands. "I wish we could. So what do we do now? Call the police? Try to find out if he's staying somewhere else in town? Or just hope he left when it looked like Thorn had skipped town with the jewelry?"

"Jewelry?" Bev's expression could only be described as worried.

LuAnn brought her up-to-date as quickly as she could, keeping the story vague and general.

The woman was shaking her head long before she finished. "If Brick thinks there's a score to be had—and at Tory's expense—don't count on him leaving without making an attempt for it. That's what my gut says, and I've learned to trust it."

That dark cloud Bev had spoken of feeling before bullied its way into the room. LuAnn whispered a prayer against it. Maybe they couldn't fight a decades-old greed. But she knew Who could.

As LuAnn walked Bev to the door a few minutes later, she forced a smile to her lips. "I appreciate how you never tried to poison Laura against her dad," she said. "A lot of women aren't so generous. Though Jake seems a bit wary of him."

Bev's smile was affectionate. "Jake's a good guy. He was afraid Tory would hurt Laura's feelings, but he adores her so much, he couldn't bear to be the thing standing between them, so to Marietta they came. He gets a little grumpy when anyone upsets her, but when I left the hospital, all that grumpiness was focused on whoever did this to her dad. He said, 'No one hurts my family and gets away with it.' Looks like he's accepted Tory as family, finally. And in Jake's mind, that's that."

With a smile and a little wave, Bev opened the door and stepped outside.

LuAnn hoped and prayed that Bev was reading him right. And if she thought about it in the right light, his attitude at the hospital yesterday could have been on *behalf* of Thorn and not *because* of him.

She hoped. But it did little to make her lighter as she shut the door quietly against Bev and the night.

CHAPTER SEVENTEEN

I bet this is referring to it." McKenna tapped her pointer finger on the photocopy on the table. "The date's right."

"You think?" LuAnn bent over the copy of Prudence Willard's journal. She'd been sipping her morning coffee while reading through McKenna's collection of notes and copies, while their guest looked through theirs. Good thing she was the only guest this morning, as they'd commandeered the café as Research Headquarters.

They hadn't spent much time on this side of things last night. McKenna was exhausted after her long day of travel, and the Inn Crowd had been distracted with the Thorn side of things, so they'd been happy to bid her a good night.

Bev Thornton—who really did still go by her married name—had gone to the police station and told them her fears. They'd promised to keep an eye out for Marshall Bricker as they made their rounds, and to check into his release from Leavenworth. She'd left them a voice mail on the inn's line with an update and to let them know she was staying at Laura and Jake's house.

Shaking off those thoughts, LuAnn refocused her attention on the papers spread on the café table before them. Janice and Tess had looked up from their seats at the two-top beside them, the collection of papers currently far too big for one table alone.

"Here." McKenna tapped a journal entry.

A wire came today, assuring us that T is safe with L's friends. It is sore consolation, given all that passed here as she was on the train headed north.

Why are we, Thy creation, so eager to believe the worst of each other, Lord? So quick to judge what we don't understand? And now all I can do is cry out, "Father, forgive me!" I know Thee will. But I fear that poor girl will forever hate me for the role I've played in all this.

Her beloved is forever gone, into Thy arms. A few short days ago, I wondered at his intent, at his soul. Now I know that within him was the purest of devotion, bought at the highest of costs.

And heavy in my hand is the legacy he charged into my care. I will hold these tokens until T comes for them. And if she does not…then I will bury them in the place that looked on while he proved himself once and for all.

Forgive me, Father. Forgive me for my inability to do anything that day. Forgive me for my suspicion, that led us there. Forgive me for judging a man's heart, when that belongs only to Thee.

Forgive me.

Conviction spread through LuAnn. She took another sip of her coffee as she finished reading the entry from May 5, 1862. She thought back to her devotion from just a couple of days ago: *Do not judge, or you too will be judged.* She thought of the people she'd met in the last few days. Jake, Marshall Bricker, McKenna. She'd let her first impressions of them—her *judgments* of them color her attitudes toward them. In every instance, her judgment had been the exact opposite of the truth. Jake wasn't an angry man who resented his father-in-law. Marshall wasn't a polite gentle giant. And McKenna wasn't a hoity-toity snob who didn't care if she inconvenienced others. *Just as You forgave Prudence, Father, I know You'll forgive me. Help me see people through Your eyes and not my own.*

She looked up and saw Tess and Janice staring at her, questions in their eyes. She blinked away her tears and cleared her throat. "You're right. The dates coincide with Tilla coming, and she could well be the *T. L* could be Lewis Humphreys."

McKenna put a finger to her mouth and moved to almost chew on her nail before she stopped and lowered her hand again. She didn't look quite so professional today—her hair was down and wavy, her slacks had been traded for jeans, and she wore a T-shirt that proclaimed MY KID'S SWEETER THAN YOUR KID. "But it doesn't give any clue as to where Tilla went."

"It implies that the treasure didn't go with her though, don't you think?" LuAnn tapped the *heavy in my hand* sentence. "Sounds to me like Lewis had them and left them with

Prudence. That could explain why they were in our basement. That must have been where he was killed."

"True." McKenna didn't get distracted by mention of the jewelry though. Her brows remained knit. "But I still hope I can figure out where Tilla went, where she ended up. Oscar's journals say he was certain she headed for Toledo, though he never says why he's so sure. That's where I've been looking for some clue that she'd been there. But that doesn't make sense to me. Why would she have gone the long way, especially if she knew Oscar was on her tail? Maybe the Toledo information was false, meant to lead him astray."

"Maybe." Finding evidence of one escaped slave anywhere would be like looking for a needle in a haystack, though. LuAnn rose. "This requires more coffee. Refill?"

"Bless you." McKenna handed over her empty cup.

LuAnn took their cups over to the carafe and filled them, exchanging them for Janice's and Tess's next. She was still pouring the fragrant brew into their cups when the phone in the lobby pulled Tess from the café. LuAnn set her cup before the now-empty chair and paused to put a hand on Janice's shoulder. "You okay?"

Her friend shrugged. "Still worried about Thorn. And severely creeped out at the thought that he could have been attacked in our basement." Her words were quiet, her gaze flashing to McKenna.

Not that the woman, thoroughly absorbed in another page from Prudence's journal, seemed to be aware that they were even still in the room.

"Me too," LuAnn whispered. Her gaze drifted to the scrap-book borrowed from the Bickertons. It sat open to that other journal entry, the only other evidence they had that Lewis Humphreys had died. Here. Also in the basement, if Prudence's intent was to bury the jewelry in the literal place where he'd died. LuAnn couldn't suppress a shiver.

From the lobby, Tess called out, "Folks coming today will be here early! I'm going to run up and double-check their room."

"Okay!" LuAnn hollered back.

"Y'all are bellowing like a bunch of billy goats!" Winnie shouted, with a laugh, from the kitchen.

LuAnn smiled and resettled with her coffee and all those words spread out before her and tried, with the three sources they had, to piece together what must have happened back in 1862.

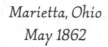

Marietta, Ohio
May 1862

Something had gone wrong. So very wrong. Prudence didn't know what it was, but when she saw the sheriff shaking the single hand of the slave hunter, a chill skittered down her spine. She spun away, back toward Riverfront House. The basket on her arm was filled with bread—her supposed purpose for coming, as the cook was still a bit under the weather. But she'd wanted to make sure those men weren't following the train to Cleveland.

She wanted to make sure Lewis Humphreys hadn't run the opposite direction, into the arms of the Confederacy.

The Confederacy. It wasn't a cause she could sympathize with, not given the slave-holding rights they held at their core. It wasn't a cause she'd thought the sheriff likely to be swayed to either, hence why Jason had ventured into those offices yesterday. But the sheriff was shaking hands, smiling in that wicked way, with those two men.

The words from Proverbs 6 that Jason had read aloud that morning while they breakfasted filled her mind again. *"These six things doth the LORD hate: yea, seven are an abomination unto him: A proud look, a lying tongue, and hands that shed innocent blood, An heart that deviseth wicked imaginations, feet that be swift in running to mischief, A false* witness that speaketh lies, and he that soweth discord among brethren."

Proud looks had those two men aplenty. As to the rest, she could only pray against it and continue on her path.

"Psst. Mrs. Willard."

She started at the voice and, pretending to stumble a bit and check the heel of her boot, made sure no one was watching her as she ducked into the alley. Lewis Humphreys stood there in the shadows, half-crouched behind a crate. "What are thee doing?" she snapped in a whisper.

He motioned her closer. "Is he still out there?"

"Who?" But she knew who he meant, and she joined him behind the crate.

"Oscar Garrison. Tilla's brother—and master." If he was set on betraying Tilla, he hid it well behind the apprehension in his eyes. "Apparently he decided to hunt her down himself. He paid me a visit yesterday afternoon."

"Did thee return the jewelry?" This she breathed so quietly she feared even he wouldn't hear her.

Lewis's larynx bobbed when he swallowed. "I offered him the story we came up with and said I'd stashed the gems. I didn't have them on me—I hid them the night she gave them to me, so I wouldn't be seen with them if anyone caught me crossing back to the plantation."

Then he'd left them somewhere on this side of the river? What place could possibly be safe enough?

"He didn't believe me." Lewis leaned closer so he could whisper as well. She fancied she could smell the fear rolling off him. "He said he knew well Tilla wouldn't part with them, not as long as she had breath left in her. He means to kill her, Mrs. Willard, if he finds her. Even if I give him the jewels, he'll keep hunting for her. He said he knows his father loved her more than him, and he'll have his payment for the affections that should have been his."

Prudence let her breath out. She'd thought it the gold they would seek. Not the life of one too-lovely, too-charming girl. "We ought to try though. Perhaps it will at least distract him."

Lewis nodded. "Happily, as soon as it's dark and I can retrieve them. If we have that long."

"Why would we not?"

His gaze pulled toward the street again. "I've been following him all morning. He's bribed the sheriff. Which means he could learn all too soon that Tilla was on that train to Cleveland, if he shows a picture of her."

Prudence gripped her basket. "What then?"

"I'll try to stop him, somehow. Not easy, given that he doesn't trust me. I swear, I think he knows I was scouting for the Union, before Tilla showed up."

She straightened a bit. "I beg your pardon?"

"I was all set to rendezvous with my contact next week." He shook his head. "But Tilla's more important. I'll get the information to them another way."

Her throat suddenly felt like a desert. Was it possible that he'd had those troop movements on him, not to betray the Union troops to the South, but to meet up with them?

What had they done?

"Look, I need you to do something for me. I hate to ask it, but it's for her." He pressed a paper to her hands. "You work at the hotel, right? Garrison's in room twelve. I'll make sure he stays out here, if you could find a way to slip into his room. He's always kept a journal, writes in it every evening. It'll be in his room. If he knows she's on that train, it'll be in there. Can you do that?"

Jason would object. She knew he would. And yet the thought that they had misjudged this young man...Prudence nodded. "Give me twenty minutes. I will meet thee back here."

She didn't pause to see his nod, just bustled back onto the street, aimed for the hotel, as if she'd only stepped into the alley to retie her boot. It took her only a few minutes to traverse the distance along the street, to let herself into the servant's entrance, deposit her bread on the table in the kitchen, and give the cook a single look that said much. Having escaped slavery herself not long ago, Prudence knew her friend would understand.

The usual bustle filled the hotel, but Prudence had long ago perfected the art of slipping in and out without being noticed. No one ever thought anything of seeing her in these halls and rooms anyway, not given how she'd worked here before and still filled in when necessary. No one stopped her as she slipped into the room Lewis had indicated, helped along by the skeleton key she kept always in her pocket.

Her breath wanted to catch when she realized what room Oscar Garrison had been assigned—one of the few through which the secret ladder went. He wouldn't have found it. Couldn't have. But still, it quickened her pulse.

No time for such sentiments. She clicked the door shut behind her and hastened to the small secretaire in the corner, where a leather-bound book caught her eye. A flip of its cover proved it to be filled throughout with handwriting rather than type. *I thank Thee, Heavenly Father.* She turned the pages briskly until she found the last ones with writing upon them and scanned the words.

An account of his arrival in town, his meeting with Lewis—colored with some appellations that made her skin crawl and proved that Lewis had been right in his assessment of Garrison's opinion of him. He suspected his sympathies had always been with the North, as evidenced by his fondness for Tilla.

I should have known when I caught them embracing by the cemetery in this very town that he'd been ensnared by her. That lying minx wrapped him around her finger just as she had Father. I ought to have buried him then and there beside his great-grandmother.

Prudence shook her head at the acid dripping from the words but didn't stop reading. Thankfully, she saw no evidence of his having discovered Tilla's whereabouts, either while she was still here or since she departed on the train.

They had only to keep it that way.

Commotion in the hallway grabbed her attention and made her shut the journal before she registered that it was

Lewis's voice. Shouting an argument against being manhandled, no doubt for her benefit.

Her feet acting before her mind even paused to consider, she headed for the hidden ladder in the closet. She'd managed to climb in and secure the cover again before the door flew open. Fearing that if she moved downward they would hear a creak and investigate, she remained still.

"I've had enough of your antics, Humphreys! Tell me where she went!"

Prudence's fingers tightened around the rung of the ladder.

"I told you, I don't know. I only saw her for a minute—as soon as she recognized me, she ran. I managed to grab her bag, but there was no hint in there where she was going." He was sticking to the story they'd devised, but it did little to put Prudence's heart at ease.

Garrison growled. "Keep an eye on him," he spat. "I'll be back in a minute."

There must be a third person, likely the other hunter, in the room. And Lewis was likely bound, or at least had a gun held on him.

The door opened, shut.

Then came the sound of something striking flesh, a grunt, and a thud, like a grown man hitting the floor, hard. Prudence barely contained a gasp. Did *keep an eye on him* mean to knock a body out in their dialect?

But it was Lewis who said, "Aren't so tough, after all, are you, Hank?"

He was all right. Heaving a sigh, she swung the trap door open and then pushed the closet door as well. "Lewis!"

He jumped, slapping a hand to his chest. "What the—"

"Follow me. We must get thee to the basement. From there, I can lead thee to safety."

In a glance, he seemed to size up where she was, and how. "Is that a ladder?" At her nod, he shook his head and pointed down. For the first time, she noted the red staining his pant leg. "Took a bit of a tumble when he caught me. I don't think I can handle a ladder. Are there stairs to this basement?"

She nodded and told him quickly how to find them. "Hurry," she then added, though the word was surely unnecessary. He was already shoving aside the prone figure of the guard and opening the door to the hallway.

Prudence refastened the door and hurried down the ladder, through the darkness, until her feet touched the familiar earthen floor of the basement. The smell of damp and mold crowded her nose, but to her it meant safety. She knew this basement as well as her own house, every inch and nook and cranny.

All the servants would be busy in the rest of the hotel this time of day, so she had no worries as she made her way to the main stairs. Within moments, an uneven step came down them. With only the dingy light from the windows to guide them, she motioned Lewis to follow her.

"There is a tunnel," she whispered. "It will lead thee under the road and to the river. If thee will wait in it until dark, thee will be safe."

"I can't thank you enough, ma'am. From the river, I can take my boat back to the plantation and then get away. Meet Tilla."

Crashing and banging and hurried footsteps interrupted, and terrifying light spilled down the stairs. Prudence dashed toward the corridor between the servant quarters.

"You think you can get away from me so easily, Humphreys?"

Lewis muttered something and made a lunge into the hallway—obviously too late. He'd been seen. Heart pounding, Prudence motioned him to hurry. They could still make it into the tunnel, they could—

Lewis shook his head. "If I follow you now, they'll find the tunnel. I won't ruin the whole operation." His voice was too low to be heard by anyone else, but time was still of the essence. He shoved something at her.

Blindly, she took it. "Come."

"No. Go. Get that to her. The Lord warned me this morning to write it. And the other... well, I shouldn't have. But I wanted her to have it." Something flickered across his face and then flitted away. Resignation settled. He stepped back out into the main part of the basement, hands up. "Thought there'd be a basement door."

Prudence edged away, silent and aching. He could have made it. But he was right. It would have put a halt to this stop on the railroad. She glanced down at the bundle in her hands. A folded piece of paper and a small black bag. Clutching them, she slid without a sound into the last room on the left and eased the door closed. But she didn't go into the tunnel. Not yet.

Not when she heard the sound of something striking someone again. And this time it was Lewis's voice that cried out in pain.

"Tell me where she is! *Tell me!*"

Prudence closed her eyes. As she listened to blow after blow. As she whispered prayer after prayer. As she heard, time and again, that young man protect his beloved with every breath in him.

Prudence shook the contents of the bag into her hand. The bracelet from the set that should rightfully have been Tilla's. And two loose emeralds.

"Where—" A blow. "Is—" Another. "She?"

"Toledo!" It's all he would say. And then he said nothing.

CHAPTER EIGHTEEN

LuAnn nearly dropped her coffee cup when her phone squawked at her. She growled and snatched it from the table, tapping the button to talk. "I'm going to disable this thing, Tess, I swear I am. It about gives me a heart attack every time you page me!"

Beside her, McKenna laughed.

So did Tess, from wherever she was above them. "Sorry." *As if.* "Could you bring up a few granola bars? I hadn't noticed the basket was depleted. I was giving the bathroom another once-over."

Needless, but there was no point in arguing with Tess over such things. LuAnn tapped again. "Coming right up." Another tap to stop.

McKenna leaned close. "Interesting. What app is that? I have a walkie app, but you have to hold the button the whole time."

"Wokka Tokka." LuAnn made a face at her phone as she stood. "That's why Tess wanted it. Drives me nuts."

"I can't get mine to work, honestly." Janice looked a little bashful about it as she pulled out her phone.

"Want me to take a look?" McKenna held out a hand with all the confidence of a generation born with technology in its rattles.

"No. You don't. Be grateful yours is broken." Grinning, LuAnn headed for the kitchen and the granola bars. When she swung back out a minute later, Janice and McKenna were huddled over the phones together. "Don't say I didn't warn you."

"Is it okay if I access the app on yours, LuAnn, to test Janice's?"

LuAnn waved as she jogged to the front of the café. "Have at it, crazy people." Not slowing for the steps, she'd managed a little bit of cardio to offset the morning's sugar intake by the time she heard Tess humming on the second floor. LuAnn added her harmony as she came in and refilled the goody basket.

"There. All done." Tess emerged from the bathroom with a satisfied smile, and they headed back down the stairs.

The front door flew open when they were still halfway up the staircase, and a wide-eyed Laura blew in on the breeze, her eyes finding them immediately. "He's awake! Mom just called!" Without another word, she vanished again.

"Praise the Lord!" LuAnn flew down the remaining stairs, Tess keeping pace. She detoured to the café long enough to scoop up her phone and nearly collided with Janice, who was already rushing out.

McKenna stood. "But—"

"We'll be back soon! Sorry!" Knowing their guest would understand—and that Winnie would help her clean up the mess of papers before the café opened for lunch in an hour—LuAnn charged out the door behind her friends.

The machines still beeped. The halls still smelled of antiseptic and food. But it was a normal room they all crowded into, and Thorn's eyes were open. LuAnn couldn't stop saying, "Thank You, Lord," as she found a spot, sandwiched between Tess and Jake.

"When did they move him out of ICU?" Janice asked the room at large.

"This morning, after he regained consciousness." Bev sat at the bedside, Thorn's hand clasped in hers. She sent an apologetic smile at Laura. "I know, I know, I should have called you the minute he woke up. But you were here until two, sweetie, and you needed some sleep."

Laura, teary-eyed as she perched on the bed holding her dad's other hand, just smiled. "I don't care. All that matters is that you're awake, Dad. You're going to be okay."

Thorn offered a bruised and battered smile. "My treasure," he murmured, eyes locked on her.

"Oh." LuAnn pressed a hand to her heart. "So sweet."

Jake chuckled beside her. "Still like to know who did this to you, Thorn."

LuAnn looked from Jake to Bev, whose gaze was still latched on to Thorn's swollen profile. Maybe he had been more concerned *for* Thorn than *about* him, after they found him here.

It seemed to take effort to swallow, and Laura had to put a straw to his lips so he could drink before he attempted any more words. "I...letter. Pocket of my...my work shirt."

"Hmm?" Laura slid the plastic cup back onto the side table. "What letter?"

"Work shirt."

"Okay." Obviously happy to do his bidding, Laura reached for the plastic bag drooping on the floor, where, apparently, his street clothes had been stashed. She pulled out one of the button-up work shirts that Thorn favored on the job and fished a folded piece of paper from the pocket.

It looked old. Fragile. Yellowed. Laura frowned as she unfolded it. "What's this?"

"Found it. Brick was loose, so I..." He paused, coughed, and looked at Janice. "Urban...archaeology."

LuAnn couldn't help but smile along with her friends. "Do you remember what happened, Thorn? After that? You found the jewelry."

"Bracelet. Letter." He moved his head on the pillow and winced. "I don't know. My phone? Something...a text." His eyes opened wider and fastened, this time, on Bev.

She gave him a tight-lipped smile. "Brick. I know. Lar has your phone. You saw that, I take it?"

"Yeah. Then..." He reached up and touched the bandage wrapped around his head.

"Was he there?" Janice clutched her hands together. "Bricker? Was he at the inn?"

Jake tensed.

Thorn's eyes clouded. "I don't think so. I just...I don't know. Can't remember anything after the text."

"Maybe you were so surprised you jumped up? Hit your head?" Bev stroked her thumb over his knuckles.

"Maybe. I don't know. Just remember thinking I had to keep him away. From everything. Then…" He winced again.

Likely an accident, then. And, injured, he stumbled out of the basement, trying to protect them in whatever way he could. Maybe not in ways that would have made sense normally, but he'd been minutes away from a coma, after all.

"Guys?" Laura had eased back down onto the edge of the bed, her eyes on the paper. "This is from 1862."

"What?" LuAnn shifted, though she couldn't well move to Laura's side without elbowing a few friends out of the way. "Wait—was that with the bracelet, Thorn? Is it from Lewis Humphreys? Or Tilla?"

"Lewis, *to* Tilla," Laura answered, awe in her tone. "And it may just be the sweetest thing I've ever read, even though I don't have a clue who either of those people are. 'To my beloved Tilla. I write this fearing the worst, even as I pray for the best. Your brother has found us already, and though I will do all in my power to protect your destination from him, a whisper in my spirit this morn warned me to take the time now to write to you, lest I lose my chance. I will endeavor to return the bulk of the jewelry to him, as I swore I would. But as I secured it upon leaving your side, I couldn't bear to strip you of the entire legacy your father left you. I kept these for you, beloved. I pray you never need to sell them, as you'd been planning, but rather that they will remain a token of his love. If the worst happens,

241

I trust our mutual friend will get this to you. If you've need of the rest and your brother hasn't claimed it, look for it in the place where first I kissed you and confessed my love. Which shall always remain yours, Lewis.'"

"So the rest of the jewelry was never in the inn." LuAnn looked to Janice and Tess. "Just the bracelet and that one emerald—Prudence hid that, apparently unable to get it to Tilla. But the rest is still wherever Lewis hid it."

Tess's purse squawked. Hand flying to her heart, she jumped and reached for it. "What in the world?"

"That's the Wokka Tokka alert." LuAnn frowned. "But who...?"

"It says Janice." Tess looked from her still-squawking phone to their friend, who was most certainly not activating hers.

Janice's eyes grew. "I left my phone at the inn!"

Tess swiped her phone and tapped. "Who's this?"

"McKenna! Sorry, I didn't mean to eavesdrop—LuAnn, your phone was still in walkie mode. I tried to tell you as you were leaving. But anyway! I walked back into the room and heard the letter being read, and I know where the jewelry is! Oscar's journal—he mentions finding the two of them together outside the cemetery where Lewis's great-grandmother was buried in Marietta. I'd already looked that up—she's at Mounds Cemetery. You remember that drawing that I said might be by Tilla?"

The hill, the gravestones, the fence. LuAnn's eyes widened. "The hill! Of course!"

"Great-grandmother Humphreys is buried on the east-most edge, close to the fence. With a little luck, I'll find that tree and have the treasure dug up before you can say, 'Oscar Who?'"

Tess laughed and tapped her talk button. "Hang tight, McKenna. We'll be back soon and will help you. Who knows how much digging you'll have to do—or how many irate caretakers you'll have to talk down."

"Oh, don't worry about me. I'm already all but out the door, and your friend stopped by and offered to help when he heard me yelp in victory."

Tess tapped again. "My friend? Who?"

"Marsh. I'm leaving Janice's phone here for her. See you guys at the graveyard! Ta!"

The whole room seemed to jerk, to surge forward. Tess was already tapping. "McKenna, wait! McKenna!" She tapped off and paused, but no answering voice sounded.

Thorn tried to push himself up. "Brick. We've gotta stop him. He'll—"

"We who, buster?" Bev held him down with a finger on his shoulder. Just one, proving his weakness. "You're not going anywhere. We'll call the police."

"And we'll go." Jake shouldered his way from their ranks.

"Honey." Laura took a step forward.

Jake held up a hand. And right beside him, up close, LuAnn could see the pure love in his eyes. "You stay here with your dad, babe. I've got this." He shot a heavy look at Thorn. "No one messes with my family. Right, Dad?"

Thorn sagged against the pillows, nostrils flaring. "Don't hurt him too bad. Just let them send him back to Leavenworth."

Jake laughed and headed for the door. "Anyone else coming?"

LuAnn and Tess hurried after him, Janice a more hesitating step behind. But there. LuAnn fell in beside Jake, matching her stride to his. Something about Thorn's reaction niggled. Why wasn't he concerned for Jake's safety, when he knew what kind of man Brick was? "What is it exactly that you do, Jake?"

He grinned at her. "I run an online martial arts academy. Record the videos in the basement gym—though I'm behind. Haven't put one up since the live stream on Friday."

"Friday." Janice sighed and jogged a step to keep up. "What a day that was."

"Right? I just got done shooting and came upstairs to find Lar covered in peas, and it's like we haven't had time to breathe since."

He'd been filming. A live stream. Verifiable evidence of where he'd been, if LuAnn had still needed it. Which she didn't.

Brad was right about him, at least—he was just a guy wanting to protect his family.

He pulled keys out of his pocket and jiggled them. "I'll drive."

A storm had blown in while they were in the hospital—of course, as if the weather weren't willing to let mere humanity solve a problem without creating a few new ones of its own. It was mostly gusting wind and a few fat drops of rain, but LuAnn caught the grumble of thunder in the distance as Jake jammed his car into Park and they all spilled out.

He'd gotten them as close to the eastern edge of the cemetery as possible, and they only had to run for a minute before the lay of the land looked familiar—the view Tilla had captured in her drawing. The mound rising, the gravestones, now rounded with age more than they'd been in the picture. The fence.

The tree, small in the drawing but now towering. Sheltering the two figures from those fat drops of rain.

"I'm going to circle around." Jake motioned them to continue on their path while he jogged off at an angle.

LuAnn prayed such tactics were unnecessary. That it wasn't Marshall Bricker. Or that he had changed, had softened, was just a tired man ready to bury the hatchet and not out for any nefarious purposes.

Once Jake was out of sight, LuAnn nodded to Tess, who called out, "McKenna! Find anything yet?"

McKenna spun around. Her hair was caught up in a ponytail now, and her face was wreathed in a smile. She waved with her left hand. In her right, she held a piece of what looked like pointed rebar. "Hey, girls! I think so! We've been poking. Already dug up a few rocks." She laughed as she indicated a few small piles of dirt and stones. "This one feels different though. Sounded metallic, didn't it, Marsh?"

Hope one dashed. Marshall Bricker offered an easy smile as he leaned on the shovel. "It did." He tipped his ball cap toward them. "Afternoon, ladies. I was coming back through town and thought I'd stop and see if you'd heard anything from Thorn. Your lovely friend here told me he was in the hospital, in a coma."

"I was heading in to check with your cook about details to give him when I heard the letter over the walkie." McKenna poked the rod into the ground again. "Listen to that. I bet it's some kind of metal box."

"Let's see. Better back up, miss."

LuAnn pressed her lips together as Marshall forced the shovel into the dirt. Came *back* into town, did he? She watched him as he moved, trying to gauge his height. Where would he come on Thorn's old truck? Right where the vandal had, she'd bet. And he wore that ball cap.

"How exciting." Janice grinned, just like they'd agreed in the car that she would. "You should have seen the look on Thorn's face when you said you knew where it was!"

There, a hitch in Bricker's movements. "I thought he was in a coma."

"Just woke up this morning." LuAnn shifted a bit, ready to give him a roundhouse kick to the jaw if he made a move before Jake could reach them. Or the police, who Bev said she'd call. "My romantic heart likes to think it was because he heard Bev's voice."

"Beverly's here?" He tossed a heaping shovelful of earth aside and paused, his gaze hard and cold as it settled on her. "Thought they split."

"They did. But when their daughter told her he was in the hospital, she caught the first flight out." Tess shifted closer to

McKenna. Her brows knit when she glanced down into the growing hole. "I think I see something. Or maybe it's a rock."

"That ain't a rock." Seeming to ignore the Bev news, Bricker turned back to his work with renewed vigor. Digging didn't seem to be a chore to him—but then, they still did hard labor at Leavenworth, didn't they? A minute later he paused and laughed. "Definitely a box!"

McKenna looked as though she may well dance a jig. "I can't believe it. All these years. All this time." She dropped to her knees, heedless of the dirt quickly turning to mud as the rain increased.

LuAnn caught a glimpse of Jake, edging toward them from the north, coming up behind Bricker. Better keep *him* from catching a glimpse too. She shifted closer, leaning down to watch as McKenna jiggled the box loose of the soil. "Lucky you came by when you did, Mr. Bricker. Good to have some muscle around, especially since our usual laborer is a bit out of commission."

"Happy to be here. In fact..." He cast his gaze upward, at the clouds that continued to rumble and spit at them—faster now. "Why don't you ladies get out of the rain? Miss McK and I will get the box free."

"Are you kidding?"

"Not a chance."

"We're staying right here till that thing is open."

He looked none too happy at the trio of responses that bombarded him. His attention went back to the hole. "Want me to dig some more around the edges?"

"No." *Grunt.* "I think…" *Grunt.* "I've…*got it!*" McKenna gave a tug mighty enough that she and the box both tumbled back into a mud-splattered heap that the professional-looking woman of twenty-eight hours before never would have borne.

But then, the professional-looking woman was obviously just a front that McKenna Garrison knew how to put up well. This woman, the one with a T-shirt bragging about her daughter and mud under her nails from a historical treasure hunt, was far truer.

Jake, unheard over the rising splatter of rain, edged closer still, going from tree to tree.

LuAnn, Tess, and Janice all huddled close to McKenna, ignoring the rain that fell in earnest now. It was warm, and they would dry.

McKenna lifted the lid of the box. It caught a little but not much. And then she gasped.

For a moment, LuAnn imagined it was empty. Or filled with something different, something someone else had buried. Or with rocks, a trick.

But no. Yellow gold glinted up, and deepest emeralds, and winking diamonds. A tiara. A necklace that looked so heavy she could scarcely imagine a slave wanting to carry it on her escape. A ring. A brooch.

"Whoa." Her voice awed, McKenna drew the necklace out. "That painting didn't do it justice. My insurance policy is going to need one major inland marine addition."

"Oh, I don't think so." Bricker's voice was all friendliness and warmth. Which made a marked contrast with the metallic *click* that followed it. "Your insurance won't know a thing about it, sweetheart."

Janice's fingers dug into LuAnn's arm. "Gun. He has a gun."

She could see that, and had the moment she looked up at that click. He'd taken a step back so that he could encompass them all in the sweep of it. No doubt he figured that three old women and a wisp of a thing like McKenna wouldn't put up much of a fight.

He grinned a wicked grin. "Put the necklace back in the box, McKenna, and hand it to me. That's a good girl. No one gets hurt."

"What are you doing?" McKenna's hands shook as she lowered the jewels back down. "You're their friend. You said—"

"Words are easy, sweetheart. Now scoot that over. I might not be able to get what I came to Marietta for, but this'll do nicely as a consolation prize. Nicely indeed." He motioned with the barrel of the gun. "Scoot it over, then step back with them."

McKenna obeyed.

Tess lifted her chin. "I'm going to be glad to see you taken out, *Brick*."

"Oh yeah?" Maybe he had a snappy comeback on the tip of his tongue. If so, he never got it out. In the next instant, lightning flashed and Jake pounced with it. A silent leap, a tackle, a roll.

Jake was up, Marshall was scrambling to his feet. A foot kicked out, the gun went flying. More kicks, a few well-placed jabs, and the elder was sprawled on his back, groaning.

A siren wailed.

Marshall Bricker stained the air with a string of curses.

Jake pressed a forearm to his throat and exerted enough pressure to shut him up. "There are ladies present, loser. Watch your mouth."

LuAnn was beginning to like this young man.

Chaos ensued as the police descended—the kind that resulted in the bad guy getting cuffed and escorted off in a police car and the box of jewels getting sealed in an evidence bag. A nearly frantic McKenna was promised they'd be returned, but she insisted on riding along to the station with them.

After they'd all been cleared by the police, Jake ushered them back to his car.

LuAnn fell in beside him once more. "Online martial arts, huh? Don't suppose you offer live lessons?"

Behind her, her friends laughed. "You are a freak of nature, LuAnn," Tess said.

"Hey. I've already got a good roundhouse." She paused to demonstrate the kick.

Her friends laughed still more, but Jake was impressed. "You've got good form. Did you take kickboxing?"

"Now and then. Mostly I've focused on stretches and exercises I can do at home."

"That flexibility would serve you well, if you really wanted to learn. And I did have a studio in California where I gave lessons. Didn't want to start that up here unless I was sure we were going to stay a while."

Janice stepped up beside them too, her brows raised. "And?"

"And..." He grinned. "I think I'd be hard-pressed to ever peel Laura away from that cute Victorian house. So I might as well start looking for a property."

LuAnn looped her arm through his and brushed away a rivulet of rain from her face. "I know just the guy who can help you find that."

Chapter Nineteen

LuAnn held out the scrapbook with a smile. Brad hadn't come in very far—he was on his way to a late showing, but the aunts were eager to get their scrapbook back so they could add a new page to it.

Brad took it with a grin in return. "I'm glad to hear about Thorn's improvement. Tell them if there's anything I can do, just let me know."

LuAnn nodded. "I will. Right now they're dealing with the aggravation of having had a wallet stolen and everything that means. So I think at this point, just finding Jake studio space is all they're asking."

"I have a few places to show him tomorrow." He reached for the door. But then paused and looked back. "I never wanted to doubt Thorn," he said, blue eyes warm. "I just didn't want you guys to be hurt. You're my friends."

She could understand that. Still. What was a girl to do but quirk a brow and say, "I don't need defending, Bradley Grimes. I'll have you know I'm taking karate now." She exaggerated the pronunciation, trying to make it sound authentic.

He rewarded her with a laugh and a shake of his head. "Not the kind of *hurt* I meant."

"I know. But there's no protecting against the other kind."

He smiled and opened the door, scrapbook in hand. "We have to try though, don't we?"

The light in the stairwell didn't flicker or refuse to work when they switched it on, which no doubt gave Janice immense relief. LuAnn smiled when Thorn flipped it on and off a couple of times.

"This was acting up on Friday, wasn't it?"

"Yeah." Tess nodded and led the way down the stairs. "Robin fixed it for us the other day. Since your doctors stubbornly refused to let you check out on Thursday, like you wanted to."

Thorn grunted—and gripped the railing hard as he descended. The white bandages that had wrapped all the way around his head in the hospital had been removed, the swelling had gone down for the most part, but the bruising had simply gotten uglier. It was yellow and green, and hideous enough that LuAnn couldn't blame little Paisley for crying when she saw him the other day.

In days gone by he no doubt still would have been in the hospital this Monday, just over a week after he vanished. But between his own stubbornness and the hospital's need for his bed, he was checked into the Getty Care Facility instead—and no doubt the hovering care Laura, Jake, and Bev provided would see him well in no time. Or crazy. One or the other.

For now, it was the three women of the Inn Crowd hovering as he made his way slowly down the steps to see if being back in the basement jogged any more memories.

"I figured Robin could take care of it. She's a smart girl. Can fix most anything." He gained the floor with a palpable sigh of relief from the rest of them.

Thorn shot an aggravated but amused look at them. "I'm not an invalid."

Janice gave him her sternest look. "Don't you fuss with us, Tory Thornton, after the scare you gave us. Our concern is well placed."

"Humph." But he accepted the cane LuAnn handed back to him. He wouldn't need it long, the doctor said. Just until his balance fully returned.

They made their way slowly to the elevator, which was working again too. Robin—with the help of a specialist via phone—had seen to that the day before. But they hadn't actually used it yet. The car still sat here where it had been last Friday, open and waiting to give Thorn whatever answers it could.

LuAnn wanted to ask if anything else was coming back to him, but she bit back the words. Marshall Bricker had sworn up, down, and sideways that he hadn't attacked Thorn. Hadn't even seen him at all since he came to town. He said he'd sent the text, made a call, and figured he'd split.

"So you saw the loose brick." Tess motioned to the wall, the panel still removed. "And investigated."

"Yeah. Found that box, with the letter and the necklace." Thorn leaned into the opening. "Seems cleaner in here."

LuAnn laughed. "Thanks to LuAnn Sherrill's Amazing De-Webber."

"Patent pending." Tess grinned.

Thorn put a hand on the crossbeam inside the wall. "I think... I think I was looking for more. When Brick's text came in." He patted the beam. "I suspect this baby's responsible for the first blow. Then..." He pivoted, looking toward the elevator, and at the floor where his toolbox had been. They'd let Robin move that, given the tripping hazard. "My tools were here?"

"That's right." Janice indicated the spot with her toe.

"I fell. Into it, maybe, or over it. That's still cloudy. I have an image of the elevator gate. Grabbing it, pulling myself up."

"That would account for the blood." LuAnn showed him where she'd found the fingerprint—since scrubbed off. "You were trying to stem that, though—with your shop rags."

"Don't remember that part." He squinted at the elevator in a way that made her think another headache was coming on, as they had every other day. "But I remember thinking I couldn't let him come here. To threaten Laura, and you guys. And then that bracelet—of all the times to find something like that. Gold. Bev told you about Brick and the gold."

"Yeah." Tess nodded.

"I kept thinking I had to hide it. I think I meant to take it to my truck. Then return his text. Deflect, convince him I wasn't here. I must have dropped the bracelet though, and stashed the phone instead." He shook his head. "I obviously wasn't thinking clearly. But my goal was only to keep everyone, everything safe from him."

"We know." Janice patted his arm.

They did. All doubts about Thorn's intentions had vanished, given the vile words Bricker had been spewing to the police. Anyone who knew that man would want to protect his family from him.

LuAnn held out an arm toward the elevator. "How about a ride back up, Thorn?"

He glanced at the stairs—usually his preferred method—and nodded. "Yeah. I think it's time for some more medicine."

A few minutes later they'd turned him back over to Jake, who helped him out to his car. LuAnn stood by Tess and Janice, watching the men with a lifted hand.

"Any new memories?" McKenna slipped up beside them. She'd gone home for the weekend but then returned. Apparently she was going to be camping out here until the jewelry was released, which was fine by them. A room always full, and a new friend to trade notes with. At least for another week or so.

"A little. Nothing earth-shattering." Tess closed the door against the wind that gusted in, chilly today.

"Well. I have something pretty earth-shattering. At least to me." With a grin that shouted Little Girl in a Candy Shop instead of Professional Woman on a Mission, McKenna held up a piece of paper. "My contact in Cleveland just faxed this over. I gave her your number Tess—I didn't think you'd mind."

Tess laughed. "Of course not. What did she find?"

With a flourish, McKenna flipped the paper around, displaying a grainy image of…LuAnn stepped closer. A woman, middle-aged and still beautiful. She wore her hair pulled tightly back in a bun, an impeccable white blouse, and a tailored skirt in a dark color. Around her were a collection of girls in white dresses, their races as different as their ages. And behind her, a building over whose door was a sign, barely legible.

"What does that say? Something *home…*" LuAnn squinted still more and wished she had her glasses handy.

"Humphreys Children's Home. It's Tilla. She started an orphanage in Cleveland. Assumed Lewis's last name, apparently, and started this in 1870." Pure pride beamed from McKenna's eyes. "The article says she never married, but she mothered dozens of children over the years. She waited there, where they must have agreed to meet up again, even when he never came. And she made a difference. She lived selflessly. Her wards remembered her as being a woman of deep faith, who always taught them to forgive, love, and care for others above themselves."

"Wow." LuAnn reached out to touch a finger to the black-and-white image that told a story far beyond words. "I guess she forgave Prudence, then. I wonder if Prudence ever knew that?"

"I hope so." Janice blinked a few quick times and sniffled. "Happy ending to a sad tale."

"Yeah." LuAnn smiled at McKenna, at her friends.

They all went back to work, slowly, thoughtfully. Tess to her office, McKenna to the temporary work station she'd set up in the kitchen, where Winnie could entertain her with stories from her family history. Janice to the cleaning on the third floor. LuAnn headed upstairs to her laptop to take care of some of the emails she'd volunteered to handle that morning.

Those didn't take too long. And then she was looking back at the email from a week ago, in her personal work account. The one she hadn't answered, but hadn't deleted either.

Phillip Whitman.

She drew in a breath, pursing her lips. Sometimes you just didn't know about a person. Whom you could trust. Who had changed. Who hadn't. Who was worth giving a second chance, and who would just hurt you again. Sometimes you had to leave the judging to Someone far wiser, Who could see into the human heart.

Her phone squawked. She didn't jump, just laughed and swiped and tapped. "What now?"

Tess laughed too. "Got a minute?"

"Always." Sometimes you didn't know… She thought of McKenna, Jake, and Brick. And sometimes you did. She clicked the box by *Phillip Whitman*, dragged it to the trash can icon, and watched that piece of her past blink away. She stood and went downstairs, her mind returning to McKenna's discovery. "I wonder…" she murmured to the wallpaper. "How could Tilla afford to open that orphanage?"

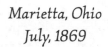

Marietta, Ohio
July, 1869

"Are thee sure?" Prudence looked into the beautiful eyes of the woman she hadn't seen in five years. The words she'd spoken, the story she'd finally told still lingered in the air of the farmhouse kitchen. Outside, Moses shouted with laughter. From the barn came the bang of a hammer on a plow.

Tilla Humphreys smiled. "I'm sure. I don't want it. When I realized he wasn't coming, when I saw in the paper he was reported as defecting to the South, I knew. I knew he was gone. And I knew how he'd want me to live without him. I don't need those reminders of my past."

Given that she'd long since hidden the letter, bracelet, and that one emerald in a wall of the hotel, Prudence wasn't keen to argue. But she reached into her pocket, fingers finding those familiar articles she always kept there, every day. The skeleton key that had once opened the door to each room in the hotel—though maybe it didn't any longer, she didn't know. And a small, smooth stone, warm from where it rested against her.

She pulled it out, letting it gleam green as a spring promise in the sunlight. "At least take this. There were two—I kept this one out. Just in case you came by one day."

Moving slowly, Tilla reached out and took the emerald. "I don't even know what to do with it. I've gotten used to living on little."

Prudence closed the woman's fingers over the emerald. "Do good. Do for others. Like he did."

A smile slipped onto Tilla's lips far more beautiful than any Prudence had seen on her before. "With the Lord's guidance, I will. For him."

Dear Reader,

I admit it—I have a love for treasure stories. I love to read them, watch them, and write them. So when I sat down to lead our Inn Crowd into a hunt for missing jewelry, I was in many ways in my element...but of course, I also had to search for the real treasure they'd be finding. In this case, new friends and new understanding of old ones, and the honor of making the Lord real to one hurting young woman.

As I wrote *Greater than Gold*, the news was, as it too often is, filled with allegations and startling confessions from respected figures. Yet again I heard all the *I never would have thought!* reactions from heartbroken fans and followers, even from those closest to the people. And I realized anew that sometimes we really can't know a person's deepest heart. Sometimes all our trust is betrayed.

But at other times, *most* times, we *do* know—we know who the Lord has put in our lives and in our hearts to love and nurture. And even if these people sometimes surprise us, for good or for ill, that's just part of the experience of loving them. Much like the holes left by grief, those surprises are part of the lacework of our lives.

I hope you enjoyed our ladies' story in this installment, that you had fun seeing familiar characters pop up, and also meeting some new ones. It was a true pleasure to get to lead them through a new adventure!

Until next time,
Roseanna

ABOUT THE AUTHOR

Roseanna M. White is a best-selling, Christy Award nominated author who has long claimed that words are the air she breathes. When not writing fiction, she's homeschooling her two kids, editing, designing book covers, and pretending her house will clean itself. Roseanna is the author of a slew of historical novels that span several continents and thousands of years. Spies and war and mayhem always seem to find their way into her books... to offset her real life, which is blessedly ordinary. You can learn more about her and her stories and sign up for her newsletter at http://www.RoseannaMWhite.com/.

THE STERNWHEEL FESTIVAL
IN MARIETTA, OHIO

Every year on the weekend after Labor Day, the quiet little town of Marietta comes to life, and crowds flock to her on land and water. Because every year on that weekend in September, the Sternwheel Festival is held.

Hands-down Marietta's most popular attraction, the Sternwheel Festival is a time when the rivers are teeming, once again, with paddle wheel boats—most of them faithful re-creations, but some of them genuine vessels from centuries past—and the town is teeming with tens of thousands of merrymakers who have come to enjoy the boats and the celebration.

From Friday evening through Sunday, the town has non-stop events and entertainment. There are car shows and beauty pageants, bands of every imaginable style, and more food vendors than you could possibly decide between. There are fireworks and boat races, sunrise services and coronations. And through it all, a blend of history and modernity that keeps the crowds coming back again, year after year.

For photos of the celebrations of years past and information on the next Sternwheel Festival, visit http://ohioriversternwheelfestival.org/.

Something Delicious from our Wayfarers Inn Friends

Peanut Soup

Ingredients:

  ¼ cup (½ stick) butter

  1 medium onion, finely
    chopped

  2 celery sticks, finely
    chopped

  3 tablespoons flour

  8 cups chicken stock
    (reduced sodium)

  2 cups creamy peanut
    butter

  1¾ cups light cream or half-
    and-half

  Finely chopped peanuts for
    garnish

Instructions:

Melt butter in a soup pot over medium heat. Add onion and celery and cook until softened, stirring often, 3–5 minutes.

Stir in flour and cook 2 more minutes.

Pour in the chicken stock. Increase heat to high and bring to a boil, stirring constantly. Reduce heat back to medium and cook, stirring often, about 15 minutes or until it begins to thicken.

Pour through a strainer into another large bowl or pot, pushing on the vegetables to get as much flavor from them as possible. (As an alternative, you could put the soup into a blender to get rid of any chunks.) Discard any remaining chunks. Return soup to pot.

Whisk peanut butter and cream into soup. Warm over low heat for about 5 minutes, but do not boil. Garnish with peanuts, serve warm.

Read on for a sneak peek of another exciting book
in the Secrets of Wayfarers Inn series!

A Flame in the Night
by Virginia Smith

The aroma of cumin from the day's butternut squash soup
lingered in the kitchen at Wayfarers Inn, though the café
had closed several hours ago. The mood of those gathered
around the table was at complete odds with the room's cheerful atmosphere. Janice Eastman slumped in her high-backed
chair, her mind reeling with the news Tess Wallace had just
delivered.

"I don't understand." Janice shook her head. "How can we
be broke?"

"We're not broke." Tess tapped the document resting on
the surface of the table between them. "We even showed a
profit last month, which Jeff says is terrific for a start-up business. It usually takes years to start making money."

Jeff, Tess's son, served as advisor to the three owners of
Wayfarers Inn on financial matters, since he was a CPA.

LuAnn Sherrill, the third member of the Inn Crowd, as
they called themselves, stirred her tea with slow circles. "That's
because most businesses have to take out huge loans to get

enough operating capital to open. Thanks to my inheritance from my father, we didn't have to borrow that much."

Janice shifted in her seat. Terms like *operating capital* made her uncomfortable. In fact, discussions of finances in general left her feeling uneducated and dull, which was ridiculous since she'd earned her living as a teacher for several decades. But Lawrence, her late husband, had always handled the money. When he passed away last year, she'd had a terrible time trying to gather all the information she needed to pay the bills, much less keep track of their modest investments. When she and her two best friends opened Wayfarers Inn, she'd been happy to leave the day-to-day financial matters in Tess's capable hands.

"So we're not broke," she said to Tess, "but we're losing money?"

"Given the number of reservations we have—or don't have—we'll be operating at a loss for the next two months."

"But the café is full to bursting almost every day." Her glance slid from Tess to LuAnn. "Aren't we making money there?"

LuAnn's features scrunched. "A little, but we didn't open the café to make money. There was never any expectation that we'd support the inn by selling soup and bread."

"I know," Janice said. "But it has become far more popular than we imagined. That's got to help."

"The café pays for itself." Tess tapped on the document again. "The income from there pays Taylor's salary and buys all the supplies. It even covers part of the utilities, but it's not nearly enough to keep the whole inn running."

"We've had a lot of business in the couple of months since we opened." LuAnn made the statement sound like a question. "We were even booked to capacity during the Sternwheeler Festival."

Tess nodded. "The revenue from that week helped out a lot. But the projections for the next couple of months, as we head into winter, are bleak. Nobody's visiting Marietta. Or if they are, they're not staying here."

"If only people knew how beautiful the area is this time of year," LuAnn said. "The leaves are at their peak all up and down the Ohio River. It's a wonderful time to visit Marietta."

"We do have a lady arriving next Friday, and she's staying for two weeks." Janice had taken the reservation on the phone herself. "That ought to help, right?"

"Definitely. And we have two more at the end of the month. But we need a steady occupancy rate of at least"—Tess glanced at the columns of numbers on the paper—"forty-four percent. That means we need to have four rooms rented at all times. And that's just to break even."

Silence fell around the table while thoughts whirled through Janice's mind. She and Lawrence had faced some lean times back when the kids were young. "We need to close off the vents in the rooms we aren't using. That'll save on the heating bill. And we've got to turn off lights. I can't tell you the number of times I've come into an empty room and found the light left on." She didn't look at Tess, who she suspected was the light-leaver-on-er.

Both her friends nodded, and then an uncomfortable expression stole over Tess's features. "I hate to even mention it, but should we consider a layoff?"

Janice jerked upright. Fire one of their friends? Taylor needed the money from his part-time job waiting tables in the café. College students were notoriously short on cash. And Winnie...her mind shied away from the idea of letting Winnie go.

"No." LuAnn's tone left no room for arguments. "I've still got money from my inheritance."

Tess leaned toward LuAnn, frown lines on her forehead. "We're not taking more of your money for the inn. We agreed on that. You've already paid for far more than you should have."

"*Pshaw.*" LuAnn flipped a dismissive hand in the air. "That's what money is for. Besides, it all belongs to the Lord. We opened this inn and the café as a ministry, remember?"

Her words served to loosen a couple of knots in Janice's stomach. "You're right. We did. So let's leave it up to God to work out."

Tess gave Janice a grateful smile. "Good idea. Would you lead us in prayer?"

Now *that* was something Janice felt entirely comfortable doing. The three grasped hands and bowed their heads.

"Lord, we're sitting here worrying over money, which is exactly what Jesus told us not to do. You know what we need, and You are more than capable of providing for us and for this inn. Please send guests so we can pay the bills and continue to welcome people in Your name. Help us not to worry or be anxious over anything, but instead to trust You even more than we ever have before. In Jesus's name we pray."

"Amen," the three chorused together.

Tess squeezed her hand before releasing it. "Thank you. I feel better."

"Me too." Lu Ann picked up the financial document and flipped it, face down, on the table. "Not only that, but I have an idea. Why don't we host a big celebration feast? You know, to celebrate the harvest like the farmers did in the old days."

"A harvest celebration." Tess said the words slowly, as if testing them out on her tongue. "Isn't that what Thanksgiving is?"

"Yes, but I don't want to wait until November. Let's do it in October. Say, the last Saturday of the month." LuAnn's voice grew animated. "We'll decorate the inn with fall colors, and have a huge meal where we thank God for blessing our harvest."

"And not just the harvest of our garden." Janice gazed around the kitchen. "We'll thank Him for the harvest of our ministry here at Wayfarers Inn."

"Exactly." LuAnn beamed at her.

Janice clapped her hands. "I love the idea. We'll invite all our families. I'm sure Stacy will help with cooking and decorating."

At least, she hoped Stacy would help and not put up a fuss. A tiny frown tugged at Janice's lips. Her relationship with her daughter had definitely improved since she'd moved from the apartment over Stacy's garage and into her cozy quarters on the fourth floor of the inn, but Stacy still tended to be a bit, well, prickly. Though she loved the idea of Wayfarers Inn, she'd never fully accepted Janice's involvement. Stacy insisted that launching a business this late in life would be a drain on all three women at a time when they should be slowing down and enjoying their retirement. Though Janice's son, Stuart, shared his sister's concern, he was far more easygoing and made a point to support the three friends in their venture. "And Stuart will come wherever there's food."

"Jeff too. I'm sure Lizzie and Michael will come and bring the kids." Tess glanced toward the giant vintage stove that resembled a fire engine in both color and size. "One thing's for certain. We could cook the entire meal at once in Big Red. No trying to juggle casseroles so they all stay hot."

An idea occurred to Janice. "Perhaps we could invite our friends as well. Like Thorn and Winnie and maybe Robin." As the last name left her lips, an excited tickle fluttered in her stomach. With luck, she could finagle things so Stuart and Robin were seated next to each other. If those two young people would actually exchange more than a few words, Janice was sure they'd see how perfect they were for each other.

An artful smile curved Tess's lips. "And Bradley, of course."

Janice glanced at LuAnn in time to see a spot of color appear on each cheek. Bradley Grimes had become a fixture in their lives since he sold them Wayfarers Inn. In particular, he and LuAnn had become close friends, though he made no secret of the fact that he hoped for more than friendship.

LuAnn ignored Tess's suggestive tone. "We must absolutely invite our friends. But I was thinking of something on a larger scale. What if we opened the inn's doors to anyone who wants to come?"

"We could charge a fee," Tess said slowly, as though turning the idea over in her mind. "That might help generate some income, but I don't—"

LuAnn held up a hand. "Actually, I was thinking of doing it for free. Kind of the inn's way of saying thanks to the community."

Tess's jaw dropped while Janice sat slowly back in her chair. A free Harvest Celebration dinner for everyone in Marietta? Of course, not everyone would come, but if they opened the doors to anyone and everyone, they might have hundreds of guests.

"But it wouldn't be *free*, would it?" Janice searched LuAnn's face. "Think of all the food we'd have to buy. How can we afford that?"

"Janice is right." Tess gave a firm nod. "We're sitting here talking about how tight our finances are, so we decide to spend a bunch of money throwing a party?" Her lips twisted sideways. "'Cause *that* makes sense."

LuAnn acknowledged the sarcasm with a dip of her head. "I know it sounds crazy, but we opened this inn as a ministry. What better way to show God how grateful we are than to welcome people to a celebration dinner?"

Tess appeared ready to argue, but a Bible verse crept to the front of Janice's mind.

"'*Give and it will be given to you*,'" she quoted.

A smile appeared on LuAnn's face, and she continued the quote. "*A good measure, pressed down, shaken together and running over, will be poured into your lap.*'"

They both looked at Tess, who continued to look stubborn. Then her expression softened, and she completed the verse. "*For with the measure you use, it will be measured to you.*'" She heaved a sigh. "Okay, I get it."

Janice rested her hands on the table. "Finances aren't my strong point, but I'm perfectly happy trusting in God's economy. If He wants to bless hundreds of people with mashed potatoes and gravy, I'm happy to dish them out."

A pained look creased Tess's forehead. "Could we at least make it a potluck? For those who can afford it, anyway. That'll spread the cost around a bit."

LuAnn tilted her head to consider the suggestion. "I don't see why not."

Janice clapped her hands, delighted. "I love potlucks! At Christ Fellowship we used to have a potluck once a month, on Communion Sunday." She grinned. "Lawrence said it boosted attendance. Some people used to stay home on Communion Sunday because the service tended to run long." Her grin faded. "I wish Pastor Ben hadn't stopped the potlucks."

The young pastor who'd taken over Lawrence's pulpit had introduced many changes to Christ Fellowship, and not all of them were well received by longtime members of the congregation. A touch of irritation niggled the back of Janice's mind. Things had run smoothly at the church for more than a decade before Lawrence's death. The two of them had operated as a team in ministry. They'd worked hard at maintaining the relationships within the church family and had learned to introduce changes slowly in order to keep people happy and in agreement with the direction the church was headed. Ben and his wife, Paige, didn't seem to understand the importance of gradual change.

She forced the disloyal thought from her mind. The young couple had treated her well, and she had grown quite fond of them both. And after all, their attention had been focused elsewhere. They'd certainly done a good job of attracting younger people to the church. Nearly every week new faces appeared in the padded pews, and the Sunday school classes were full of children. Those were good changes.

Chair legs scraped across the gleaming tiles as LuAnn left the table to retrieve a notepad from one of the drawers.

"All right," she said when she'd resettled. "Let's plan the menu."

The three exchanged smiles. Planning was one of the things they loved to do.

"Let's stay away from turkey since next month is Thanksgiving. We don't want people to be all turkeyed out," Tess said. "Ham. I like honey-baked ham."

"I'll make my butternut squash casserole." The list of ingredients formed in Janice's mind as LuAnn wrote. "And corn bread. That will keep in the freezer, so I can start making it now."

"Scalloped potatoes with lots of onions and cheese." LuAnn recorded the items in her neat script. "Anybody have a good baked apple recipe?"

Tess raised a hand. "My mother-in-law made the best cinnamon apples you've ever tasted. It's a favorite dish in our family. I'll make that."

The ding of a bell reached them through the open doorway. The front door.

Janice scooted back her chair to rise. "I'll get it. Maybe it's a walk-in guest."

"Where is everybody?" A familiar voice called from the café.

"We're in here, Marla," LuAnn shouted back.

A moment later, Marla Still charged into the kitchen. That was the only way to describe the near-run that catapulted the well-padded woman through the doorway. She marched to the center of the room, whirled to face the table, and planted her feet shoulder-length apart.

"Y'all will never guess what's happened."

Janice eyed the woman. Clearly, something had excited her, something good, judging by the toothy grin that carved dimples into cheeks the color of milky coffee and awarded them a clear view of her molars. Her eyes practically sparkled as she paced across the room with a lilting step and turned with something just short of a hop. Coarse dark hair with a liberal smattering of gray danced around her head, escapees from the tight knot gathered at the base of her hairline.

"It must be something good," LuAnn said.

"Good? It's downright fabulous." Marla's deep laugh filled the room. "It's finally happenin'. I cain't hardly believe it. I keep pinchin' myself. Go ahead. Guess. You'll never guess."

Janice couldn't hold back a giggle. How could she not laugh in the face of such exuberance? "Why don't you sit down and have a cup of tea?"

Tess cocked her head, her gaze fixed on Marla, who cavorted from the counter to Big Red as though unable to stand still. "Better make it herbal. Caffeine might send her blasting into orbit."

"Tea?" The woman pirouetted and bounded across the room again. "Who's got time for tea? I want you to guess my big news before I bust." She grabbed the back of Janice's chair with one hand and LuAnn's with the other. "Here's a hint. The Sternwheel Festival."

Janice exchanged a blank glance with Tess. Marietta's annual festival had been held over a month ago.

LuAnn ventured a guess. "You're entering next year's boat race?"

Marla threw back her head and released a peal of laughter. "Not even close. Guess again."

"Does it have something to do with fireworks?" Tess asked.

Another loud laugh and Marla bounced on her toes. "Sort of, but not the kind you think. C'mon. Keep trying."

The guessing game, and particularly the high-schoolish shenanigans coming from a woman in late middle age were starting to wear on Janice's nerves. She pasted on a smile. "I'm completely stumped."

"Me too," LuAnn said. "Don't keep us in suspense."

"All right." Marla released the chair backs and gathered herself to her full height. "I'm getting *married*!" She let out a startling shout that made Janice jump. "Yippee skippy, I'm getting hitched!"

Janice's jaw went slack. She couldn't have been more stunned if Marla had announced that she was planning to dye herself purple and parade down Front Street in a polka-dot bikini. As far as she knew, Marla hadn't been on a date in more than ten years. And Marla being Marla, she wouldn't have kept the existence of a boyfriend secret. Judging by the stunned expressions worn by Tess and LuAnn, they were as shocked as she was.

"Well, that's..." Tess appeared to grope for a word. "Surprising."

"Yes, it certainly is," LuAnn agreed. "Who's the lucky man?"

"Byron Wickham." Marla breathed the name on a sigh, her eyes sparkling like a clear sky at midnight.

The name sounded vaguely familiar. "Is he from around here?" Janice asked.

"He's from Canada, but after we're married he's going to look for a job down here. Y'all met him, though." The wide grin returned. "Guess where."

Janice took a stab at the obvious. "At the Sternwheel Festival?"

Marla pointed at her. "Bingo. He stayed over at the Lafayette, on account of he didn't know any better." She cast an apologetic glance toward the ceiling, beyond which lay the inn's beautiful guest rooms. "He came here for lunch one day and hasn't stopped talking about Winnie's gumbo since. Told me he cain't hardly wait to come back and order a big bowl of it."

Though the weekend of the festival had been crazy-busy, an image rose from Janice's memory. A tall, nice-looking black man, midfifties maybe, who asked a ton of questions about the inn's history. After lunch, he'd asked to meet Winnie to compliment her gumbo and then had succeeded in charming the recipe from her.

Tess found her tongue. "Did you know him before the festival?"

Marla shook her head, wiry gray wisps floating around her like a halo. "He came into the store looking for earplugs on account of the noise, and it was love at first sight."

LuAnn's eyebrows arched. She stood up and gestured toward her chair. "Sit down, dear. We want to hear all about it. I'll get you some tea." She glanced at Tess. "Chamomile."

Marla hesitated, her knees bent as though poised for take-off. But then, she relaxed and sank into the chair. "Well, okay. Truth be told, I could talk about Byron all day long."

Since Janice had never known Marla to be at a loss for words on any subject, she settled back and prepared to listen.

"I was working the photo counter at Walgreens, and the store was packed. Always is during the festival." Marla's eyes grew dreamy and distant. "I was printing a one-hour order and I saw him wandering through the cough and cold aisle, looking kind of lost. I've got to tell you girls, he is one good-looking man. About took my breath away. Tall, shoulders wide like a football player, and skin the color of Hershey's best. No." She closed her eyes and continued in a dreamy tone. "Not Hershey's. Ghirardelli. Rich and dark and delicious."

The description conjured a clearer image in Janice's mind. Yes, that was the man she remembered.

LuAnn returned with a clean mug, the tag of a tea bag dangling over the rim. "Love at first sight, huh?"

"It was for me. Took Byron a week or so to come around. He went back to Canada, where he lives. He's an accountant in a big firm there, Godfrey and Associates." With a grin the size of Texas, she watched steam rise from her mug as LuAnn poured water from the kettle. "But he couldn't forget about me. And then *bam!*" The grin doubled in size, though Janice wouldn't have thought it possible. "Our wedding's going to be October 20th."

Tess's eyes went wide. "But Marla, that's in eight days."

"Don't I know it? Fast, but neither of us are getting any younger."

Janice forced her face to remain impassive. In her years as a pastor's wife, she'd cultivated a calm demeanor that masked any amount of concern, worry, or even shock. "But Marla, you barely know him. Marriage is a lifelong commitment. How can you be sure he's the right man for you after such a short time?"

"I know him better than if we'd been sweethearts for years," Marla assured her. "Not a single day has gone by when we didn't talk on the phone. Last month I got me a tablet with Facetime so's we could see each other every day."

"Phone calls and video chats are hardly sufficient to get to know a potential spouse," Tess said.

"Nonsense." Marla picked up the tag and swirled her tea bag in the mug with the force of a whirlwind. "We aren't teenagers, you know. We didn't spend all that time mooning at each other. We talked about serious stuff. Our goals and our childhoods and our beliefs." She dropped the tag and picked up the mug, then caught Janice's eye over the rim. "He's a good Christian man, my Byron is."

"Well at least you discussed the important things," LuAnn said.

"Of course we did. We can't afford to waste time. And we both want a big wedding. A big church wedding." The wide grin returned and Marla directed it toward Janice. "And I want you to help me with it."

Surprised, Janice slapped her hand to her chest. "Me?"

"Yes, you. You've planned some of the most beautiful weddings I ever saw at Christ Fellowship. You know exactly what to do in that church, how to have it decorated, and where all the flowers should go."

It was true that Janice had helped many a bride enjoy their dream weddings in that church over the years she and Lawrence ministered there. But that was her former life.

She spoke slowly, allowing hesitation to creep into her voice. "Maybe it would be better if you asked Paige to help you."

"*Psht!*" Marla flipped a hand in the air. "That young thing? She's still wet behind the ears, her and Pastor Ben both. I like them, don't get me wrong. But this is *my* wedding. And I want everything perfect. Not only perfect but big. Flowers everywhere. The organ turned up full volume. And bells." Once again her eyes sparkled. "I want those church bells tolling, telling everybody all over town that Marla Still's done got herself a husband."

Despite her misgivings, Janice completely understood why a woman in her fifties, who never expected to get married, would want to celebrate her big day in a big way. But this whole thing just felt wrong. To marry a man she'd known only a month and met only once in person? Janice needed to think about this, to pray about this.

To cover her conflicted thoughts, she voiced the first thing that came into her mind. "Those bells haven't rung in years."

"I know it. But for my wedding I want those bells ringing." Marla set her tea mug down on the table with a thud and shot out of the chair. "I've got to go. I have news to spread, and I'm spreading it all over town." She headed toward the doorway and then stopped. "One more thing I nearly forgot. Byron and his friend are coming to Marietta tomorrow, and they're planning to stay until the wedding. I told him they just have to stay here because y'all run the best inn in the whole state." An anxious expression crept over her features. "You do have openings for them, don't you? Oh, and for Byron's family a few days before the wedding? There's a whole bunch of them."

Janice exchanged a glance with her friends. Was this God's answer to their prayer?

"Of course we will make room for them," LuAnn assured the woman.

"I knew I could count on you." She looked down at Janice. "This wedding's going to be one to put at the top of the best weddings you ever arranged. And besides, after you get that belfry cleaned out, the church bells can ring again."

Then she was gone, leaving the three in the kitchen in a stunned silence.

"My goodness," LuAnn said. "That was certainly a shocker."

Tess picked up a napkin and wiped up the tea that had splashed out of Marla's mug. "At least this man is a Christian."

Janice wasn't so sure. "A lot of people claim to be Christians. I've seen enough fakes in my years of ministry alongside Lawrence to know just because you park yourself in a garage and call yourself a car doesn't mean you are one."

LuAnn picked up the deserted mug. "Aren't you a sourpuss?"

Yes, Janice supposed she was being pessimistic. But she couldn't shake the idea that Marla Still was making a mistake of epic proportions.

A Note from the Editors

We hope you enjoy Secrets of Wayfarers Inn, created by the Books and Inspirational Media Division of Guideposts, a nonprofit organization that touches millions of lives every day through products and services that inspire, encourage, help you grow in your faith, and celebrate God's love in every aspect of your daily life.

Thank you for making a difference with your purchase of this book, which helps fund our many outreach programs to military personnel, prisons, hospitals, nursing homes, and educational institutions. To learn more, visit Guideposts Foundation.org.

We also maintain many useful and uplifting online resources. Visit Guideposts.org to read true stories of hope and inspiration, access OurPrayer network, sign up for free newsletters, download free e-books, join our Facebook community, and follow our stimulating blogs.

To learn about other Guideposts publications, including the best-selling devotional *Daily Guideposts*, go to ShopGuideposts .org, call (800) 932-2145, or write to Guideposts, PO Box 5815, Harlan, Iowa 51593.

Sign up for the
Guideposts Fiction Newsletter
and stay up-to-date on
the books you love!

You'll get sneak peeks of new releases, recommendations from other Guideposts readers, and special offers just for you . . .

and it's FREE!

Just go to Guideposts.org/Newsletters
today to sign up.

Guideposts.

Visit Guideposts.org/Shop
or call (800) 932-2145

Find more inspiring fiction in these best-loved Guideposts series!

Mysteries of Martha's Vineyard

Come to the shores of this quaint and historic island and dig in to a cozy mystery. When a recent widow inherits a lighthouse just off the coast of Massachusetts, she finds exciting adventures, new friends, and renewed hope.

Tearoom Mysteries

Mix one stately Victorian home, a charming lakeside town in Maine, and two adventurous cousins with a passion for tea and hospitality. Add a large scoop of intriguing mystery and sprinkle generously with faith, family, and friends, and you have the recipe for Tearoom Mysteries.

Sugarcreek Amish Mysteries

Be intrigued by the suspense and joyful "aha!" moments in these delightful stories. Each book in the series brings together two women of vastly different backgrounds and traditions, who realize there's much more to the "simple life" than meets the eye.

Mysteries of Silver Peak

Escape to the historic mining town of Silver Peak, Colorado, and discover how one woman's love of antiques helps her solve mysteries buried deep in the town's checkered past.

Patchwork Mysteries

Discover that life's little mysteries often have a common thread in a series where every novel contains an intriguing whodunit centered around a quilt located in a beautiful New England town.

To learn more about these books, visit Guideposts.org/Shop